Startled, Mic [ ] *his attention riveted to the screen.*

He saw the photo of the familiar farmhouse, his parents holding hands by the porch, and then the snapshot taken by the barn of the three of them, Michael standing between Hannah and little Katie, with a big sheepdog seated by his feet.

Rex—the dog's name had been Rex.

And then he swallowed down a lump in his throat....

There she was, a slender, dark-haired woman with dimples as deep as his own. His mother—older, of course, but instantly recognizable. Michael rose to his feet, his heart pounding.

"They told me you died," he said aloud to the empty room.

Dear Reader,

The weather may be cooling off as fall approaches, but the reading's as hot as ever here at Silhouette Intimate Moments. And for our lead title this month I'm proud to present the first longer book from reader favorite BJ James. In *Broken Spurs* she's created a hero and heroine sure to live in your mind long after you've turned the last page.

Karen Leabo returns with *Midnight Confessions*, about a bounty hunter whose reward—love—turns out to be far different from what he'd expected. In *Bringing Benjy Home*, Kylie Brant matches a skeptical man with an intuitive woman, then sets them on the trail of a missing child. *Code Name: Daddy* is the newest Intimate Moments novel from Marilyn Tracy, who took a break to write for our Shadows line. It's a unique spin on the ever-popular "secret baby" plotline. And you won't want to miss *Michael's House*, Pat Warren's newest book for the line and part of her REUNION miniseries, which continues in Special Edition. Finally, in *Temporary Family* Sally Tyler Hayes creates the family of the title, then has you wishing as hard as they do to make the arrangement permanent.

Enjoy them all—and don't forget to come back next month for more of the best romance fiction around, right here in Silhouette Intimate Moments.

Leslie Wainger,
Senior Editor and Editorial Coordinator

Please address questions and book requests to:
Silhouette Reader Service
U.S.: 3010 Walden Ave., P.O. Box 1325, Buffalo, NY 14269
Canadian: P.O. Box 609, Fort Erie, Ont. L2A 5X3

MICHAEL'S HOUSE

PAT WARREN

Published by Silhouette Books

America's Publisher of Contemporary Romance

If you purchased this book without a cover you should be aware
that this book is stolen property. It was reported as "unsold and
destroyed" to the publisher, and neither the author nor the
publisher has received any payment for this "stripped book."

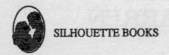 SILHOUETTE BOOKS

ISBN 0-373-07737-8

MICHAEL'S HOUSE

Copyright © 1996 by Pat Warren

All rights reserved. Except for use in any review, the reproduction
or utilization of this work in whole or in part in any form by any
electronic, mechanical or other means, now known or hereafter
invented, including xerography, photocopying and recording, or in
any information storage or retrieval system, is forbidden without
the written permission of the editorial office, Silhouette Books,
300 East 42nd Street, New York, NY 10017 U.S.A.

All characters in this book have no existence outside the imagination of
the author and have no relation whatsoever to anyone bearing the same
name or names. They are not even distantly inspired by any individual
known or unknown to the author, and all incidents are pure invention.

This edition published by arrangement with Harlequin Books S.A.

® and TM are trademarks of Harlequin Books S.A., used under license.
Trademarks indicated with ® are registered in the United States Patent
and Trademark Office, the Canadian Trade Marks Office and in other
countries.

Printed in U.S.A.

PAT WARREN,

mother of four, lives in Arizona with her travel-agent husband and a lazy white cat. She's a former newspaper columnist whose lifetime dream was to become a novelist. A strong romantic streak, a sense of humor and a keen interest in developing relationships led her to try romance novels, with which she feels very much at home.

Prologue

Michigan
September 10, 1978

It's several weeks since I left the hospital, and I seem no closer to finding my children than I was during the two years I spent as a patient there. Each night, I return to my small apartment to eat alone, to count my meager money supply and to weep. Charles Dutton, the private investigator I hired, has come up empty-handed, as well. But today, he offered me a slim hope—the name of a man who's been successful in locating children who've been kidnapped or otherwise taken from their custodial parent. Mr. Dutton tells me that Sloan Bradford is a little rough around the edges, but what choice do I have? He's my last chance to find Michael, Hannah and Katie. I plan to look him up tomorrow, and I pray he's the answer.

September 12, 1978

I must finish this quickly, then pack and meet Sloan. We leave for Mexico tonight.

How I wish it were my three we hope to find south of the border. The man I need to help me has a problem of his own to solve first, and I've agreed to assist him. His ex-wife and her latest lover have kidnapped Sloan's seven-year-old son and he's learned they're headed for the rugged mountainous country of Durango, just north of Mazatlán. Sloan is unfamiliar with the area and doesn't speak the language, but I know both. We've made a deal, as he calls it, although he was reluctant to include me, for there is the likelihood of danger. I don't care about my own safety, for, if I help him, he will put all his efforts into finding my children after our return. He appears to be a man of his word.

He's a formidable man—tall, with wide shoulders and piercing blue eyes—and totally focused on bringing back his Christopher. I know just how he feels. Sloan hates needing and accepting help, as do I. But the ends will justify the means: for both of us, I pray. The authorities in Mexico will be even less help than the police locally have been. The mountain people are suspicious and often unfriendly to outsiders. Our mission is not easy.

I hate to delay the search for my own, but I've explored every avenue and been unsuccessful. My only hope lies in this brusque, determined man. I must trust him, despite my misgivings. I will write down my thoughts as frequently as I'm able.

May God go with us.

Chapter 1

San Diego, California
December 1995

He was winded from his run, and thirsty. Michael followed his white sheepdog, King, inside, bumped the door shut with his hip, grabbed a bottle of crystal-clear water from the fridge and took it into the living room at the back of the house. The windows that looked out on the Pacific Ocean drew him, as always. He drank deeply, then drank in the view.

Flopping into his favorite easy chair, he glanced at his watch. He had time before his shower to relax a bit. A note propped on the end table caught his attention. He picked up the single white sheet and read the brief message.

"I taped a segment of an important show for you. Watch it before I get home. I know you'll want to talk about it then. I love you."

Michael smiled. She was always doing little things like that, surprising him with one of his favorite golden-oldie

movies, searching out a special bottle of wine, taping a
sticky note to his shaving mirror if she left the house first.
It was only one of the many reasons he loved her.

King ambled in and lay down by the hearth to rest after
their run. Another long swallow of the cooling liquid, then
Michael reached for the remote and clicked on the large-
screen television at the far end of the room. Selecting Play,
he started the tape.

He'd seen the television show before: "Solutions." It was
one of those that encouraged the viewing audience to call
in if they had any information on reenacted crimes they
presented or if they could help reunite families torn apart
by a variety of circumstances. The filmed segment, according to the debonair host, was about a search for three
siblings who'd been separated over twenty years ago.

Leaning his head back, Michael took another drink as
the voice informed the audience that Child Protective
Services had taken the children from their farm home in
Frankenmuth, Michigan, after their father had been killed
in an accident and their mother had to be hospitalized due
to a life-threatening illness. Startled, Michael straightened, his attention riveted on the screen.

He saw the photo of the familiar farmhouse, his parents
holding hands by the porch, and then the snapshot taken by
the barn of the three of them, Michael standing between
Hannah and little Katie, with a big sheepdog seated by his
feet. Rex. The dog's name had been Rex. Swallowing down
a sudden lump in his throat, he wondered who had brought
this to the attention of the show's producers.

Then she was there, a slender, dark-haired woman with
dimples as deep as his own. His mother—older, of course,
but immediately recognizable. Michael rose to his feet, his
heart pounding. "They told me you died," he said aloud to
the empty room.

He listened as the woman named Julia told how she'd
been searching for her children ever since she'd gotten out
of the hospital two years after the separation. Her eyes were
shiny with unshed tears as the host implored the viewing
audience to call the number at the bottom of the screen if

they knew the whereabouts of any one of the three Richards children.

Shakily, Michael noted the number, then sat back down. He stared at the screen as the segment ended and they moved to a commercial. Now he understood why she'd filmed this for him and why she knew he would want to talk about it, he thought, as he hit the Off button.

His mother, Julia Richards, alive. Could that be? Why had the authorities lied to him? Where were Hannah and Katie after all this time? So long ago. He'd been only fourteen that fateful summer.

Leaning back, Michael let himself remember.

San Diego
September, two years earlier

"Michael's House," Michael said into the phone.

In Colorado, the woman on the other end frowned and gripped the receiver tightly. She felt her eyes fill yet again as she brushed back a lock of hair. She had to stay in control. Mom was crying enough for both of them. "Hello. I just found a slip of paper in my sister's jacket pocket with this phone number and name on it—Michael's House—both words capitalized. Would you be Michael?"

"Yes, I am. And who would you be?"

"Fallon McKenzie." A faint hope stirred in her heart. "I'm looking for my sister, Laurie." Who was this Michael? Laurie had never mentioned him. "Is she there with you?"

Michael cradled the portable phone to his ear with his shoulder, walked to the kitchen counter and poured himself a mug of fresh coffee. "What does she look like?"

"She's five-four, slender with long chestnut-brown hair and big dark eyes. She usually wears jeans and loose shirts, probably tennis shoes. She just turned sixteen and she's...she's shy and sweet." Fallon struggled to keep her voice steady.

The woman with the intriguingly husky voice had just described about fifty percent of the teenage girls Michael saw every day. The other half were blondes. But he heard the emotion in her voice and softened his own. "No, sh isn't here. What made you think she might be?"

Feeling the disappointment, Fallon sat down heavily a her sister's desk in the typical teenager's room, wall post ers of hunks contrasting with a collection of teddy bears o the bed. "As I explained, because of the note with you name on it. I recognize your area code and, to my knowl edge, Laurie doesn't know anyone in San Diego. Is she friend of yours?"

"I wouldn't say so."

"Can you explain where she might have gotten you number?"

Michael was used to calls like this. He fielded several week ever since he'd opened his halfway house several year ago as a haven for troubled teens. While he always coop erated with the police, he didn't give out information on hi young guests indiscriminately to just anyone. And cer tainly not over the phone.

He took a sip of hot coffee. "No, I can't. She could hav heard about us any number of ways. Is she in trouble? Ha she run away from home?"

His voice was deep with a hint of impatience that cause Fallon's already strained nerves to bunch and tighten. Hov had he guessed so readily? Her imagination, activated b too little sleep and too much stress lately, had her conjur ing up frightening images of Laurie alone in a strange city exposed to thieves, drug dealers, white slavery. Exactly wh was this *us* Michael referred to? "What connection do yo have to runaway teenage girls?"

He caught the fear and understood her concern. "I'm th director of Michael's House, which is a safe place for youn people, the ones who've left home under, shall we say, less than-ideal circumstances. And because of those very rea sons, they can't return."

She studied the slip of paper. "How do kids know abou your place?"

"They hear about us through word of mouth, posters i bus stations, flyers around town, ads in the newspapers."

Fallon was taken aback. "Are you saying you take these kids in, even advertise for them, and keep them from the parents who love them and are searching everywhere for them? Don't you know what agony you put their mothers and fathers through, not knowing where their child is?"

Michael sighed. It was discouraging, but he knew how much easier it was for a relative to blame an outsider than to handle the responsibility themselves. "Look, Ms. McKenzie, I don't keep anyone here against their will. Teenagers leave home for a variety of reasons, but mostly because of some intolerable situation. They come to us with limited education, and practically no money. They're often frightened and heartsick. Some have been abused. Suddenly they find themselves on their own, afraid to trust strangers, where merely surviving can take all their wits and energy. Some really terrible things can happen to kids living hand-to-mouth on the streets."

He let his words sink in before continuing. "Michael's House offers an alternative, a chance to get their lives back on track. If they truly want to return home, we give them assistance. If not, we help them start over and direct them to programs that will allow them to eventually be self-supporting. Instead of condemning us without checking out our place in person, you might be asking yourself why it is that your sister ran away in the first place."

Fallon felt her rush of anger drain away, because the man was on target. She'd been asking herself that very question since receiving her mother's nearly hysterical phone call three days ago. Actually, Laurie had been gone two weeks before Fallon had been informed because Mom had felt that surely her younger daughter would walk back in at any moment. Only she hadn't.

So Fallon had asked for a couple of days off from work and driven to Colorado Springs to see how she could help. Since then, she'd questioned nearly everyone Laurie knew and still hadn't a clue where she might have gone. The cryptic note she'd left propped on her dresser had revealed very little. "Mom," it had said. "I need to get away for a while. Please don't worry about me. Love, Laurie."

Her mother had said that there'd been no serious arguments lately that might have precipitated Laurie's departure. Fallon had been raised in the very same household and, although she'd experienced moments of rebellion as a teenager, she'd gotten over them. She couldn't picture her shy sister—who was every bit the dreamer their father had been—preferring to live on the streets rather than in her lovely room.

"I'm sure the teenagers who come to your place are as you describe, troubled and in need of help." She heard the defensiveness in her tone and cleared her throat, wanting him to understand. "But my sister's not like that. Our mother's a very loving woman and her husband, although strict, is a good person. Teens are highly emotional and sometimes blow small things out of proportion. They overreact, and a misunderstanding becomes a serious conflict from their viewpoint. I know Laurie will realize that and want to come home. After all, it's not as if she's been abused." Why did her voice lack conviction, then?

Her mother's husband, she'd said. A stepfather. Michael found himself wondering if Laurie had left because she hadn't gotten along with the strict stepfather. He'd encountered that sort of thing more times than he cared to recall. Would her sister not know this, or was she in denial? "Verbal abuse can be as damaging as physical abuse, Ms. McKenzie."

"I'm aware of that." She'd been ten when Roy Gifford had married her widowed mother, and had received more than one tongue-lashing from him before she'd left his house in Colorado Springs for college in Denver on a full scholarship. But abusive, verbally or otherwise? No, she wouldn't call Roy's Rules, as she'd tagged her stepfather's many edicts for proper behavior, abusive. They were an annoyance but not impossible to abide by. She'd never been able to love Roy, but after all, he had stepped in and raised two daughters fathered by another man. She didn't agree with Michael's supposition that all teenage runaways had serious problems. "Thank you for your time. I'm sure Laurie will come home any day now and—"

"She was here," Michael said softly.

Fallon all but stopped breathing. "What did you say?"

Michael drained his by now lukewarm coffee and sat down at the large oak table in the dining room. "It was about ten days ago, a rainy evening."

"Why didn't you tell me that sooner?"

"You asked if she was here now. She's not, not anymore."

"Oh, God," Fallon whispered.

"She came in with another girl, a tall, thin blonde named Emma, I believe. The two of them were pretty wet. She had a piece of blue yarn tied around this long ponytail and she was wearing a small opal ring set in gold on her right hand. She has a slightly crooked eye tooth, on the left side, I believe. She said her name was Laurie. We don't press for last names."

Fallon realized she was holding the phone in a death grip and forced her fingers to unclench. She'd given Laurie an opal ring last Christmas. "Was . . . was she all right?"

"She wasn't sick physically, if that's what you mean. At least, not that I could see." The girl had looked younger than sixteen, with huge, wary eyes that wouldn't meet his, and her hands had trembled noticeably.

"She's not there anymore, you said. How long did she stay?"

"She had dinner with us, took a shower, then washed and dried her clothes. We have a laundry room, honor system, a quarter a load. She carried a beat-up green gym bag with Colorado on it in white letters. She and her friend shared a room for the night, but they were gone before breakfast."

Taking in a steadying breath, Fallon leaned back in the chair and closed her eyes. The man, it seemed, was quite observant. "I don't suppose you know where they were headed?"

"Probably back out onto the streets."

"But why?" Her voice was thick with frustration. If only she could understand. "Why would she leave your place, too?"

Michael shrugged. "Maybe because we have rules here, too. No drinking, no drugs, no fraternizing. Regular health exams, vitamins, daily showers, clean clothes, everyone doing their fair share of the chores. We also insist that they enroll in some sort of school, that they get at least a high-school diploma or equivalent. If they're addicted to something, they have to be willing to quit and accept counseling. That sort of thing." She was quiet so long, he wondered if what he said was getting through to her. Did she think that he, too, was too strict? "None of us can live without some sort of rules."

Fallon let out a ragged sigh. "I agree." Why couldn't Laurie see that? She'd been rebellious from childhood on, but to actually run away with no discernible reason? She was so inexperienced, so sheltered. How could she possibly survive on the streets? "I'd like to leave you my parents' phone number and if she returns, or if you happen to spot her somewhere, you could call here collect and—"

"No. I don't do that."

Her temper, so close to the surface these days, had her rising from the chair. "Look, I'm willing to pay you."

"That's not it. It's a matter of trust. The kids who come here know we won't turn them in. If they leave, it's because they want to, not because someone makes them."

"But they're underage. You have no right—"

"Don't talk to me about rights." Annoyed, he walked through the archway into the kitchen and set his coffee mug down on the counter. He knew better than to lose his temper with a relative of a runaway, his training and experience telling him how tough it was for them to understand. But sometimes, they got to him. "You see, I believe that kids have rights, too—to two parents who love them, who don't abuse them, don't leave them, but care for them. But how many have all that? Too damn few. If you don't believe me, come see for yourself. A couple of days here might just open your closed mind. If you really want to find your sister and if she's in San Diego, I'll help you find her. But once she's found, if she doesn't want to go back with you, I won't let you take her."

His gruff manner didn't put her off as much as his message shocked her. "Why wouldn't she want to come back with me? We love her."

"You tell me. And if you all love her so much, why did she leave in the first place?" Michael heard the kitchen door open and saw Dr. Paul Ramirez saunter in. "Got to go. If you decide to come, we're in the book." He hung up.

Feeling suddenly drained, Fallon replaced the receiver and stared for several minutes at the piece of paper with Michael's phone number written in Laurie's youthful handwriting. Perhaps this wouldn't be so difficult if she could understand *why* her sister had left in the first place. Certainly they all knew that Laurie could be impulsive, but what teenager wasn't? Annoyance with parents was also common among that age group.

Gazing out the window, Fallon swallowed uneasily. Laurie had called unexpectedly one evening and all but begged Fallon to let her visit, if only for a few days. But Fallon had been about to leave on a trip to New York on business. Since Laurie had sounded more bored than upset, she'd sloughed her off, promising to let her visit at semester break instead. While Fallon was in New York, Laurie had run away from home.

Where are you, honey? she asked silently. *And why did you run away?*

Pocketing the note, she left her sister's room and went downstairs to talk with her mother and Roy.

Michael's House was the only residence in San Diego that catered strictly to young people, according to the agent who rented a car to Fallon. He gave her a map, circled the area of Twelfth Avenue near San Diego Community College and told her that the place she wanted was near the Neil Good Day Center for Men, the House of Rachel, which took in women, and The Storefront, which attracted mostly bilingual occupants.

Placing her suitcase in the trunk of the red Mustang, Fallon realized it was much warmer in California in mid-September than it had been when she'd left Colorado early that morning. She removed her tweed blazer, laid it across the passenger seat and got behind the wheel, letting out a weary breath.

The day had started off badly with a scene at the breakfast table, her stepfather adamantly forbidding Fallon to go after Laurie, which had set her mother to weeping again. She'd known last night when she'd talked with both of them that Roy Gifford considered Laurie irresponsible and reckless, not worth the trip. If that hadn't been enough, his demanding tone had further irritated her.

Although she knew it upset her mother, she'd reminded Roy that she was twenty-six and had been on her own since age eighteen. Thanks to her scholarship and the jobs she'd managed to hold while studying, she hadn't cost him one cent since leaving his house. And, while he had supported her from age ten till then, she firmly maintained that he could no longer dictate her behavior.

If she'd been hesitant at all about going to San Diego, Roy had made up her mind for her with his vehement outburst. She'd called her manager at Breuner's Department Store where she was one of the head buyers and asked for a leave of absence. She was determined to find Laurie whether their stepfather liked it or not.

Now, here she was, studying the map, looking for the house for runaways under the supervision of the man she'd spoken with yesterday. It took her some time, but she finally located the address. However, there was no sign identifying it as Michael's House. Still, this had to be it.

Parking the Mustang in front, Fallon got out and looked up at an imposing building three stories high with a large porch in a neighborhood that could only be classified as "undergoing renovation." There was a tired-looking school with a fenced yard a block over and a small park across from that.

On the porch, she read the hand-painted sign over the arched doorframe: Welcome. Please Come In. A nice touch. She pushed open the heavy door and stepped inside to a small, tiled foyer. At the desk behind a waist-high counter was seated a tall black woman with wonderful cheekbones, wearing a white nurse's uniform. She looked up as Fallon approached, her smile distracted.

"This is Michael's House, isn't it?" she asked. "The agent where I rented my car directed me to this address, but I didn't see a sign out front."

"There's a small brass nameplate, but it's hard to spot. Michael doesn't like large signs." Opal's dark eyes appraised the young woman, noting the leather shoes, fawn-colored slacks and matching silk blouse, the expensive haircut. The overall impression, she thought, was elegant and unexpected in this neighborhood. And, having worked for Michael since the day he first opened his doors, Opal had seen them all.

Too young to be a parent of one of the teens, she decided. Yet the young woman's eyes were shadowed with worry. The nurse gave her an encouraging smile. "I'm Opal. How can I help you?"

"I'm Fallon McKenzie. I've just flown in from Colorado. I spoke with Michael yesterday and sent him a fax requesting an appointment at four." She glanced at her watch and saw that it was ten after. "Is he available?"

Opal ran long, slender fingers over her hair, worn pulled back into a tight bun. "I believe he's out back with some of our residents, playing basketball. I'm sure he won't be long. You can have a seat over there, if you like." She indicated the area through the archway where a piano stood in one corner and several couches and chairs were arranged in conversational groupings, as well as a pool table off to the far side.

Basketball? The director of this so-called house for run-aways was playing basketball with the kids?

Fallon glanced into the rec room, then down the hallway that led toward the back of the house. She could hear voices shouting and cheering. "Would it be all right if I went out and watched the game?" It would give her a chance to study the kids who were currently staying here. And it wouldn't hurt to be able to scrutinize Michael before actually meeting him.

"Sure," Opal said. "Right through there."

A tall dark-haired man wearing a suit came bustling through the front door at that moment. He was carrying a large cardboard box and greeted the nurse-receptionist warmly. "How are things, Opal?"

She smiled broadly. "Hi, Dr. Paul. What've you got for us?"

"Some surplus bandages and sterile wipes, plus a mess of cheese-and-cracker packets for Michael's Balboa Park runs."

"We can always use those," Opal said, taking the light carton from him and placing it behind the counter.

The man's brown eyes swept over Fallon appreciatively, and he stuck out his hand. "Hello, I'm Paul Ramirez."

She couldn't help but respond to his friendly manner, reaching to shake his hand and introducing herself.

"Are you here to see Michael about that teaching position that's open or about one of our guests?" Paul asked. "I'm the on-call physician and all-around medical consultant as well as his best friend."

"I'm looking for my sister. I have an appointment with Michael."

He smiled, revealing very white teeth. "All right. Don't let me hold you up. Nice meeting you, Fallon."

"Same here." She started down the hallway, listening to Opal ask the doctor if he was planning to stay for dinner. They seemed pleasant enough. Why, she couldn't help wondering, did they need a doctor and nurse on call?

She passed a doorway on the left and saw a huge dining room opening onto a big kitchen where a dark-headed woman enveloped in a snowy white apron was busy at the sink while a very pregnant teenage girl was shucking corn. On the right was a doorway to a laundry room with half a dozen washers and dryers, two pay phones and a soft drink machine. Two side-by-side lavatories were across from a paneled office where a balding man could be seen using an adding machine.

Fallon shoved open the back screen door.

The basketball court consisted of a large concrete area with two freestanding hoops at opposite ends alongside a building that looked like an aluminum storage shed. Stepping outside, she walked over to stand in the shade of a flowering jacaranda tree where she could watch unobserved.

There were seven boys and three girls ranging in age from probably twelve to eighteen, shifting positions—guarding, shooting, dribbling, racing from side to side—the game in progress. And there was no mistaking the man in charge: the referee, who had to be Michael, with a whistle dangling from a chain around his neck.

He wasn't exactly what she'd been expecting. Several inches over six feet and lean, with broad shoulders and a flat stomach beneath a black knit shirt and white shorts, he resembled a runner with his long, muscular legs. His hair was very blond and had that appealing wind-blown look, the length just barely touching his shirt collar. She saw him swing about and noticed startlingly blue eyes in a tanned face, his expression one of utter concentration. He flashed a smile as the ball whipped through the basket from center court, and she spotted two deep dimples that softened the hard masculine lines of his features.

No, he wasn't what she'd expected.

A scrappy Hispanic boy had the ball next, dribbling low to the ground, guarded by a tall, gangly kid who was all arms and legs. Michael's attention on the duo was absolute as he trailed along the makeshift court with them. Impatient and anxious, the taller boy shouldered the smaller one, batting the ball away and bouncing it to a teammate. The players swiveled about and headed for the opposite basket, but were halted by Michael's shrill whistle.

Fallon heard the foul called, then saw the gangly kid make an obscene gesture as he lined up alongside the free-throw line. Michael's whistle sounded again. He stopped the action and took the boy aside. While the others exchanged looks and nervous whispers, Michael talked quietly to the surly kid who stood with hands on his skinny hips, his eyes downcast. Finally, looking chagrined, he nodded to Michael before walking over to the Hispanic boy. He said a few words she couldn't hear and extended his hand. The boy shook hands with him, and the game resumed after the free throw.

Fallon reached for a tissue from her purse and patted her damp brow as she watched, reluctantly impressed by Michael's cool control on the court. She wasn't sure what exactly she'd expected from their brief phone conversation, but it hadn't been someone so obviously in top physical condition, a man who could easily be labeled "all-American handsome," and yet was amazingly low-key and patient, although he appeared to be only in his thirties.

His comments to the kids were a mixture of praise and warning, of instruction and approval. Yet there was no recrimination in his deep voice even as he reprimanded. Rather, his tone was amicable but with a definite ring of authority.

She studied the kids and found them to be a mixed bag of ages and sizes. A couple of the older boys looked tough, one with his head completely shaved and sporting an earring while several others had shoulder-length hair and one wore a buzz cut. Hair always seemed to be a personality statement with kids, Fallon recalled from her own teen years; an act of defiance that often became a bone of contention with adults. Their clothing was casual—shorts and knit shirts—and noticeably clean. Two of the girls were fairly decent players, but the third looked bored and disinterested.

"Try that again, Jamie," Michael yelled out, tossing his hair out of his eyes before throwing the ball to the shortest kid.

A junk heap of a car rattled down the side street, followed by a barking dog. Behind Fallon, the screen door banged shut after two boys came out, lighting cigarettes as they walked toward the adjacent two-story building. A jet dipped low overhead on its way to Lindbergh Field International Airport. She couldn't help noticing that Michael's gaze never wavered, his attention never strayed from the game and the kids playing, despite all the distracting sounds around them. What made a man so focused? she wondered.

Fallon tried to picture Laurie in this setting, perhaps involved in an impromptu basketball session. Her sister had never gone out for sports in school, perhaps because their stepbrother, Danny, had tried out for everything and excelled in all of them. *And* kept his grades up. Why hadn't she noticed sooner that living in the shadow of Roy's overachiever son for most of her life had probably caused Laurie to quit trying?

The teenagers Fallon was watching seemed very much like kids she'd glimpsed at shopping malls in Denver. Had Laurie been here long enough to realize that she might have it in? Or had she left this place, too, because she feared the competition?

Fallon shifted the strap of her bag to her other shoulder, then rubbed her forehead, which felt warm and sweaty. Perhaps if she'd had something to eat this morning instead of quickly downing a glass of juice and half a cup of coffee, she wouldn't feel so shaky. But the tense scene with Roy had put knots in her stomach and chased away her appetite.

After he'd stomped out of the house, Fallon had called a cab to take her to the airport, unwilling to ask her mother to drive in her upset condition. The rest of the day hadn't been much better. The first plane took off late, causing her to have to run, barely making her connecting flight in Phoenix. After landing in San Diego, she'd had to wait forever for her bag, and then for the courtesy van to the car-rental lot. She'd planned to check in at a nearby motel before driving to Michael's House, but a quick glance at her watch had changed her mind.

Now, here she was at half past four, hot, hungry and headachy, with more tension waiting for her, most likely. Stepping backward, she leaned against the brick wall and closed her eyes, suddenly feeling faint.

"Are you all right?" a deep voice at her elbow asked.

Startled, Fallon looked up and into those piercing blue eyes she'd noticed minutes ago, and blinked, feeling disoriented. "I think so." It was the heat. She wasn't used to

it. She took a couple of steps, wondering why her legs felt
so rubbery. "I..."

"Here, let's get you inside." Michael bent, slipped one
arm under her knees and the other around her back, and
carried her inside.

Chapter 2

She felt ridiculous.

Settled on the corduroy couch in the office she'd passed earlier, Fallon felt embarrassment flush her face. "I don't know what came over me," she said in explanation, in apology.

"I thought you were going to faint there for a minute." As he sat on the edge of the couch, holding a cold cloth to her head, Michael's face wore a worried frown.

"I *never* faint," she insisted. What must he think of her? Lord, what a way to begin an interview.

"How long since you've eaten, dear?" Opal stood by the two chairs that faced a sturdy, slightly scarred desk, leaning against the nearest one.

"I didn't have anything today. I was in a hurry." Feeling mortified, she tried to sit up. "I'm not used to your heat here, I guess. We're into fall back home."

"It's unseasonably warm for September this year," Michael said, removing the cloth from her head. Part of the problem was the proper little high-necked, long-sleeved blouse she was wearing. He thought about telling her to undo a couple of buttons, but decided she wouldn't like the suggestion.

"Still, I'm going to get you a nice cold glass of orange juice and some crackers." She glanced at Michael. "I wouldn't be surprised if her blood sugar's down."

"That won't be necessary, really." Fallon swung her legs to the floor, sitting all the way up. "I'm fine now."

As if she hadn't heard, Opal left the room, a woman with a mission.

Michael stood. "Let her fuss. She enjoys it." He'd been studying her sporadically for the last quarter of the game, noticing the tension in her flushed face, the interested way she shifted her gaze from one player to the next. He'd gotten the fax and knew who she was. Her shadowed expression had revealed very little, but her green eyes were huge and vulnerable. He'd been surprised at the shock of physical awareness he'd experienced when he'd held her in his arms. "You must be Fallon McKenzie."

"Yes, and you must be Michael. Again, let me apologize for causing so much trouble."

"No trouble, honestly. If you're sure you're all right?"

"Absolutely." She brushed her hair back with both hands, noticing that they were less shaky. He was studying her so intently that she was finding it difficult to normalize her breathing—whether because of the episode outside or his nearness, she couldn't be sure. Despite her confusion, when he'd carried her in, she'd felt a quick, sensual tug such as she hadn't known in years.

Opal brought the juice and crackers on a tray and Fallon had to admit, the cold drink tasted wonderful. Sipping, she looked around, noticing that his office was functional, with no frills. The floor was red Mexican tile, lending a bit of color to the room, and wooden blinds painted white hung across the wide window. The Serenity Prayer was framed and hanging on one wall, a soothing seascape on the other.

Michael walked over to the credenza and grabbed a white terry-cloth towel, mopping his brow with it. It was warm outside today, but then, he'd been running around for an hour. The young lady whose color was finally returning had been standing in the shade for only about ten minutes. He turned and saw their resident cat, a yellow tabby, jump up and settle on her lap.

He pulled a chair around and straddled it, then sat facing her. "I should introduce you to Thomasina."

It was relaxing to stroke the cat whose yellow eyes closed in ecstasy as Fallon scratched behind its ears. They'd never had pets when she was a child; they'd moved around too much when her father had been alive, and animals were strictly forbidden after Roy had come on the scene. Now, she wondered why she hadn't bothered to get one since living alone. "Odd name for a cat."

"Yeah, well, it was originally Thomas, as in tomcat. Then one day she presented us with a litter of six kittens."

She didn't want to smile or to be charmed, but she did—and was. Maybe because she'd been through such an emotional wringer over the past couple of days, to say nothing of the last dozen hours, and welcomed a moment of levity. Her eyes rose to his face and she saw his own smile deepening his dimples.

With no small effort, Fallon brought her attention back to why she'd come. "I hope you don't mind, but I have to ask. What's basketball got to do with helping runaway kids?"

"Quite a lot." The question didn't surprise him. He'd heard it before. "For one thing, sports help get rid of excess energy that might otherwise explode in a fight. We also take a group bowling weekly and have regular softball games.

"But there's another, more important reason. I use sports to teach kids about life. Not everything goes your way in a game every time, no matter how good you are. Michael Jordan missed some shots, lost some games. Not everything goes your way in life, either. Michael Jordan lost his father to a senseless act of violence. All his money and fame couldn't prevent the loss. It's an important lesson to learn, for kids and adults."

"I see." Fallon agreed with his philosophy, but she thought it was time to get to the point. "I don't want to take up too much of your time." Carefully, she disengaged the cat and reached into her leather bag, passing him the photo. "Is this the girl who came here calling herself Laurie?"

Couldn't miss the resemblance, Michael thought immediately. The girl was younger, of course, her face more immature, less interesting than her older sister's. But they both had the same slender build, the almost-delicate bone structure beneath flawless skin and a sensuous shape to their lips. Then there was that thick chestnut hair—Laurie's quite long, while Fallon's was chin-length. And green eyes the shade of moss growing on the black rocks along the coastal waters. "Yes, this is Laurie."

Thank God. A genuine lead at last, Fallon thought. The moment he'd described the opal ring on the phone, she'd been fairly certain.

Michael handed back the picture and let his eyes roam her face. "Your sister's lovely, but you're beautiful."

His comment had her frowning, not wanting to acknowledge the attraction she hadn't been expecting. She hadn't interrupted her life and come all this way for a flirtation. "I'm here to find Laurie and nothing else."

"Don't worry," he said easily, again flashing that dimpled smile. "I won't let the fact that I find you attractive keep me from helping you."

Fallon hoped he meant it. "Tell me about the night she was here, please."

Michael draped the towel around his neck and leaned back. "I told you most everything I know on the phone. She was here scarcely twelve hours. I haven't seen her since." He saw Fallon flinch and softened his tone. "Did you find out why she ran away from home?"

"Not specifically. We've conjectured a great deal, my mother and I."

Not the stepfather, he noted, and wondered why she hadn't mentioned him. "And what have you come up with?"

Not nearly enough. That evening after she'd talked with Michael by phone, she'd quizzed her mother, asking if Laurie had ever mentioned a blond friend named Emma or a desire to visit California. But Jane Gifford had been as puzzled as she.

Roy, on the other hand, had jumped in enthusiastically, calling Laurie a selfish, inconsiderate girl without a responsible bone in her body, a sharp contrast to *his* always-perfect son. Danny had graduated from high school with a 3.9 grade average. Danny had been appointed to the U.S. Air Force Academy with a full scholarship, sponsored by Roy's pal, Fred Englehardt, a state senator. Danny had never given them a minute's trouble, whereas Laurie was barely pulling in C's and always finding herself in hot water.

She'd never heard Roy rave on so. If it hadn't been for the sight of her weeping mother, Fallon knew she would have let loose with how she *really* felt about his tirade.

Fallon put Laurie's photo away and glanced up at Michael. "We haven't come up with much. I learned yesterday that Laurie wanted to attend a private school in another town for her last two years. The students there have to pay tuition, room and board. Roy Gifford, our stepfather, decided the cost was prohibitive. Still, I can't believe that alone would make her leave." If she'd known about Laurie's request, perhaps she could have helped pay the cost. If she had allowed her sister to visit that last weekend, they could have worked something out.

Michael watched her from under lowered lids, noticing the conflicting emotions playing across her features. This was one troubled woman, and he wondered if her problems stemmed from her sister's leaving or from something else.

Fallon rubbed at the headache now pounding above her eyes. "Laurie had only attended a week's classes in the new semester. I talked with her high-school counselor, her teachers, several of her classmates, plus the druggist where she worked part-time. She'd mentioned nothing to any of them and, although a couple mentioned that she'd seemed

quieter and more withdrawn since starting the fall term, n
one thought she had serious problems.''

"Was she the sort of girl who confided in people and, i
so, who would that person be?''

Guilt and regret had Fallon's cheeks flushing yet again
"At one time we were close, or so I thought. But I live i
Denver, some sixty miles from her, and I don't get back a
often as I probably should. And Mom, well, she's not a
good listener.''

Which was truly an understatement. Fallon had never
blamed her mother for marrying Roy Gifford after her
father's death. Her father, Jim McKenzie, had been a
handsome, robust, fun-loving Irishman, well liked by al
who knew him. But he'd been a dreamer, a man who wen
from one low-paying job to the next, dragging his weary
wife and two daughters along from city to city, always cer
tain that one day his ship would come in.

But it hadn't, and Jim had been killed in a head-on col
lision, with no insurance on the car or himself. Unskilled
Jane had limited job choices and they barely got by.

So the following year, when Jane met Roy Gifford at a
Parents Without Partners mixer dance and soon after de
cided to marry him, Fallon had hoped their lives woul
improve. And they had, to some degree, although neither
she nor Laurie had ever truly taken to their stepfather.

"What about her friends?'' Michael asked, drawing he
out of her reverie. He had a feeling that her sister's run
ning away was causing Fallon McKenzie to face a few none
too-pleasant facts.

She shrugged tiredly. "I talked with her best friend, Tina
and all I got out of her was that Laurie seemed unhappy
and told her she planned to leave. No details. I also checked
with her bank and she's withdrawn everything from he
savings account—a whopping hundred and sixteen dol
lars.'' Fallon sighed tiredly. "How long can she last or
that?''

He detected a small tic in the delicate area beneath he
left eye. It was probably because she was exhausted an
worried. He could also hear the self-recrimination in he

voice. "Don't wrap yourself in guilt. You wouldn't be here if you didn't care about your sister. It's often difficult to spot a troubled teenager even if you live with one. Did either your mother or stepfather mention noticing anything different about Laurie recently?"

"I'm not sure what you mean by different."

"Oh, like any sudden weight gain or loss, a disinterest in school, difficulty in sleeping, maybe a new boyfriend. Did she seem withdrawn, argumentative, more emotional? These things can indicate a change in her life, such as drug use or possibly sexual experimentation."

"No, absolutely not." Fallon shook her head adamantly. "My sister's not like that. She wouldn't touch drugs and the only dates she's been on have been in groups. Football games with the crowd, ice skating, that sort of thing."

She was certainly in denial, Michael thought. He wondered what it would take to make her see. "Any teenager in today's world can be tempted, Fallon." Actually, it had always been thus, he wanted to add, but thought better of it.

"You're wrong. Not Laurie. She's sweet, shy, innocent. I... I don't know why she left, but I feel strongly that if we—no, *when* we find her and I talk with her, everything will be all right and she'll want to go back home to the people who love her."

Even after all these years of dealing with runaways, Michael found himself amazed at the simplistic solutions people thought would fix a problem that had mushroomed to one of major proportions by the time a kid ran away. Maybe Fallon just had trouble remembering her own teen years. Or had she never rebelled? "Laurie's younger than you by, what, six or seven years?"

"Eight, actually." Fallon tucked her hair behind one ear, wondering when this day would end and why it couldn't end happily. She wasn't a Pollyanna, believing that she would fly in and find Laurie on the first street corner, as Roy had accused her of being. Yet now, tired, hungry and hurting, she found the task overwhelming.

Michael rose and went behind his desk, found a bottle o.
aspirin in a drawer and handed it to her, noticing she hadn'
eaten the crackers. "Here, this might help."

She smiled her thanks, thinking him very perceptive. Ei
ther that or she really did look as bad as she felt. She
quickly swallowed two pills with the last of her juice, then
looked up at him. "How on earth can I find her? I . .
Please, can you help? I've visited San Diego before, but i
don't know the city well. I don't know where to begin. I'l
pay you."

Shaking his head, Michael sat back down. "I don't ac
cept money to find runaways. That's not how it works. In
order to know where to begin, I need to know more abou
your sister—her habits, her likes and dislikes, her dreams
Those things are the key. Why don't we start with her
childhood, your family life, anything you think might help
us?"

Us. Oddly enough, the fact that this stranger had joined
with her in her seemingly hopeless search lifted her spirits.
So she told him about Jim McKenzie, who'd run out of
dreams and died much too soon, and Jane, who hadn't
been able to cope alone with two young girls. And she ex
plained about Roy, and why her Mom had been attracted
to him, trying to stick to the facts only. And about their
stepbrother who was so perfect, such an overachiever that
both she and Laurie had felt unable to compete.

"It was hard not to like Danny, especially then. He was
four when Roy married Mom—this adorable blond, blue
eyed little boy with a sunny disposition. He was quite nat
urally the apple of his father's eye and soon, Mom's little
darling, as well. She'd had a stillborn boy between Laurie
and me and had hoped for a son."

"And did you take to Danny, too?"

"Yes. I was ten, so there was really no competition be
tween us. Laurie's the one who had the problem with
Danny. *She'd* been the youngest and cutest and suddenly,
she had to share the limelight with a kid who could do no
wrong. So she tried getting attention with one escapade af

ter another to get Mom and Roy to notice her. Unfortunately, she only made them mad."

"You think it was years of jealousy over Danny that caused Laurie to run away?" Michael asked.

Fallon's frown was thoughtful. "I really don't think so. Finally, he's out of the house and not competing with her on a daily basis. He left for the Air Force Academy in mid-August on a scholarship. Why leave now?" She noticed that Michael listened with that same absolute concentration she'd observed during the basketball game. She waited while he digested all she'd told him.

"I have the feeling that you're leaving out a couple of things," Michael finally said.

Perhaps it was her fatigue, or maybe her natural reluctance to reveal any more personal information to a relative stranger, but suddenly, Fallon felt she should know more about this man who'd so far been asking all the questions. She'd seen him with the teens and felt he had their respect, probably hard-won. She'd briefly glimpsed the facilities of Michael's House and come to the conclusion that, on the surface at least, he had a decent operation, here.

And she wasn't too tired to notice that he was enormously attractive and very self-assured.

But it was that very self-assurance that put her off a bit. She'd been up against that sort of confidence in men before, and found the inevitable arrogance behind it difficult to handle. Perhaps Michael wasn't altogether like that, but she needed to learn more about him and this place.

Michael saw the hesitancy on her expressive face and waited. He was nothing if not patient.

"Forgive me if I seem wary, but this is all pretty new to me. I'm admittedly not an expert on teenagers. I'd like to know something about your credentials, about what makes you qualified to work with these kids, before I tell you more about my sister and my family. I feel awkward discussing private matters with you on such short acquaintance without some background on you and your staff—how you're funded, what sort of programs you offer and where the kids go from here."

He nodded, not in the least offended. "You have a valid point. I've got a degree in clinical psychology and—"

"I don't see a certificate on the wall." Pointedly, she glanced around again. "This *is* your office, right?"

He gave her his slow smile. "It's in one of the drawers. I can dig it out, if you like. I find that a number of framed diplomas hanging on the wall puts people off, especially the kids, and doesn't prove much except that you took the courses and graduated. I don't feel I have to prove anything with certificates because this place speaks for itself."

She had yet to decide if that was so. He was almost obsessively low-key, with the discreet sign outside and his diplomas stuck away in drawers. Curious.

"I have on staff a visiting doctor, twenty-four-hour nursing available and access to free legal advice."

"Yes, I met Dr. Ramirez when I arrived and, of course, Opal."

"Right. I have a full-time bookkeeper and Donovan, my right-hand man who's mostly a jack-of-all-trades. We hold classes all day long taught by qualified instructors, some giving lectures, others with hands-on work. We discuss addictions of all kinds, sex education, health care, the basics of job hunting and applications. We cooperate with local schools, with foster homes and GED certification programs. Nearby is a local Alcoholics Anonymous, Alanon and Narcotics Anonymous that hold daily meetings. We conduct large group discussions and smaller, round-table talks where they can bring up any subject and it's all confidential. We're in touch with runaway hotlines across the country and help reunite when that seems appropriate. For the others, we tell them it's a jungle out there and we teach them how to survive."

"How long have you been open?"

"Eight years altogether. Five at this location and three in a rented storefront that we quickly outgrew." He checked his watch and saw that he had time. "Would you like to take a look around? I can give you a quick tour, if you're up to it."

Fallon *was* interested, mostly because Laurie had somehow heard of Michael's House and had come here. She didn't have a lot of time to waste, but it was apparent that she needed help to find her sister in an unfamiliar city, and Michael seemed to be the only game in town. Besides, she didn't want to insult him by refusing to tour the facility he seemed quite proud of. "I'm fine and yes, I'd like that."

With his hand on the small of her back, he guided her down the hallway. "The main house is pretty old, but it's structurally sound. A San Diego businessman needing a tax write-off donated it to us and a crew of volunteers helped renovate it. This whole neighborhood's in the throes of urban renewal, but it goes slowly." Stopping at the winding staircase, he glanced up. "The second floor is where our classrooms are, six of them, plus a small lounge and a larger multipurpose meeting room. We have four bedrooms and baths on the third floor, one that I use occasionally. The others are reserved for special guests or to accommodate an overflow."

Fallon turned and suddenly realized that he'd moved and was directly behind her as she stood with her hand on the newel post. Unnerved by his nearness, she stepped to the side, clearing her throat. "How many kids can you handle?"

She smelled a hell of a lot better than he probably did after refereeing in the hot sun, Michael thought. He inhaled her scent before answering. "The two-story building you probably noticed out back was built after we finished remodeling here. It can sleep forty kids, two to a room, with shared baths." He led her into the dining room where two boys and a teenage girl were gathering plates and silverware.

The table was vintage, undoubtedly also donated, but made of solid oak and could easily seat eighteen. "I guess when you have a full house, you have to have two sittings."

"Sometimes even three. Some kids wander in just to eat."

"You don't turn any of them away?"

"Never." He strolled through the archway where the smell of fried onions teased the nostrils and the woman wrapped in a white apron was transferring grilled burgers onto warm buns while ears of corn were cooking in a huge pot on the stove. "Fallon McKenzie, meet Sukey, the best cook this side of the Mississippi."

The slender woman shifted her dark eyes to the newcomer, then back to Michael. "Just *this side* of the Mississippi?" she asked, her smile widening.

Sukey looked to be on the far side of forty and not fighting it, Fallon thought as she greeted the cook. "It smells wonderful."

"Good to meet you, and I hope you'll join us for dinner," Sukey invited.

Michael seconded the motion. "We try to come up with menus teenagers typically are drawn to, but Sukey makes sure she serves healthy things like cereal, fruit and vegetables, too. She can disguise broccoli so that even George Bush would ask for seconds." He knew that afternoon classes would end soon and the hungry mob would be descending, so they left the kitchen.

As they retraced their steps, more questions occurred to Fallon. "I don't imagine any of these kids have much money. Who pays the bills, buys the food and supplies, and pays the teachers?"

He'd been expecting this one. "Mostly donations and a couple of sizable grants from the private sector. We have a large garden on the side lot and an arrangement with several markets to pick up day-old stuff. Part of my job description is fund-raiser. I give speeches at Rotary Clubs, Optimist meetings and various corporations, raising money wherever we can."

"So you're strictly nonprofit?"

"Absolutely."

Fallon had to admit that the man had her even more curious than the operation he ran. "What about you? Do you take a salary?"

She was certainly persistent. He smiled. "Not as such, though I take out some expenses. I am what might be called well connected."

Fallon frowned, realizing she didn't even know his full name. "How's that?"

"My name's Redfield. Michael Redfield." He waited, watching her and knew the moment the information clicked in.

"As in Redfield Boulevard, the street I drove in on from the airport? The last time I was in San Diego, it seems I remember reading that the boulevard was named after some judge or politician. Right?"

"Judge Jonathan Redfield."

So he came from a wealthy family. That intrigued more than it explained. "With all that, you chose to work with runaway kids in the inner city? Why?"

Michael wished he had a dollar for every time he'd been asked that question. He wondered if even Jonathan understood. He surely wasn't going to let this woman he'd just met, attractive and intelligent though she was, look into his heart and discover what made him tick. He gave her a crooked grin and shrugged. "I guess I just like kids."

Uh-hmm. There was something more there, something hiding behind that flash of dimples. "How many kids would you say have been through Michael's House over the past eight years?"

"Hundreds. Well over a thousand. I've lost count."

Fallon paused outside his office, anxious for the answer to her next question. "And what is your success rate, honestly?"

"If you mean how many runaways' lives have we helped to straighten out, I'd say we're hovering around a sixty-percent success rate."

She raised a questioning eyebrow. "That's all? Just sixty percent?"

Irritation flickered across his features, then was gone just as quickly. "That's damn good. Check around if you don't believe me." He walked inside and sat down at his desk. She hadn't a clue, not the smallest idea how good a record that was. He was suddenly annoyed that he'd allowed her to make him defensive. "You came to me for help, remember? I didn't go looking for you, begging you to let me assist you. If you're looking for some facility that has a higher success rate, go to it and good luck." He picked up a file folder and pretended to read it.

She'd certainly hit a nerve, Fallon decided as she followed him in. "Look, I think it's wonderful if you can help sixty out of a hundred kids find their way back. But I honestly don't believe my sister is one of those lost kids. She isn't on drugs or in trouble with the law or whatever. She doesn't need to be in a place like this to straighten out, terrific as it might be. I believe that Laurie feels inferior to Danny, is annoyed at Roy's constant harping and she's probably angry with me for not allowing her to visit me in Denver more frequently. So she ran away to prove a point, to make us sit up and take notice."

Feeling confident of her facts, of her analysis of why Laurie had split, she nevertheless still had to locate her. "Now all I have to do is find her and reassure her, and I'm sure things will once more return to normal." She saw that his eyes had lost some of their welcoming warmth, but she'd come too far to back down. "Will you help me find Laurie or are you too busy?"

Michael rose and walked around the desk until he was standing very close to her. "How do you *know* she isn't on drugs? You told me you haven't seen her in months. Or possibly in trouble with the law? Do you know how many teenagers shoplift, for instance—some in order to eat, but others just for the thrill of it or to get attention? Or how about this? Maybe she's pregnant and too frightened to tell anyone. You admitted you're no longer her confidante. What have her grades been like recently? Maybe she ran because she's flunking out and afraid of Roy, the stepfather who's so strict."

He saw that he had her attention now. "Any or all of those could have her scared and wandering around an unfamiliar city all alone. And you come here, calm and confident, sure that you'll run into her after a quick look

around, then give her a hug, tell her you love her and she'll
return home, happy as a clam. Get real, lady. Face some
facts, even if they're not sugar-coated. You can't help your
sister with your head stuck in the sand.''

Fallon felt a shiver race down her spine, a mixture of
shock and awareness. The sheer maleness of him so close
to her that she could feel his breath warm her cheeks as he
spoke was as unnerving as what he said. She stared up at
him wide-eyed, as he reached for her hand, gliding his
thumb along the sensitive skin of her wrist, causing her
pulse to skitter, his eyes boring into hers.

She couldn't step aside since her back was to his desk.
And she needed to—needed some distance from his pene-
trating gaze, his wrenching words and the underlying tension that was suddenly between them. What on earth was
happening here? This was ridiculous. She'd come here to
find her sister, not find an overwhelming attraction to a
man who thought he knew all the right answers.

Fallon cleared her throat nervously. ''You're right, I
suppose. I really *don't know* if any of those things are so
with Laurie. I just have this gut feeling that—''

''Do you know why most young people get into drinking and drugs and trouble with the law?'' Michael asked,
unwilling to abandon the discussion even though he was
suddenly struggling with an irrational urge to pull her into
his arms, to see if she tasted as good as she smelled. ''Because of low self-esteem. How's Laurie's self-esteem? Does
she have a good self-image?''

His question had Fallon recalling an incident in early
summer when she'd taken Laurie shopping in her store.
Nothing she'd tried on suited her, she'd told Fallon, and
everything made her look too fat or was too frilly or the
wrong color. *She* was the problem, not the clothes, Laurie
had dejectedly told her sister. When Fallon had tried to tell
her that she had a cute figure and was a pretty girl, Laurie
had stood firm, insisting she was too short, bordering on
fat, and almost ugly.

Tugging her hand free of Michael's, Fallon finally managed to step aside. ''I guess maybe Laurie has a fairly

common problem with self-image," she admitted. "Like a lot of teenage girls, she doesn't think she's very attractive."

It had been a mistake to move so close to her, Michael realized belatedly. He could still smell her scent, still see the pulse in her throat throbbing. Was it due to the subject matter or his nearness? He picked up the discarded towel to give his hands something to do as he searched her face. "Did you go through that stage?"

A rather personal question, Fallon thought, but decided to answer anyway. "Naturally. There aren't a lot of confident young girls walking around."

"Nor teenage boys," he answered, turning away. "It's a rough time of life for all of us." He swung back. "Amazing that we survive it, don't you think?"

A knock at the door had them both looking up to find Opal with her hand on the knob. "Michael, Sergeant Damien's on the phone. Says he's got Daryl down there again. If you won't sign for him, they're going to send him to Juvenile this time."

"Thanks, Opal. Tell him I'll be right there." After the nurse left, he turned to Fallon McKenzie, his look appraising. She'd come a long way and he hated for her trip to be in vain. But if she didn't go about her search the right way, she would never locate her sister. And if she didn't understand runaways, even if she found Laurie, she wouldn't be able to reach her. "I need to grab a quick shower and change clothes, then go down to the police station. Daryl's a runaway, probably picked up for his same old offense, shoplifting. I think it might be a good idea for you to come with me."

Fallon was exhausted, utterly drained, from her restless night, the emotional turmoil and the encounter with Michael. All she wanted was a hot meal and a clean bed. Wearily, she looked up at him. "Tell me why I should go."

"Because I think you'll understand better how things work with runaways if you see for yourself. Afterward, if you still want me to, I'll help you find Laurie." Provided she followed his game plan and not her own agenda.

It would seem he had her over a barrel. If she didn't agree, she would be on her own. The prospect held little appeal. She sat down in the chair. ''I'll wait here while you change.''

Chapter 3

Police headquarters in downtown San Diego at Fourteenth and Broadway was a sleek, modern high-rise that resembled a tall, silver box. As Fallon followed Michael through the lobby and into the elevator to the fourth floor where Juvenile Division was located, she couldn't help noticing that several police officers and plainclothesmen walking by greeted Michael with a wave or a word.

"You must come here a lot," she commented as they turned the corner.

"More often than I like," Michael said as he reached the familiar office. The door was ajar, but he gave a quick knock anyway before walking in. The sergeant was on the phone and acknowledged their presence with a nod.

Fallon took the chair Michael indicated alongside the one he settled his tall frame into. She hadn't ever visited a police station before and found it to be as institutional looking as so many other government buildings, despite this one's newness. Beige seemed to be the color of choice and there was a lingering smell of unwashed bodies and stale smoke that permeated the place. More than that, the ringing phones and people hustling up and down the hallways gave the place an air of increased anxiety on a level that was almost palpable.

She took a moment to study Sergeant Sam Damien, who sat behind his nameplate. Even seated, he seemed quite short, with a balding head, round face and intelligent blue eyes behind glasses framed in black. His voice was extraordinarily deep, seemingly out of place in a man of his small stature. But his handshake, when Michael introduced them after he'd finished his call, was firm and his smile friendly enough.

"Are you working with Michael and his kids, Ms. McKenzie?" the sergeant asked, finding himself sitting up a little taller, sucking in his stomach.

"Not exactly," Fallon answered.

"Her sister's a sixteen-year-old runaway," Michael explained.

Sam's expression softened momentarily, then he became the cop again. "If you want to give us a picture or a description, I can have my guys look around."

"Thank you." Fallon glanced at Michael. "I'd hoped to get some flyers made up tomorrow, using the picture I showed you."

Michael nodded. "Fine, we'll do that." He turned back to Sam. "So, what'd Daryl do this time, as if I can't guess?"

Sam leaned back in his groaning desk chair. "You got it, only it wasn't food he stole this time." He glanced down at his notes. "A pair of fifty-dollar running shoes from one of those sidewalk sales at the mall. Only reason I didn't book him was because I promised you I'd call if he ever showed up here again." The sergeant ran a chubby hand over his bare scalp. "That and the fact that the tennis shoes he had on when we caught him were ragged and full of holes."

Michael ground his teeth. "So, the first time he stole to eat and this time because the pavement still gets pretty hot during sunny days and he was down to bare skin." He swung his eyes to the grimy window, feeling the frustration. "Did you ask him what happened at the foster home we arranged for him to live in?"

"Yeah, but he wouldn't say anything except he didn't like it there." Sam gave a snort. "Like he's got a lot of choices."

"Okay, Sam, what can you offer me? Will you release him to my custody and see if I can get through to him this time?"

Sam straightened to the music of his protesting chair.

"Okay, but I have to tell you, it *is* the last time. If the kid can't learn from you, he'll have to learn from us."

Michael stood. "I appreciate it, Sam. I'll do my best."

"I know you will." He held out a slip of paper. "This is the name and address of the store owner. We talked him out of pressing charges, but someone's got to pay for Daryl's new shoes."

Nodding, Michael pocketed the paper. "I'll take care of him. Is Daryl in Holding?"

"Yeah." Sam picked up the phone. "Wait for him downstairs and I'll get him released." He glanced at the woman with the green eyes and fleetingly wished he were twenty years younger and a foot taller, like Michael. "Nice to meet you. Bring those flyers by and I'll personally see to them."

Fallon smiled. "Thank you, Sergeant."

"Yeah, thanks, Sam." Michael ushered Fallon out into the hallway. At the bank of elevators, he pushed the button.

"Can you tell me a little about Daryl?" Fallon asked. She'd watched and listened and had a million questions.

"He's fourteen. Been on the streets three years. Abandoned by both parents, which probably was all for the good since they were raving alcoholics—mean drunks who used to vent their temper on him. Daryl got into the system and was placed in a foster home, his younger brother into a different one. The brother adjusted. Daryl never has. He runs away repeatedly, lives hand-to-mouth, steals to eat, as you heard."

His words were clipped and angry, but she knew it was directed at the system, the fates or whatever, not at the boy. "How did you run across him?"

The elevator arrived and Michael stepped in after Fallon. "He knew about our place from the other kids, but he didn't show up until he was desperate. He'd caught a cold sleeping in the park and it worked into pneumonia. His clothes were like rags, he was starving and sick. We fixed up his body, but his mind was still troubled. We arranged another stay with a foster family, but he didn't stick it out for long."

On the main floor, they walked to a bench. Fallon turned to him, noticing a muscle in his cheek clench. "I don't understand. Why would he want to go back to life on the street?"

He knew she wasn't asking just about Daryl, but about Laurie as well. "You have to understand the mind of a juvenile runaway. They're filled with terror at being suddenly alone. The feeling of abandonment, of having no one to go to, doesn't go away. They're afraid to trust *anyone.* It isn't as if they choose to be on the street, but often it's the lesser of two evils. There are plenty of foster parents who are sincerely interested in helping kids, but others are in it for the money. All of them have rules, naturally. A kid who's known the freedom of the street, dangerous as that is, has a hard time with rules."

"We talked about this on the phone, that *all* of us have to follow some rules."

Michael drew her down to the bench. "Sure, but try telling that to one of these kids. He walks around neighborhoods where kids live in nice houses with parents who care, who buy them bikes and cars and good food, provide them with TVs and VCRs and fun vacations. He doesn't have any of that, and most of the time, it's due to nothing he personally did. It's the luck of the draw that his parents died, or were drunks or got divorced or just cut out. He's frustrated at the injustice of it. So maybe he steals a car so he can feel like the other kids."

"He steals a car? But that only compounds his many problems."

"Right on. But for that brief time, he's king of the hill behind the wheel of that powerful car. He's just like the kids he envies, for a change. Oh, sure, the fantasy ends, but the feelings don't go away. Then when he gets picked up, his freedom's really gone. Now he's living with even more regrets. And he's filled with impotent rage because he didn't get a fair break in life. When he's released, the cycle repeats."

Fallon leaned her head back against the stucco wall. "What about the kids who have parents at home who gave them material things and love and attention? Or at least tried to."

Michael met her eyes and knew that it was Laurie she was picturing. "One thing you're going to have to come to grips with is that Laurie didn't run away because she didn't like the dinner menu or the color of her bedroom curtains. We don't know what prompted her yet, but I guarantee you, she has a reason. And when we find her, it isn't going to be any easier to remedy her situation than it is Daryl's. Offering a kid love isn't enough."

Before Fallon could refute his analysis, the door alongside the bench opened and a uniformed policeman came out, his hand on the arm of a young boy. Daryl looked younger than fourteen, Fallon thought, with his slim frame and baby face. But his eyes as he gazed up at Michael looked old and world-weary. She'd been expecting defiance, given his history, but was surprised that he looked as if he was having a hard time fighting tears.

"I'm sorry, Michael," Daryl said, his voice cracking with a mixture of puberty and emotion.

Michael put his hand on the boy's shoulder, his touch light but unmistakably reassuring, then he turned to the officer. "You've got some papers for me?"

"Right here."

He signed for Daryl, then led the way out to the blue van.

Fallon insisted on climbing into the back seat so that Daryl could sit alongside Michael up front. He introduced them as he turned on the engine, but she could barely hear the boy's mumbled "Hi." She couldn't blame him for not feeling chatty.

If even some of what Michael had told her was true, the kid was frustrated and embarrassed. Fourteen. Good God, at that age, he should be starting high school, worrying about homework, trying out for football. He should be joking and laughing instead of hanging his head low. He should be tanned and healthy instead of thin and pale. He looked in desperate need of love and affection.

She turned to gaze out the window at the dark streets, feeling emotions clogging her throat. What kind of world were they living in where boys like this one had to steal to eat and have a decent pair of shoes, or where girls like Laurie preferred living on the streets to the sort of home Fallon had thought was not perfect but far from terrible?

For the first time since she'd gotten her mother's frantic phone call, Fallon began to wonder if perhaps something awful had happened to Laurie to make her leave.

They rode in silence the short distance back to Michael's House. The van wasn't new and Fallon wondered if, given the surrounding neighborhood, Michael deliberately used an older vehicle that was less apt to be stolen or stripped. Or perhaps there wasn't enough in the way of donations to pay for a new van.

Michael stopped in front of the quiet house, shut off the motor and turned to Daryl. "I signed for you. That means I'm responsible for you. I want your promise that you won't make me regret that decision."

After a moment, Daryl raised his head. "What do I have to do?"

"You have to go in with me, get cleaned up, eat something and take a room assignment. You have to enroll in school *tomorrow* and no cutting classes. You have to follow our rules."

Daryl thought that over for a long moment. "You going to send me to another foster home?"

"Before I answer, I want to know why you left the last one."

Daryl took even longer answering this one. "The woman was okay most of the time, but the man yelled all the time, even at his own kids. He had a lawn service he'd started and he made all of us work cutting grass, after school and all day Saturday, until dark. I told him I had these allergies where my eyes almost swelled shut and my nose ran all the time. He told me to stop being a baby and do my share or he'd call and report me. I cut out of there before he could."

"If he'd reported you, you could have told your story. Well, never mind now. These foster parents, they didn't hurt you physically, did they?"

"No. They just weren't for me."

What would be for him? Michael wondered. Like himself, Daryl had lived in half a dozen foster homes without feeling *at* home. That thought made his decision for him. "I'm going to let you stay with us, but you've got to promise me—no running and no more stealing. You study hard and keep your nose clean." Then, because he saw the quick relief on Daryl's face, he again touched his shoulder. "Will you do it? Will you hold up your end and not let me down?"

Daryl blinked rapidly, his eyes downcast. "Yeah, okay."

Michael swung around and saw that Fallon had been watching them with avid interest. "Wait here. I'll be right back."

"I should go." She pointed to the Mustang parked ahead of the van. "That's my rental. I need to check into a hotel or a motel. It's getting late and—"

"We have to talk," Michael insisted. "And you need to eat."

Fallon brushed her hair back from her face. "I'm too tired to eat, honestly."

Michael opened his door. "You're going to eat if I have to spoon-feed you." He saw temper move into her eyes and softened his tone. "You're running on empty, Fallon. You need to refuel. The body, even one as well made as yours, wasn't intended to operate on sheer determination. Besides, I missed dinner, too."

He turned toward her and held out his hand. "Give me your keys. I don't want to leave your car there on the street with your bag and all in it."

"But I..."

Impatience whipped through him. "It's only a little after seven. Will you please relax? I'll be back in a couple of minutes." He stepped out of the van.

Daryl opened his door, then glanced back at Fallon, a small smile hovering around his mouth. "He's real bossy, but he's a helluva guy." He jumped out and followed Michael up the steps.

Fallon stared after them, trying to decide whether she was terribly annoyed at Michael's take-charge manner or terribly impressed at the way he'd handled the boy. She sat watching the two figures, noticing them pause before opening the door, talking quietly on the shadowy porch. Then she saw something that had her peering more closely out the window. Michael opened his arms and Daryl closed the gap between them. As if it were the most natural thing in the world, the tall man hugged the young boy.

They went inside then, and Fallon moved up to the seat Daryl had vacated. She felt as if she'd intruded on a private moment, but she was glad she had, for she suddenly realized something important: Michael cared.

Despite his bossy ways, he honestly cared for these kids, some who very likely had no one else to care about them. She hadn't been prepared for that, thinking that he was probably a stern taskmaster in order to win the respect of these streetwise kids. And he was, but he was much more. She also hadn't been prepared for the way what she'd just witnessed had shifted her opinion of Michael Redfield.

As Daryl had told her, he was a hell of a guy.

Fallon heard her stomach growl in anticipation as the waitress wearing the name tag "Dolly" placed a large plate containing a fat cheeseburger and a huge serving of fries in front of her. Dolly put the exact same meal in front of Michael, seated on the red faux-leather booth across from her, before setting down two glasses of ice-cold milk.

"Anything else I can get you?" Dolly asked, her smile aimed at Michael.

"Thanks, Dolly. I think this is just what the doctor ordered." He gave her a friendly wink.

Fallon shook her head. "No doctor on earth would order this meal. I can hear my arteries screaming already." But she picked up the enormous burger with both hands, all but salivating at the delicious aroma of onions.

"You can eat tofu and carrot sticks tomorrow," Michael said. He'd ordered for them, thinking she needed something substantial and forbidden. "Besides, milk is healthy, isn't it?"

"*Skim* milk is. This glass is loaded with butterfat."

Michael chewed appreciatively, then swallowed. "Maybe this stuff will kill you, but I don't want to die eating wheat germ."

They ate in silence for several minutes in the last booth of the small neighborhood sandwich shop. Michael knew both waitresses and the owner, Roberto, who donated day-old bread and buns to his place regularly. He usually took his meals at the house since he spent so much time there, but he'd wanted to get Fallon away from there tonight, wanted to hear if she'd learned anything on her trip to the police station. Privacy was often hard to come by at Michael's House.

He decided to let her bring up the subject, fairly certain that she would. He didn't have to wait long.

Fallon couldn't believe that she would eat three-quarters of the huge burger practically before taking a deep breath. She took a sip of her milk, studying Michael as he ate with gusto.

Unruly was the word for his hair, which gave him that untamed look. Adding to that impression was the set of his mouth and the determination in his dazzling blue eyes. She had the feeling that Michael Redfield was a man who called the shots in everything he did.

"You were pretty terrific with Daryl," she began, picking at her fries now that the main thrust of her hunger was appeased.

Michael shrugged off her compliment. "It's not readily apparent, but that kid's got potential. The last time he was with us, he expressed some interest in art, so I took him up to one of the vacant rooms on the third floor where I keep some paints and a couple of canvases."

She remembered the seascape in his office. "Did you do the one on the wall behind your desk?"

"Yeah, I doodle around with it. Frees my mind, you know. So I let him go to town. You should see the painting he did. A mountain lion standing on a rocky crevice, very detailed, very beautiful. He didn't copy it from a picture, either. Daryl told me that once, a while back, he'd been taken camping by the foster family of the moment and they'd spotted a mountain lion. He liked the 'reined-in power' of the animal. His words, not mine."

Fallon set aside her plate and leaned back, sure she couldn't swallow another mouthful. "So you bailed him out tonight because you feel he has potential as an artist?"

Michael finished munching on his fries and concentrated on wiping his fingers as he answered her. "Not exactly, although that's possible. I think he's got potential as a person. He's not really a thief but someone who's had a rough go. Not to excuse the theft, but to understand the boy's motive. Who among us would starve rather than steal half a dozen apples—his last run-in with the law. I think Daryl's basically a good kid." He smiled at her. "And, as I said earlier, I like kids."

Thoughtfully, Fallon planted her arms on the table and leaned forward, her eyes on his. "I think there's more. I think you relate to that abandoned boy with such empathy because of something else." She'd been thinking about this since they'd pulled away from the house, wondering what made Michael so sensitive to a young boy's feelings—enough to know he needed a hug more than a hot shower. She couldn't reconcile his compassion with the fact that he'd grown up privileged.

Of course, she knew that many wealthy people were philanthropists and helped those less fortunate in a variety of ways. But Michael didn't just contribute money, from what she'd seen. He worked with these kids, went fund-raising for them, ate with them and shared a room in the house with them. He made deals with the police on their behalf and offered medical assistance.

She believed that he cared, but she also suspected there was more to him than she'd so far been able to figure out.

She hesitated, knowing the question she wanted to ask was quite personal, yet she decided to plunge in anyhow, realizing that he would have done the same. "Were you adopted, Michael?"

She saw a flicker in his eyes—something that came and went so quickly, she wasn't sure if she'd imagined it. "No. My mother and father both loved me very much. Don't make a drama out of my defense of Daryl. It happens to be my job." Turning, he signaled the waitress for the check.

That was the second time Fallon felt she'd hit a nerve with him. She couldn't have been mistaken twice. "Let me pay my share," she said, reaching for her purse as Michael gave the waitress several bills.

"Nope. Tonight, I pay. Tomorrow, you can buy my dinner." He slid out of the booth.

"I'm not going to be around tomorrow. I've got to get busy and find Laurie." She followed him outside to the van.

He held open her door. "Get in. We have an errand to run."

Fallon sighed wearily. "Look, I've gone to the station with you and I've eaten like you ordered me to. Enough's enough. I'm exhausted and I . . ."

He climbed behind the wheel, started up and swung out into traffic. "This won't take long and I promise you it will be worth your time."

She had to call an end to this soon, Fallon decided as she fastened her seat belt. The man ordered her around like one of his runaways and overrode her every objection. She needed his help in finding Laurie, but she'd had it with his commanding manner. They'd only just met a few hours ago and she felt as if he would take over her life if she let him.

Perhaps if she hadn't lived with a domineering stepfather or been engaged to a man like Jeff Raynor who wanted to make every decision for her, she might not have felt quite so reluctant to go along with Michael's many whims. She realized that he had numerous connections she could use in her search and that he knew the city inside and out. Still, just a few hours with him, and she was beginning to get that smothered feeling. Maybe if—

The van jerked to a stop at the edge of a large park. Becoming aware of her surroundings, Fallon sat up straighter and noticed a picnic area with overhead lights, a lot of shrubbery, a running path, walkways, and a play area with swings, slides and teeter-totters. She also noticed more than a dozen young people walking or sitting on the grass, or playing catch. "Where are we?" she asked.

Michael unstrapped himself and moved to the back of the van where several boxes were stacked. "Balboa Park. I come here several evenings a week. It's a gathering place for teenagers. Not all of them are runaways or street people, but a majority are." He shoved open the sliding van door. "I pass out donated food, blankets, sometimes jackets and socks, bandages, something to drink—whatever usable donations people give us. Everything gets picked up." He stepped out, then grabbed two of the boxes. "It won't take me long. You can wait here or walk around, if you like. Maybe you'll spot your sister."

That prompted her like nothing else would have. Trailing slowly along, she watched Michael leave a box on a picnic table, removing the lid. Several kids wandered over right away, others hung back, eyeing both of them suspiciously. Carefully, she scanned the faces, looking for a familiar oval face and long chestnut hair.

Michael tossed a pile of blankets on a stone ledge, then went back for a case of drinks. Fallon noticed two teenagers in an intimate embrace on the grass, oblivious to everyone around them. Three others sat smoking on the grass, their eyes in the light of the streetlamps looking jaded and more suspicious than Daryl's had been. One girl had a gash on her forehead covered with dried blood. Fallon wanted to go to her, but the tall, skinny boy with his arm around her waist wore an open leather vest and a challenging expression that had her turning away.

She strolled on, searching, but Laurie wasn't among the lost and lonely faces that stared back at her, some in defiance, others with empty eyes. She counted more than twenty kids before she turned and started back. Of everything she'd seen and done today, this was the worst. Looking around, she spotted Michael by a burbling water fountain talking with a very young, very pregnant girl. Feeling thoroughly helpless, Fallon climbed back in the van.

A few minutes passed before Michael got behind the wheel and glanced over at her. "There weren't too many out tonight. Some evenings, there are twice as many." He saw the astonishment on her face before anger leaped into her green eyes.

"It isn't fair, all those kids out there, alone and unsupervised. A couple of them didn't look to be more than twelve or thirteen. Where are the adults—someone to supervise them, someone waiting for them to come home?"

Michael had hoped this visit would help her understand and question. He struggled with a sense of weariness as he tried to explain. "I suppose some of those kids left decent homes for whatever reason, like Laurie, but the others, more often than not, have no one. They have only each other."

Fallon sensed his frustration at life's inequities and shared it. "And they have you."

He started the van. "Yeah, but some are too far gone to accept help, from me or anyone else. Some are into drugs, prostitution, con games. I hate that, but it's a fact. It's the others I work to bring around. The ones who can still be saved. Like Daryl and Wendy over there." He motioned toward the pregnant girl curled up on one of the blankets he'd left. "Her baby's due soon. I think I've got her talked into stopping by tomorrow and having Paul check her over."

Again, Fallon felt a rush of anger. "She should be in prenatal care. And where's the baby's father?"

"She doesn't know or care. She was raped." Michael started the van and pulled away, very aware of Fallon's stunned eyes on his face.

The ride back was silent and strained. He'd given her a great deal to think about, and wondered as he glimpsed her pallor if he'd overdone it. The trouble was that Fallon McKenzie had arrived here from her safe suburban world with no idea of what she would face in trying to locate her sister. There'd been no way to pretty it up or even to tell her and have her believe. So he'd shown her instead.

And shocked the hell out of her.

He pulled the van into the side drive close to the house and got out, walking around to help her down. She was pale as a ghost as he went with her toward the back. "Are you all right?"

"I'm not sure I'll ever be all right again." She felt battered, bruised, disturbed. She was angry, upset and frightened. Not for herself, but for the kids out there. And for her sister, wherever she was. "I can't remember ever feeling so overwhelmed, so hopeless. How do you stand it?"

Michael paused at the back door. "The only way I can stand it is to know that I can make a difference. Not for everyone, but in some of their lives. We take it one day at a time. If we can help one kid get back on the right path, we've accomplished something. If not today, then tomorrow."

Fallon looked up at him and studied his strong features in a patch of moonlight. "I know you believe in your work, and I've seen that you're very good with kids. But I honestly don't feel that Laurie's like any of the teenagers I've seen—not here or in the park, thank God. She's *not* alone and had no need to run away and live on the streets. She—"

"You're doing it again." Her eyes were a deep emerald green in the silvery light. She was very beautiful, and very stubborn. "You're lying to yourself. You want to believe that your sister left on a whim, a small act of defiance because her parents changed her curfew or wouldn't let her go to that private school.''

"You don't *know* that that isn't exactly what happened.'' She was growing angry again at his stubborn insistence. Her mother hadn't been able to come up with a reason, either. How could Michael know when he'd never met Laurie, or her folks, or seen the way they live.

"Let me finish. If that had been the case, if she'd left over a minor disagreement, she wouldn't have stayed away more than a day or so. She wouldn't have asked around and had the phone number of my house for runaways in her pocket. She'd have gone instead to a girlfriend's home or taken a bus to visit you and poured out her story and been back home, safely tucked in her own bed by now.''

He shook his head, placing his hands on her arms to emphasize his point. "Laurie's been gone three weeks. She ran away for a damn good reason and frankly, I don't think she intends to go back unless that reason is removed.''

Fallon shook off his hands and turned away. "You don't know that for certain. You're guessing, conjecturing, just like me.''

"You're right. But I've got eight years of experience working with runaways. I've yet to come across a kid who left a loving, comfortable home for a frivolous reason or over a minor squabble, and stayed away for weeks.'' There was a question he'd been wanting to ask her, but he hesitated. She was tired, vulnerable and scared. Yet there seemed no point in waiting, for she had to face some hard facts soon. "Have you thought of this? Is it possible that your stepfather might have come on to her?''

"Good God, no!'' Instead of feeling angry, Fallon almost laughed. Was she so exhausted that she was becoming giddy? she wondered. "Roy's the most sexless man I've ever known. I don't believe Madonna in the nude strolling into the room would affect him. I've often wondered how my mother could stand him touching her.'' Suddenly appalled at all she'd revealed, Fallon shot a look skyward, groaning inwardly. "I can't believe I just told you all that.''

"Is that how you really feel about Roy?''

She didn't hesitate. "Yes."

"Then, why *not* say it? Besides, your opinion's safe with me. But I don't think too many men can be labeled sexless, even if you might find him so."

Fallon shook her head. "This one is. Roy's tall and skinny with half a dozen strands of hair he carefully combs over his balding head. He has pale blue eyes, thick glasses and no discernible chin. He's a nerd, a bean counter at the IRS, about as interesting as last week's newspaper. But more importantly, it's his manner, his attitude, his idiosyncrasies, his maddening self-righteousness that make him so unappealing. No, Laurie wouldn't have permitted any touchy-feely stuff. If Roy had so much as looked at her in a suggestive way, she'd have phoned me or told Mom."

Michael wasn't nearly as convinced as she. Fallon hadn't lived in her stepfather's house since she was eighteen. Many a young girl had been molested and the mother had been unaware or chose to not make waves by looking the other way. However, he could see that Fallon wasn't able to even imagine that at the moment. "It's late. We can take this up again tomorrow."

Fallon checked her watch. Nearly eleven. "I've got to find a motel. Can you direct me to one nearby?" Apparently he'd decided he would help her begin the search tomorrow.

"I have a better idea. There's a room with its own bath available up on the third floor. I've already put your car in the garage. I can get your bag and take it up. The room's clean and comfortable, I assure you. It's too late to go looking for a place tonight. Tomorrow, if you want to make a change, you can."

He was taking charge again. Why was she constantly surrounded by men who wanted to take over? Fallon wondered wearily. However, for tonight, she was just too beat to argue with him. "All right, if you're sure."

"Absolutely. Go inside. I'll get your bag."

A dim light burning over the stove cast shadows in the spotless kitchen. The rec room was empty and a sign was propped on the entryway desk. It read: In Case Of Emergency, Come Get Opal In Room 12.

Michael joined her at the foot of the stairs and led the way up. "I didn't know you had staff staying over," Fallon said.

"Some do. Opal has no family, so we built her a sort of minisuite on the ground floor of the dorm. Then there's Donovan, our handyman. He's retired but sometimes stays over when he doesn't feel like driving home. Brian, our bookkeeper, lives in the Hillcrest area not far from here, and so does Sukey who goes home to her cat most nights. Ramona does the laundry and cleaning and she has a little house in Chula Vista. Her husband's dead, but she's got several kids and grandkids. I've told them all they're welcome to stay any night they want, provided we have empty beds, and they can eat here, as well. Every one of them works hard." On the third floor, he paused outside the second door.

He was close, so close that Fallon had to tilt her head back to look into his eyes. "You're very generous."

"Just practical. Things run more smoothly because everyone's treated like family. It's not just a job for anyone. They're all committed to the kids or they don't last." He swung open the door and went inside to switch on the bedside lamp.

The first thing she noticed was that there were cabbage roses on the wallpaper. "I didn't figure you to be the floral type."

Michael set down her bag and glanced at the wall. "My mother loved cabbage roses. I thought it might make our female guests feel at home." He shrugged, embarrassed. "There're stripes in the boys' rooms. Wallpaper's easier to keep clean than painted walls."

Sheer white curtains hung at the window and, although the twin beds and chest of drawers were an odd lot, she could see that he'd made every effort to make the room welcoming. "Very homey. I like it."

"As I mentioned, the rooms up here are usually for unexpected guests and any overflow. I thought you might like this one especially. It's where Laurie slept when she was with us. We were really full up that night. I put her and her friend up here.''

Fallon swallowed hard as she walked over and ran a hand along the yellow chenille spread. *Oh, Laurie, where are you?*

Michael pulled out the drawer of the nightstand and removed something. He held it in his hand as she turned to him. ''She left this behind.''

''Oh,'' Fallon gasped. It was a pink-skirted ballerina that danced when you wound it up from the bottom of the dome. ''Our father, our *real* father, gave that to Laurie before he died. He . . . he used to call her his little princess.'' She swallowed down a sob that caught in her throat. ''I can't believe she left it behind.''

He watched her struggle with her emotions and wanted to take her in his arms and soothe away her tension. But she held her shoulders erect and her spine straight. ''Ramona found it on the nightstand tucked behind the lamp. Laurie and Emma left when it was still dark out that morning. She probably didn't see it in her rush to leave before anyone was awake to question her.''

Fallon took it from him and held it to her, closing her eyes for a long moment. Finally, she set it down on the nightstand and brushed away a stray tear. ''I'm sorry. It's . . . it's been a long day.''

''You don't have to be tough for me, Fallon. You may not think so, but I know what you're going through.''

She blinked back more tears, lifting her eyes to the ceiling, fighting for the self-control she valued so dearly. He probably did know, as empathetic as he was. And he'd dealt with relatives of runaways for eight years, so he'd undoubtedly seen it all. ''If what you said earlier is true—that love isn't enough—then what can I give Laurie?''

She got to him with that simple, heartfelt question. He turned her around to face him. ''Let's find her first and take it from there, okay?''

''Then you will help me?'' She needed to hear him say it out loud.

Hadn't he known he would from the moment he'd seen her standing by the basketball court, her hair being rearranged by the breeze, her green eyes studying him intently? "Yes," he answered softly, and heard her audible sigh of relief. "Men have a hard time saying no to you, I imagine."

"I can't honestly say I've noticed that." Despite the lateness of the hour and the emotional roller coaster she'd been on for days, she was suddenly very aware of his nearness, the solid strength in the hands that gripped her arms, the masculine scent of him tangling her senses.

Later, Michael was to remember that he hadn't intended to touch her, although he'd wanted to. But she'd looked so lost and scared that the next thing he knew, she was in his arms and he was holding her, comforting her. She seemed a little stunned, a little slow to react. Then her arms encircled him, her touch tentative. He eased her fractionally closer, felt her cheek press into his chest. She felt soft, feminine, fragile. He bent his head slightly and inhaled the delicious scent of her hair.

Fallon felt Michael's heart beating beneath her ear, strong and steady. She hadn't thought she needed simple human contact until a moment or two ago. She drew in a deep breath, then let it out, feeling some of the tension flow from her. It seemed as if Michael, in agreeing to help her search, was taking a portion of the burden from her shoulders, lightening her load. She closed her eyes in gratitude, moving infinitesimally closer.

He liked the way they fit together, the way her breasts felt against his chest, the way her slender form pressed into him so unobtrusively. She was thinking of comfort, not sensuality, he was certain. He, on the other hand, had a little trouble separating the two. He tightened his hold on her and felt his arms tremble slightly.

When was the last time a woman had caused him to tremble? he wondered.

Finally, Fallon eased back and looked up at him, surprisingly unembarrassed. She saw him smile, the dimples deepening, and she smiled back. "Thank you," she whispered.

Her response surprised him. No one had ever thanked him for a hug before. Reluctantly, he stepped back. "I'll be in the room across the hall. The key's in the door, so lock up." Hand on the knob, he turned back. "Sleep well."

"You, too, Michael." After he left, she closed the door and turned the key. She felt drained, yet somehow better than when she'd come into the room. She walked to the bed and sat down, her eyes moving to the ballerina. Carefully, she wound it up and watched the figure spin and dance.

"We're going to find you, honey," she whispered into the quiet room. "I promise you."

Chapter 4

Fallon was an early riser. By five, she was up and dressed, down in the kitchen making coffee. She wasn't sure what time Sukey usually arrived. She hoped the friendly cook wouldn't mind, but she badly needed her morning coffee.

In Denver, the newspaper was delivered early and Fallon loved to begin her day with coffee and the headlines. The first cup got her juices flowing while she cast a critical eye on the store's ads featuring some of her buys. It was her habit to take another cup into the bathroom while she showered and dressed. Oddly, the second cup calmed her, although everyone she knew argued that caffeine wouldn't allow that.

The last spurt dripped into the pot. Fallon found a mug in the cupboard and poured. Strolling into the dining room, she sat down at the big, empty table and sipped. Her thoughts were skittering every which way, another reason she'd gotten up early. She'd fallen asleep from sheer exhaustion last night right after her shower, yet her sleep had been restive rather than restful.

She wondered how things were going back in Denver. Craig Miller, the manager over all the buyers, had been polite and seemingly understanding when she'd called to request more time off. But he was new on the job and she didn't know him well. She had no idea how to gauge his tolerance level. She certainly didn't want to lose her job, and hoped she could keep her absence within the bounds of reason. Barring that, she hoped Craig would understand how important it was for her to find Laurie.

Taking the last swallow, Fallon rose to pour another cup. She expected that Michael would awaken ready to help her begin searching. She'd brought a good picture of Laurie from home. Probably they should go to a print shop first, have flyers made up using the photo and distribute them around to places like that park where teens gathered, and also drop some off with the sergeant.

Fallon glanced up at the wall clock, thinking she should phone her mother and update her. Too early, of course. Besides, she would rather call when she knew Roy had already left for work. Her mother always seemed repressed when he was around. For the umpteenth time, she wondered how Jane Gifford could live like that. Even the financial stability she'd so desperately craved after Dad's death wouldn't be worth it, in Fallon's estimation. It was a trade-off, she supposed, with her mother getting the rough end of the bargain.

She stood at the window, looking out at the dormitory-style building next door. She could see signs of movement, blinds opening, a shade rising. Naturally, she had no idea of the usual daily routine at Michael's House. She guessed that the kids would have breakfast, then the instructors would arrive and classes would begin on the second floor. It was a big operation, when filled to capacity. And over it all presided Michael Redfield.

She barely tasted the coffee she drank as thoughts of Michael flooded her mind. She pictured him refereeing the basketball game, offering food and blankets and hope to the kids in the park, talking with compassionate authority to Daryl in the van and then hugging him on the porch.

And hugging her in the room.

The embrace hadn't been sexual, although she would have to be dead not to be aware of him as a man. It had been brief and undemanding. But when she'd turned off the light and snuggled down on the pillow, she'd closed her eyes and felt his arms still around her, still comforting her.

Silly, Fallon told herself as she drained her cup. He wasn't interested in her any more than she was in him. Michael had his hands full with his young guests and their many problems. And she had a few worries of her own, with a sister missing, a mother anxious and a stepfather highly annoyed at all three of them.

She turned back to the counter and was pouring her third cup when she heard a sound behind her.

"I see you share my addiction," Michael said as he walked over.

"Good morning." Fallon glanced over her shoulder. He was wearing scruffy running shoes, black jeans and a black knit shirt that made his hair look even blonder. His eyes were like blue pools in his tanned face. She felt her mouth go dry and found herself annoyed at her reaction to him.

Reaching into the cupboard, Michael grabbed a mug and held it out as he checked the time. "Sukey's not here yet?"

"I haven't seen her."

Before he took the first sip, he angled his head and looked her over from head to foot. He knew she hadn't had much sleep, yet she looked like something a man locked away for years might dream up. Her skin was the shade of a fresh peach with that terrific hair curving around her face. Her huge green eyes were cool, measuring. He gulped the hot liquid and nearly scalded his tongue.

She was wearing another silk blouse, this time with a skirt, and heels. Despite the fact that he thought her legs were sensational, she was dressed all wrong. "Did you plan on looking for your sister today?"

"I'd hoped we could start as soon as you're ready."

He put on a frown. "Don't you own anything, you know, casual? I mean, that's a great outfit, but we're going to be doing a lot of walking, probably not in the best parts of town. You look like you're dressed for high tea at the Del Coronado, not strolling the streets of the inner city.''

She glanced down, trying to see herself through his eyes, and laughed.

''What?''

''That's pretty funny, considering that I'm the head buyer for one of Denver's largest department stores. Casual clothes for women, that is.''

''So, that's it, then? This is as casual as you get?''

He looked so taken aback, she almost laughed again. ''I have some jeans in my bag. And a cotton shirt. Would that be better?''

''Lots. And shoes. Do you own a pair of sneakers?''

''Yes.'' She set her cup down and placed her hands on her hips in mock challenge, trying to keep the annoyance out of her voice. ''Anything else?''

Michael stepped closer. ''Are those earrings real gold? And that chain you're wearing?''

Automatically, her hand went to touch the chain. ''Yes, why?''

''It'd be better if you left them locked in your room.'' He saw her irritation and let out a whoosh of air. ''Look, I know this is all new to you. But we're going to be rubbing elbows with some questionable people. I don't want to get into a wrestling match with some punk with a knife while I'm trying to defend your jewelry.''

Fallon's expression sobered. ''It's that bad an area?''

''It's no suburban paradise like you're used to.'' Michael poured himself more coffee.

His cocky, know-it-all manner rubbed her the wrong way. ''How do you know what I'm used to?''

Mug in hand, he stepped closer until he was right in front of her. ''Tell me I'm wrong and I'll apologize.''

Her eyes stared into his for a long moment. She wasn't about to let him intimidate her. She needed him, but not that badly. And his habit of moving into her space was getting on her nerves. She stepped aside. ''I don't imagine you apologize readily or often.''

His smile was as arrogant as his words. "Only when I'm wrong, and that's not often."

The back door swung open just then and Sukey came bustling in, muttering to herself. "Cops in this town got nothing better to do than to hound taxpaying citizens." Tossing down her purse, she grabbed her apron from a hook on the wall and began wrapping it around herself. "All kinds of criminals out there, but do they go after them? No, sir. They hide behind hedges and zoom out scaring poor widow ladies half to death."

Michael's smile warmed. "Did you get another speeding ticket, Sukey?"

The tall woman fumbled with the apron ties. "That cop just didn't have his quota of tickets for the week passed out, that's all. I was going three, maybe four, miles over the speed limit and he comes racing after me, sirens blazing like I'm some sort of bank robber or something."

Winking at Fallon, Michael set his cup in the sink. "How many miles over was that again?"

"Five. Six, tops. Made me late was what he did." She opened the refrigerator and took out a large package of bagels, then began slicing them to toast.

"Has this happened before?" Fallon dared to ask.

"Every few weeks, right, Sukey?" Michael teased. "Around here, we call her Old Lead Foot."

Sukey swatted her dish towel at him. "Who you calling old?"

A sound from behind them had all three turning toward the back door. Through the screen, they could see a young woman wearing an open raincoat, clutching her abdomen nearly bent in half.

"Help me, someone, please." The voice was weak, pitiful.

Michael was the first to respond, rushing to open the door. "Wendy!" He caught her just as her legs gave out and she cried out in pain. "My baby!"

Fallon recognized the pregnant young girl he'd been talking to in the park last evening.

"It's all right, Wendy," Michael told her. "I've got you."

"Bring her in on the couch, Michael," Sukey said, holding the door open.

He glanced down at the porch floor and shook his head. "I don't think we have time, Sukey. Her water's broken. I'm going to take her to the hospital. Call Paul and tell him we're going in."

Wendy moaned. "Am I going to lose my baby?"

"You did the right thing coming here, Wendy," Michael assured her. "We're going to get you the help you need." He managed to get a firmer grip on her and started down the steps.

Fallon realized he'd given her an answer without directly answering her question. "Do you want me to go with you?" she asked from the doorway as Sukey hurried to the phone.

"No need," he called back over his shoulder. "Wait for me and we'll go as soon as I get back."

From the porch, Fallon watched him help the frightened girl lie down on the bench seat, then climb behind the wheel. The van backed out quickly. She went inside just as Sukey hung up the phone. "Well, quite an exciting morning around here."

"Not that unusual," Sukey answered, setting out several pitchers of juice, then reaching for a carton of paper cups. "You'd be surprised how often Michael has to make a hospital run with one thing or another."

Fallon heard voices, doors opening and slamming, a couple of shouts and the sound of feet on the porch. The kids were arriving for breakfast. "Can I help you?" she offered.

"Sure. There's margarine and cream cheese in the fridge to go with the bagels. I'll set out the fruit bowl."

Fallon had so many questions she would like answers to, about Michael and his operation. She wondered how talkative Sukey was. "That was Dr. Ramirez that you called?"

"Yes, ma'am. Those two been friends forever and a day."

Fallon set the table, then lined up the large boxes of cereal on the sideboard along with pitchers of milk. "They grew up together here in California?"

"They been pals since their teens, I know." Sukey moved to the table as the kids streamed in and noisily pulled out chairs. "Hats off at the table, guys," she instructed. "And no smoking in here. Josh, put that out right now."

The boy shot her a look, but he went out back and threw away his cigarette.

Sukey spotted the newcomer. "Daryl," she said, touching his shoulder lightly, "good to have you back with us."

Fallon saw the boy give her just a hint of a smile, then look up to catch her eye. She smiled at him, but he dropped his gaze to his plate. Poor kid, always having to adjust, she thought. But he looked better this morning with clean clothes and his hair washed.

Elbows akimbo, Sukey surveyed the table. "Your eye any better, Lisa?" she asked a dark-haired girl. "I don't think so. Better have Opal take a look." She scanned each face in turn. "Where's Roxie this morning?"

"She's not feeling good," a short blonde answered. "Opal said she should stay in bed until Dr. Paul comes this afternoon."

"I'll make another pot of coffee," Fallon offered. She had to put her curiosity on hold as Sukey saw to her young guests. Sukey apparently was much more than the cook, for she had a word or comment for every one of them, Fallon noticed.

It wasn't the usual gathering. Teenagers were typically loud, somewhat rowdy, chattering in between bursts of laughter. These kids were much quieter, almost subdued, some hardly saying a word. They had more than breakfast on their minds.

Opal arrived and passed out vitamin pills. Fallon noticed that several kids got other medication as well, but she had no idea what. One youngster who couldn't seem to stop coughing was taken aside for additional medicine. Nearly all of them drank coffee, although personally, Fallon thought several looked quite young. And all but two of the kids went out back to light up afterward.

A man who looked to be in his sixties with a gray beard arrived and was introduced to her as Nolan, one of the instructors. He had a friendly, open manner and joined the kids outside, announcing that the round-table discussion would be starting in the assembly room upstairs in ten minutes.

Helping Sukey clean up the kitchen, Fallon couldn't help throwing out an observation. "It doesn't seem as if the Surgeon General's warning has had an impact on these kids. They all smoke like little chimneys."

Sukey was bent low, loading the dishwasher. "They got to have some outlet, I guess. Smoking cigarettes isn't good, but it's better than smoking pot."

Fallon swiveled around. "Pot? They smoke pot?"

"Not no more they don't, but yeah, sure, some of them did. And other drugs, too. But here, they have to stay clean and sober. That's the main rule and we make 'em stick to it. They have to take regular urine tests. Caffeine and tobacco is their substitute. Legal drugs, I call them. Opal and Dr. Paul try their best to wean them from those, too. But these kids, they got some big problems if they been on the street a long while, and even before. I suppose they need a crutch, like most of us." She straightened and closed the dishwasher. "But, if they stick around here long enough, we get 'em good and healthy."

Fallon reached for a twist tie for the trash bag, wondering if Laurie had encountered any drug dealers. "I'll bet you do."

"Ain't for lack of trying if we don't." Sukey poured herself a cup of coffee before starting on the luncheon menu. "I hear your sister's out there somewhere."

Fallon nodded. "I sure wish I knew where. Do you remember seeing Laurie here?"

"Sort of. Michael described her to me. Looks a lot like you. She ate supper with us that one time. We had a real bad rainstorm that night. She didn't have much of an appetite, as I recall, and she was real shy. Hardly said a word to anyone.''

Gazing out the window, Fallon felt a shiver take her. ''It's such a big city out there. It has to be very frightening, living on the street. I don't see how these young kids manage.''

''They manage 'cause what they got where they come from is worse, don't you know?'' Sukey sighed. ''Too many people who shouldn't be having children have 'em anyway, I say. These kids, they know they're not wanted and it eats at 'em. They feel in the way, like a burden. So they leave, hoping to find better. Only most of 'em don't.'' She downed the rest of her coffee and tasted bitterness.

Fallon's curiosity nudged her. ''How did you get into working here, Sukey, if you don't mind my asking?''

''I don't mind. My husband, Jack, was a good man most of the time, 'cept when he drank and then he could be real nasty. Times like that, he'd hit anything or anyone got in his way. One night when he was like that, our son Rodney tried to talk to him, get him to stop. Jack beat him up real good, and me, too. Rodney ran away. I looked all over, trying to find him, but I didn't get to him in time. Somebody robbed him of the few dollars he had, beat him some more and left him to die next to a Dumpster in an alley. He was fifteen.''

Instinctively, Fallon reached out and touched her arm. ''Oh, I'm so sorry.''

''Yeah, me, too. Happened a long time ago, but it still hurts. I left Jack after that and went to work cooking at this Oriental restaurant. My grandmother was Asian and taught me a lot of good recipes. Then one day, I heard about Michael's House. Good things, fine things. I came and offered to work for him. Been here ever since. Ain't nobody ever say nothing bad about that boy, not around me. He's a lifeline for some of these kids. If my Rodney had had a place like this to run to, he'd still be alive today. Michael, he's one in a million.''

She had him sounding like a saint, Fallon thought, and wondered if everyone who worked with Michael felt the same. He did seem to inspire loyalty. "I imagine his father's very proud of all the good he does."

Sukey's wrinkle-free face attempted a frown. "His father?"

"Yes, Judge Redfield."

The cook shook her head. "Judge Redfield's not Michael's father." The phone on the kitchen wall rang and Sukey moved over to answer it.

Fallon vaguely heard Sukey's conversation while she pondered what she'd just learned. Michael had told her he wasn't adopted. He'd also said that his mother and father had both loved him. *Had* as in past tense. Was the judge an uncle, perhaps? Odd that he wouldn't have just said so.

Sukey set the receiver on the counter, looked over and saw the concern on the young woman's face, misreading her frown. "Don't you worry none. Michael will find your sister. I've got to hunt down Nolan. Someone looking for him. 'Scuse me." Sukey left the kitchen.

Fallon decided to go upstairs and change so when Michael returned, she would be ready to go in more acceptable casual clothes, as he'd so graciously requested.

Three hours later, though, at eleven, Michael still hadn't returned. Why hadn't he at least called, knowing she was waiting? Fallon wondered, steaming. If Wendy's baby had been so close to being born when they'd left, what had he been doing all this time since? Of course, Wendy probably had no one else and was undoubtedly frightened. She felt ashamed of herself for begrudging the poor young girl Michael's support just because she wanted to get on with things.

But then, patience had never been Fallon's strongest suit, a fact she was embarrassingly aware of. However, time was being wasted and she had precious little of it to fritter away, pacing. There had to be something she could do while she waited.

She removed Laurie's picture from her purse and paused to study it. Such a sweet face, so innocent looking. She closed her eyes on a prayer that her sister was all right. Then she hurried downstairs, stopping at the front desk.

"Opal, would you please tell Michael that I've gone to get some flyers made up and I'll be back soon?"

The nurse looked up from her ledger. "He called a while ago and left a message for you. I thought you'd left the building."

"I was upstairs. What's the message?"

"That he's delayed and you're to wait for him."

Irritated, Fallon frowned. How long, exactly, was she supposed to sit and wait? The man had an infuriating habit of giving orders and expecting instant obedience. Well, she wasn't one of his staff. "Would you happen to know if there's a print shop around here somewhere?"

"There used to be one up on Cedar that we used occasionally a while back. I don't know if it's still there, though." Opal took her measure. "Michael's not going to like it if you don't do as he asked."

"He doesn't *ask,* Opal. He *commands.* Thanks for the information." Fallon rushed off.

Her lips pursed, Opal watched the young woman hurry down the porch steps. She wouldn't want to be in Fallon's shoes when Michael finally returned, she thought. Miss McKenzie had come here for his help, then gone off on her own because she was impatient. She would soon learn that rushing out without a plan would get little if any results.

Opal sighed audibly. Funny how people so frequently showed up expecting to find someone who'd been gone for weeks just by strolling outside and gazing about. Not her problem, she decided, and went back to work.

In her Mustang, Fallon spread out the city map and found Cedar Street. It took her a good twenty minutes to locate Quick Print since she was unfamiliar with the area and its many one-way streets. Inside, she found a very helpful fellow, Larry, who spent quite a bit of time with her helping design her flyer on their computer. When she had the text just right and the photo placed as she wished it to appear, Larry went to the back and reduced it to fit and ran a sample copy.

Fallon thought the finished product looked great and told him so. She sat down to wait while he ran five hundred copies, which cost just a little more than one hundred would have. It seemed a lot, but she wanted to flood the area with Laurie's picture. *Someone* had to have seen her somewhere.

Armed with the box of flyers, she next walked to a nearby hardware store Larry recommended for some heavy-duty clear tape that she would need to tape the flyers onto trees and poles. Larry said nailing them in place would mean some people might rip them off and rain would soak them off. Tape was best. That done, she placed a handful of the flyers and the roll of tape into the bag, leaving the rest in her parked car, and set out on foot.

It was obvious from the people she'd glimpsed through the print-shop window and now strolling the sidewalk that this was an area frequented by some of the homeless. She might as well begin here, putting up the flyers whenever she saw a likely spot. But first, her stomach reminded her that she'd helped with breakfast at seven that morning, but hadn't eaten anything herself.

A coffee shop with a red neon sign blinking on and off was visible two blocks away. Fallon headed for it. She peered through the plate-glass window and saw a long counter with half a dozen stools and several booths along the sidewall. The place looked clean enough, so she went inside.

Taking the second booth, she noticed a pay phone near the door. Should she call Michael's House and see if he'd finally returned? Who knew how long he would be at the hospital or wherever else he might go? She had no right to demand that he drop everything and help her. But, by the same token, she wasn't about to take orders from him to sit tight until his return. She would do what she could without him.

A gum-chewing waitress wearing a heavy hairnet took her order for a BLT on white toast and iced tea. There were no salads on the menu, which Fallon would have pre-

ferred. Apparently, this part of town subsisted on sand-
wiches and fried food.

She checked the place out further as the waitress brought
over her tea. "Do you get a lot of teenagers in here?" she
asked the woman.

"Yeah, some," she answered noncommittally.

Fallon reached into the bag and pulled out a flyer. "Have
you seen this girl?"

The waitress peered closely at Laurie's photo. "She don't
look familiar." She handed back the flyer. "We get a lot of
folks in here. They come and go, you know."

"Sure." Fallon nodded toward the bulletin board hanging on the far wall. "Do you think I could post this up
there?"

"You gotta ask Fred, the owner."

"Thanks, I will. Are you from around here?"

The woman, who seemed to be in her late thirties, gave
her a suspicious look. "Yeah, why?"

"The girl in the picture is my sister and I'm looking for
her. I was wondering where kids her age, sixteen, might
gather around here. A particular restaurant or store or
park...you know."

The waitress screwed up her face thoughtfully. "You
could try Baileys' over on Ash. He sells fast food to go. And
the Denny's over on Front Street. Maybe the bowling alley
over on Beech. Best place is Balboa Park. Place is filled
with kids, day and night."

Fallon thanked the woman and when her sandwich arrived, she ate it quickly, anxious to be on her way. Fred, the
owner, gave her the okay and she taped her first flyer on his
bulletin board, paid her check and went out into the muggy
afternoon. Clouds had moved in, filtering out the sun, and
it looked like it might rain. But it was warm so she decided
to walk a few blocks, putting up flyers wherever possible.

In an hour, she'd posted all the flyers from her bag, taping them up in the lobby of a small slightly disreputable-
looking hotel, two more eateries, a grocery store, and a
fence that ran the length of an entire block. Whenever
possible, she asked permission, although she figured if

someone really didn't like what she'd done, they would just remove the flyer. She had plenty more.

A light rain began to fall when Fallon was still a dozen blocks from her car. Out of flyers, she started back, not rushing since the rain actually felt good and she was already quite damp. She was just passing the coffee shop where she'd had lunch when two people arguing across the street caught her attention.

A young girl with long chestnut hair pulled into a pony-tail was getting a dressing-down from a tall, thin youth with blond hair almost as long as the girl's. Fallon couldn't tell if the girl was crying or if her face was wet from the rain. But there was something familiar about the way she stood, the timber of her voice as she finally answered him back.

Fallon's heart skipped a beat. It couldn't be. Yet . . .

"Laurie?" she called out. The traffic was light, but the two young people continued to argue, apparently not hearing her. "Laurie!" she yelled more loudly.

Both of them turned then and looked at her. The boy had his hand on the girl's arm. He said something to her and the girl shook her head. Quickly, he propelled her around and they hurried off down the street.

Fallon wasn't about to give up without a closer look at the girl. "Wait!" she yelled. Finally there was a break in the slow-moving traffic and she ran across the street. She saw the boy turn and glance over his shoulder, noticing that she was rushing after them. His hand still on the girl's arm, he broke into a run, all but pulling the girl along with him.

If the young woman was Laurie, she was obviously in trouble, Fallon decided. She stepped up her pace, zigzagging amid the few people hurrying by in the rain, trying to keep the two heads in sight. If only Michael were here with her, he would undoubtedly be able to catch them, she thought, anxiety starting to grip her.

"Did you tell her I asked her to stay here and wait for me?" Michael's voice as he faced Opal revealed his annoyance.

"Yes. I even told her you wouldn't like it if she left without you." Opal kept her features even. It was uncommon, seeing Michael openly exasperated.

"Damn! She doesn't know that area. It can be dangerous."

Opal decided to tell him the rest. "She mentioned something about you not asking but ordering."

Michael saw Opal's questioning eyebrow. Maybe he was a little demanding, but Fallon McKenzie was too independent for her own good. He wouldn't forgive himself if she got hurt. "I don't suppose you know where she was headed?"

"She inquired about a print shop. I told her about the one on Cedar that we use occasionally."

A print shop. Of course. She had Laurie's picture, so she'd impatiently decided to have some flyers made for Sergeant Damien. That sounded logical, although he didn't know just how logical Fallon was.

"I'll go check it out. In case she comes back before I do, try to get her to wait for me, will you?"

Opal's face revealed her skepticism. "I'll try." Short of tying Fallon to a chair, she doubted that she could. She watched Michael skip down the porch steps and hurry into his van.

Why, she couldn't help wondering, was he so anxious to help this woman find her sister when others had come searching and he'd more or less referred them to a couple of other homes for runaways and wished them luck? Of course, Opal had to admit, most of the others hadn't been nearly as attractive as Fallon McKenzie.

Michael interested in a woman to this extent was in itself unusual. He probably had dated, for the man was certainly not a monk, but he'd kept his personal life very private and separate from Michael's House. Yet even Sukey had commented on his attentiveness to Fallon.

Interesting, Opal thought, as she dropped her gaze and went back to work.

* * *

It is beastly hot, the humidity saps our energy. Mexico is not the same country as the one I remember as a child. The terrain is more rugged, the mountains seem to loom higher, the insects are ferocious and unrelenting.

Sloan and I have devised a plan. We catch a few hours of restless sleep by day during the hottest hours of the sun and we walk at night. We left the rented car on a dirt path outside Durango and we climb on foot where no vehicle could. We carry our supplies and bedding, making the trek more laborious, but we have little choice in the matter.

Sloan finally located someone who knows Al Torres, the man his ex-wife, Monica, lives with. They have a small house deep in the mountains. I was glad to be along to interpret for him, as few people in the outlying region speak English. I'm familiar with the area we're headed toward. The inhabitants are a mixed group—some poor people, some bandidos hiding from the law. Sloan has told me that Monica and Al kidnapped little Christopher not because they want him, but for money. He showed me the note she sent him and it shocks me. How can a woman kidnap her own son, then hold him for ransom from his father? I can't imagine such a thing.

Their marriage ended bitterly, Sloan confides. Mine ended sadly, so we are both victims—a pitiful thing to have in common. He has had custody of Christopher since Monica walked away three years ago. They were better off without her, he admits; then one day, she suddenly returned. He became immediately suspicious when she asked to see the boy. But even as experienced as Sloan is, he didn't dream she would take their son.

In the late morning when the sun becomes fierce and we stop to rest, to make camp in caves or under cover of bushes and low trees, he still cannot rest easily. He thrashes, talking in his sleep, crying out Christopher's name. My heart goes out to Sloan for I, too, yearn for my children, dream about finding them, pray they are well.

We have far to go yet and little to go on but one slovenly man's directions to the house. I am ashamed of my selfish-

ness, for I want badly to find Sloan's boy so we can return home and begin looking for my children. I will help him to the best of my abilities, for he is a good and caring man.

But I count the days until my own search begins.

Chapter 5

The rain had picked up and was now falling in what could only be called a downpour. Fallon hardly noticed how wet she was as she ran along the sidewalk, her sneakers splashing in the small puddles. She had to keep the two heads, one dark and one blond, in view ahead of her. She mustn't lose sight, she told herself as she forced her feet into a burst of speed. She had to get to Laurie.

The boy's height helped, but Fallon was getting concerned at the nasty way he was dragging the girl along, apparently against her will. She seemed to be having trouble keeping up and almost slipped a couple of times. But he quickly grabbed her and kept them moving forward.

What strange hold did the blond kid have over the girl? Fallon wondered as she scooted around a skinny dog. She'd heard about pimps keeping girls in line by physically threatening them, and shuddered at the thought. He looked almost as young as the girl. Surely not.

Suddenly, they rounded the bend and disappeared from sight. A rickety truck drove by and splashed water all over Fallon's left side. Furious, she didn't stop but turned the corner and saw the two now nearly a block ahead. How would she ever catch them?

Then she saw them stop, dash up some steps and disappear through a door. She ran up to the building and read the sign above the arch: Fenwick Apartments. The place had definitely seen better days. The lock on the door had been cut out in a jagged circle. At least the tenants wouldn't have to worry about forgetting their keys. Fallon yanked open the door and found herself in a dank, dim hallway.

A small overhead bulb provided precious little light. On each side of the hall, there were three doors, all closed. At the far end was a set of stairs leading up. A radio was blaring Spanish music and a baby was crying. The smell of cabbage and fried onions permeated the walls where green paint had peeled off in great chunks. Not a soul was in sight.

Fallon hesitated, torn between wanting to pound on every door until she found the girl, and wanting to run far away from this tired old building. As she was trying to decide what to do, the tall kid's blond head appeared over the upstairs railing, his dark angry eyes peering down at her.

"What do you want with us?" he yelled.

Gathering her courage, Fallon stood her ground. "My sister. I'm looking for my sister. Her name is Laurie and . . . and she looks like the girl who was with you."

"Her name's not Laurie. Go away and stop following us." His voice broke as if he were barely past adolescence.

Fallon felt a chill race along her spine, whether because she was soaking wet from the rain or because she found herself in a tense situation, she couldn't be certain. But she wasn't about to back down on just this kid's say-so. "Tell her to come to the railing. I need to see her up closer."

The kid's eyes narrowed. "Get the hell out of here."

"No. Not until I see the girl." Fallon was being incredibly stupid, a part of her mind told her. Any moment, someone could come out of one of the apartments and put her in further danger. Yet something made her stand up to this pimply-faced boy.

"You're not ordering me around," the kid shouted, then turned and came racing down the stairs, a long board in his hand. "Get out, *now!*"

Fallon stared at the board. There were two rusty nails sticking out of it. Fear had her turning back to the door and grabbing the edge with wet, slippery fingers. She couldn't get a grip. The kid was almost on her. She tugged again and jerked at the decaying door. It opened finally, and the timing couldn't have been better. The edge caught the blond kid in the shoulder, causing him to drop his weapon and fall backward onto his rump.

Roaring mad now, he swore and tried scrambling to his feet just as the girl he'd been with came whirling down the stairs.

"What'd you do to him?" the dark-haired girl asked Fallon, her voice a shriek.

In the space of an instant, it registered with Fallon that the girl wasn't Laurie. She was shorter, her face rounder, her eyes brown. Fallon shot around the door, slamming it behind her, and raced down the steps and out into the street, certain the blond kid would come after her. She almost ran right into a blue van that was slowly cruising by. She dashed around it, nearly skidding on the wet street, glancing over her shoulder and noticing that both the boy and girl were on the stoop angrily watching her. She picked up her pace and had run half a block when she heard her name called.

Risking another glance, she saw Michael standing alongside the blue van, then running toward her. Never in her life had she been so glad to see someone. Sobs broke from her throat as she reversed and sprinted toward him. In seconds, she was in his arms, her chest heaving with hiccuping breaths as the rain poured down on them.

He held her there, motioning the occasional car to go round them, allowing her nerves to settle. Ten minutes ago, he'd run across her Mustang parked in front of the print shop, but the owner had told him that Fallon had left hours before. Michael had been driving the streets ever since, hoping Fallon hadn't gotten into trouble. This wasn't

the worst area in town, but it was far from the best. "Wha
were you running from?" he finally asked.

As if remembering, Fallon ducked her head around M
chael's shoulder and squinted at the building two doo
down. There was no one in sight on the steps or in front o
the place. The last glimpse she'd had was of the blond bo:
having retrieved his stick, standing on the top step menac
ingly, the girl alongside him. Apparently, catching sight o
Michael, they'd hurried inside.

She gave a quick shudder and stepped back from hin
"They're gone now. I owe you. Thanks." On the one hand
she was glad he'd shown up when he had. On the other, sh
hated the fact that she'd had to be rescued. And he hadn
even apologized for taking all day to show up.

Michael saw that her breathing had relaxed some, but sh
was still trembling. And she was soaked to the skin. Th
close to the ocean, the September air had cooled considei
ably with the onset of the rain and the waning afternoo
She needed to get dry, and to feel safe. Explanations cou
wait. "Come on, get in the van. You can tell me about it c
the way."

Fallon brushed damp hair from her face and saw that h
hand was shaking. It didn't please her. "On the way where
My car's back there and—"

"I saw where it's parked. I'll phone Donovan and hav
him arrange to drive it back to the house. I'm taking yo
somewhere else tonight." His arm at her back, he urged h
toward the van.

Stubbornly, she stopped in the street two feet from th
door. "You do that a lot, you know. Order people aroun
issue commands and expect people to do everything yo
say, as if you knew what was best for everyone. Like th
morning. I waited three hours for you and when you f
nally called, you didn't even have the courtesy to talk to n
in person. What did you expect me to do—work on n
needlepoint until you decided to return? I'm not on vac
tion here, you know." Nerves jangling from her close ca
she gave in to her temper. "You're not my father, n

brother or my keeper. I've been on my own since I was eighteen and I can think for myself, thank you."

He felt foolish arguing with her in the middle of the street in the middle of a downpour. Foolish and annoyed. What he wanted was to pick her up, set her inside, and be on his way. But he knew better than to get physical with her just now.

He locked his hands behind his back to keep from touching her and nodded. "All right, then. I thought we'd have time for explanations when we were in out of the rain. But now's fine. I apologize for not showing up sooner so we could begin the search together. Wendy lost her baby and she didn't take it well. I thought it important that I stay with her."

Fallon closed her eyes and tilted her head up to the heavens, wishing she'd kept still. "Oh, God, I'm sorry."

"I don't blame you for being impatient to get going, but as you apparently discovered, this can be a rather dangerous section of town. A woman alone who obviously doesn't belong here is easy prey. I wanted to spare you that. But, as you say, you can and do think for yourself."

He watched her eyes open and saw the regret there. "Now if you'd rather, you can walk back six blocks to your car in the rain and drive back to the house. Or you can get in the van and let me take you to my place where we can get out of these wet things. I'll build a fire, arrange some dinner and we can discuss what you accomplished today, and then formulate a plan. Your choice."

He watched her struggle with her conscience, between her desire to tell him to go to hell and satisfy her temper and her need to change course and turn a small measure of her problems over to him just for tonight.

The apartment door they were in front of banged open and two rough-looking men walked out, turned up their collars against the rain and started down the street, their appraising eyes boldly roving up and down Fallon. She shivered. "All right, I'll go with you. Since you asked so nicely."

Hiding a smile, well aware that her capitulation had cost her, Michael opened the van door and helped her up.

The living room of Michael's home faced the back of the property and had a wall of glass that looked out on the ocean; a sloping lawn trailed down to a sandy beach where angry waves rumbled in as the storm escalated. Wearing a huge white terry-cloth robe with a towel wrapped around her hair, still wet from the shower, Fallon stood in the large dim room watching the surge and swell of the rampaging sea. It was fascinating, beautiful, awesome. And a little frightening.

"You have your mountains in Colorado," Michael said, walking in to join her carrying two glasses, "but we have the ocean. Both are magnificent."

"Mmm, you're right," Fallon answered without turning around. "But you Californians can have them both."

"Yes, up north we have mountains and even snow. I prefer warm weather and the ocean." He held out a glass of shimmering dark red liquid. "This is port, not all that popular a wine. But Jonathan says it warms you like no other. Tonight, I think we can use a little warming."

Slowly, she turned toward him. He was wearing an unbuttoned blue shirt the color of his eyes, and tan cords. His feet were bare. His hair, damp from his shower, was very blond, lighter than the hair on his broad chest. Fallon swallowed as she took the glass. "Then here's to Jonathan," she said, meeting his eyes.

"I'll drink to that." He sipped slowly, watching her over the rim, noting that she hadn't totally calmed since the frightening incident, but she was putting on a good front. A head shorter than he, she looked fragile in the generous folds of his robe. Her feet were bare since her shoes were soaked, and her toenails were painted a bright pink. He inhaled deeply as he studied her and caught from her the fragrance of his own soap and shampoo.

King chose that moment to gallop into the room, having finished his dinner. Big, white and shaggy, as most sheepdogs are, he trotted over to Fallon and shamelessly nuzzled her hand.

She smiled, bending down to pet the affectionate dog. "I don't think King gets enough attention with your being gone so much. He's lonely."

Michael reached out to rub the thick coat. "I know. He makes me feel guilty. Paul has a house a couple of blocks over and owns a Doberman. We run on the beach with them early some mornings. King loves that, but we don't do it often enough."

The center of attention at last, King rolled over on his back, begging to be scratched. "You're something," Fallon said with a laugh, accommodating him.

"Are you hungry or do you want to wait awhile?" Michael asked. "Eldora left cold chicken and her homemade potato salad in the fridge."

She hadn't noticed his car phone the first night she'd ridden in his van. On the way to his home, he'd called Donovan and made arrangements to return her car to the house and he'd called his housekeeper, informing her that he was on his way with a guest. "You mean she whipped all that up since your call?"

"Not exactly." He led the way to the long dark green leather couch that faced the windows. King followed along, settling at Michael's feet. "She always has something ready in case I show up, which isn't all that often lately. I stay at the house two or three nights a week, depending on how things are going. Eldora's used to my crazy hours."

She was intrigued with the way his dimples appeared, then disappeared. He was beautiful to look at, even if he was bossy as hell and so sure his way was the only way. She took a sip of the wine and felt the warmth trail all the way down to her toes. She wasn't much of a drinker, but she had to admit that on a night like this, with the wind slamming the rain against the windows and the scare she'd had still fresh in her mind, the port went down well.

She hadn't felt like talking in the van, so Michael had been patient. But it was time. "Do you want to tell me who frightened you so badly that you were running down the middle of the street in a downpour?"

Remembering, Fallon shivered. "I overreacted. Stupid. I should have known better. I put myself in jeopardy for nothing."

Michael leaned back, angling sideways so he could watch her as she set her glass down, unwrapped her head and leaned forward, towel-drying her hair. "How did it happen?" he asked.

Fallon finished with the towel and sat back. Because she couldn't avoid it any longer, she told him the story, feeling even more ridiculous as the words tumbled out. "From across the street, the girl looked a lot like Laurie. About the same age, the same build, same color hair. I just had to find out, to make sure, especially when this kid was manhandling her." She draped the towel across her lap and finger-combed her hair back from her face. "I followed them into that building—not a very wise thing to do. I just wasn't thinking straight."

"Was her boyfriend waiting for you?"

"Not at first, but then he showed up and told me to leave. When I wouldn't without a closer look at the girl, he came after me with a board. A board with nails. I'm not usually so careless, it's just that I—"

"You were reacting emotionally instead of rationally. That happens when we're searching for someone we love."

Fallon took in a deep breath. "And now you're going to tell me that that's why I should have waited for you, the dispassionate one."

A frown flickered across his features. "I'm not exactly detached when it comes to runaways. But I've been at it a long time, so I've tried and discarded most of the things that don't work and kept the few that do. Which puts me a little ahead of the game."

"Actually, I'm glad the girl turned out to be someone else. I don't like to think that Laurie's under some man's control like that, even a young boy who couldn't be more than eighteen."

In the rain beside the van, she'd ranted at him about always being sure he was right, about telling her what to do. Michael didn't really feel that he tried to control people. He was curious as to why she thought so. "Control is a big issue with you, isn't it?"

Fallon took another sip of her drink before answering. "You'd have to have grown up with a stepfather like Roy Gifford to understand."

"I take it he liked to run the show." She'd told him a little about the irresponsible father who'd died and the mother who'd then married his exact opposite. But he wanted to know more, and not just to enable him to find Laurie. His curiosity extended to the woman herself, the things that had made Fallon who she was today.

"Oh, yes. Roy held all the cards and made sure we all knew it. He owned the house, had the money to feed, clothe and educate us, and so we did it his way."

"Did what his way?"

"Everything. He picked out the clothes we wore, the food we ate, the movies we saw, the books we read. Nothing happened that Roy didn't approve of." She heard the resentment in her voice and it surprised her. She hadn't consciously resented Roy while she'd lived under his roof, although she recalled being glad to be away from his strict rules. Only since Laurie had left home did the memory of the way they'd had to live begin to bother her.

"And your mother went along with everything?" He watched her take a sip of the port and wondered if it was the wine allowing her to confide more readily or if she'd begun to trust him.

"Mom was so relieved to hand over the money worries to someone that I don't think she realized until it was too late that she'd traded her happiness for financial security."

"But you managed to spend your teen years in that house and not run away. Are you so different from Laurie?"

Fallon thought that over. "I think we are different. Also, as I've said, I was older and didn't mind Danny, but Laurie developed a resentment and began rebelling at an early age."

"Roy was even harder on her because of that rebellious ness, right?"

She wrinkled her brow in surprise. "Yes, how did yo know?"

"I have a degree in psychology, remember? Most resent ful kids figure that bad attention is better than no atten tion." He leaned forward, his elbows on his knees, in thoughtful pose as he stroked King's shaggy head. Th dog's dark eyes looked up at him adoringly. "But if sh started having trouble with Roy at two, why did it take he till age sixteen to run away?" He shook his head. "I g back to my original statement—something happened t trigger Laurie's abrupt departure. Did she leave a note?"

"Yes, but all it said was that she felt she had to leave fo a while and that they shouldn't worry about her. And fo two weeks, Mom tried not to. Finally, she called me."

Puzzled, Michael thought aloud. "Two weeks, they di nothing. Not even your mother." He swung about to fac her. "And you're absolutely certain that Roy wouldn't hav molested Laurie?"

Resolutely, Fallon shook her head. "I honestly don' think so. My mother may have looked the other way abou Roy ordering us around, but not about that. And Laurie' not the type to let that go and just quietly leave. She'd hav blown the whistle, if for no other reason than to get Roy i trouble." Absently, she threaded her fingers through he hair. "No, that's not it. I sure wish I knew what it was though."

Michael wasn't convinced, but he decided not to pursu that line just now. "You mentioned this morning that yo might call home. Did you?"

"I only talked to Mom. Roy was at work. She sounde worried, but glad that I'd found a trail, weak though it ma be." Fallon struggled with a yawn. "Mom's basically good person. It's just that she had a hard life with Dad. adored my father, yet I can imagine how difficult it was a the wife of a man who kept investing in one foolish thin after another, often leaving the family with not enough t eat."

Michael leaned back, wondering if Fallon had put a charitable spin on her mother's actions because she loved her. He had a little trouble with a woman who would allow her children to be bullied in exchange for an easier life.

Fallon could see she hadn't convinced him of much, and his stubborn inability to look beyond his nose irritated her. "I know all this is hard for you to understand. You come from a very different background, different life experiences. We struggled for years just to get by. No Ivy League schools, always wearing secondhand clothes, never any frills. I understand you graduated from Stanford and lived in LaJolla. You probably celebrated your birthdays at some country club. Yes, you mingle with people down on their luck now, but your childhood was vastly different. It's amazing that you can be so compassionate with these kids when you came from such a dissimilar world."

He had turned so that he was facing her on the couch, one leg bent, his eyes questioning. "Is that what you honestly think?"

"Yes, of course. Michael, who is Jonathan Redfield to you? He's not your father, is he?" It was time to switch the focus.

Michael toyed with his wineglass. "No. I guess you could call him my mentor. We're not related—by blood, that is. But he's one of the kindest men I've ever known. I took his name to honor him for all he's done for me. And I didn't do that lightly, because I loved my biological father, too."

"Didn't that upset your parents? You mentioned that they loved you. I should think such a thing would hurt them, especially your father."

He stared at the firelight streaking her chestnut hair with red, turning her skin golden. He could think of a dozen different conversations he would rather be having with a beautiful woman in front of a fire on a rainy night. But he'd known this discussion was inevitable. "Is it that time, Fallon, when we exchange life stories?" He'd known her a little over twenty-four hours, yet it seemed much longer. Was it the intensity of the situation, the one that had brought her to him? Or did it have more to do with the obvious chemistry between them that they'd both been trying to ignore?

Scooting back, and facing him, her elbow on the back of the couch as her fingers toyed with her hair, she nodded. "Yes, I guess it is. I've already told you a great deal. Your turn."

Michael sighed, delaying. "I don't often talk about myself, my past. It seems irrelevant to what I do, to what I am." He looked toward the fire, wondering why he was considering baring his soul to someone he'd just met.

"Irrelevant? Hardly. As a psychologist, surely you know that we are what we were. No one escapes the past. It molds us even as we fight it." Hadn't she proved that to herself tonight in acknowledging that she'd probably begun resenting Roy almost immediately, although she'd consciously denied it?

"I guess you're right." He paused for a moment, gathering his thoughts. "I'm not originally from California. I was born in Michigan, in a small farming community, Frankenmuth. My father was Lance Richards. He'd inherited the farm we lived on from his father, who'd inherited it from his father. Third-generation Germans, hardworking, honest."

Fallon listened without comment, not wanting to break his concentration. She was wide-awake now, and very interested.

"My father met my mother in high school and they fell in love at first sight, he used to tell me." Michael wasn't aware of his smile as he recalled the parents he still thought of so often. "Her name was Julia and she'd been born in Mexico near Mazatlán. Her parents had migrated to this country when Mom was quite young and had opened a restaurant. She'd had a lot of adjustments to make—a new language, new customs, new people. But Dad took her under his wing and when she was sixteen, she discovered she was pregnant with me." He glanced over at Fallon, wondering at her reaction. "Needless to say, both families heartily disapproved."

"I can imagine. Thirty-some years ago, that sort of thing was even more frowned upon than now."

"Thirty-two years ago, to be exact, and you're right. But the families eventually accepted the situation and they were married. Mom quit school and they lived on the farm with Dad's folks. He was an only child, so when his parents died a few years later, he inherited the farm. And all the work that went with it. I remember getting up at first daylight and going to gather eggs in the barn when I was five or six. Later, I'd tend to the horses and work the fields, then go to school, come home and work until nightfall alongside my father."

"You were an only child?"

"No. My sister, Hannah, is four years younger and then there was the baby, Katie, eight years younger. You can't know how many hours I've sat wondering where they are, how they are."

"You were separated? What happened?"

Michael had difficulty speaking of the loss of his sisters. With no small effort, he went on. "There'd been two years of drought and Dad had had to mortgage the farm to keep going. The worry took its toll on my mother, too. She'd always been so strong, so upbeat. Suddenly she began losing weight, coughing all the time, barely able to drag herself out of bed. I was only fourteen, but I remember going to sleep at night worrying about both of them."

"That's a lot for a young boy to have to deal with."

He didn't want her feeling sorry for him—not then, not now. "I don't want to mislead you, here. We were a happy family. We didn't have a lot of money to spend on material things, but before she became really sick, my mother made that place into a home." A home such as he'd never known since. "She baked, she sewed our clothes, she made each holiday into an exciting event. And Dad always made time for us to go on picnics or to sandlot ball games and to the county fair. We laughed a great deal. There was a lot of love in our home."

"That's the way it was with us before my father's accident." Fallon was unaware how wistful she sounded.

"Then I guess you know what I mean. Just like with you, things changed because my father had an accident, too. He was fixing the tractor for the umpteenth time since there was no money to buy a new one and somehow, it ran over him." Michael could hear again his father's scream and picture the scene as he'd run across the fields, praying yet already certain he was gone. "We were all devastated, my mother especially."

"Of course she would be." Fallon noticed that he'd kept his face expressionless throughout the recital, almost as if he'd been telling a story about someone else. Until now. His eyes were dark blue and bleak. As the oldest child, and the only male, he'd probably felt the weight of the world on his shoulders, left with a mother who wasn't well and two young sisters. "How did she manage to run the farm with just your help, or were you able to hire someone?"

"It was rough. Just like your folks, they'd let Dad's insurance lapse, so there was no money. Mom got weaker, sicker, and I couldn't keep up with all that needed doing. Before long, she collapsed. They diagnosed her as having tuberculosis. They took her away by ambulance to a hospital for contagious diseases." He swallowed hard. "I never saw her again." Outside the windows, lightning flashed, then thunder rumbled as if in punctuation to the end of his childhood.

"Oh, Michael." She moved closer, her hand reaching for his.

Was it the storm, the wine or Fallon's nearness that had loosened his tongue? Michael didn't know and no longer cared. It had been years since he'd talked about his past in this way. Even Jonathan and Paul, the two who were closest to him, hadn't heard the whole story in detail; just bits and pieces, snatches of memories. He hadn't wanted their pity or even their concern back in his youth when he'd met both of them. He still wanted nothing to do with those emotions; yet somehow, with Fallon, he felt more like explaining.

Maybe because he wanted her to understand, to know that he wasn't what she thought he was, a moneyed man playing at a charitable enterprise.

"That's how the three of you got separated, then?" she gently prompted. She'd never dreamed when she'd begun questioning him about Jonathan Redfield that this kind of story would emerge. She believed Michael when he said he rarely spoke about his past. She rarely did, either. Yet she felt that in many ways, telling her was cathartic for Michael.

He twined his fingers with hers, his eyes on their clasped hands. "Child Protective Services stepped in and we were sent to separate foster homes. Like Daryl, I didn't do well in the system. I was angry at the gods for taking my parents away, worried about my mother and I felt guilty that, as the oldest, I couldn't look after my sisters."

"You were only fourteen," she reminded him.

"Yeah, but I'd been left the man of the house six months earlier when Dad had died. I'd been doing a man's job on the farm and still going to school. I felt I let them down. The worst part was that no one would tell me anything. I wasn't allowed to visit my mother because the whole hospital was quarantined. They wouldn't reveal where my sisters were or I'd have found a way to go to them. I remember that time as being filled with anger, ready to fight at the drop of a hat. Small wonder that one foster family after another found a reason to get rid of me. I was branded incorrigible."

He'd said the last almost with a hint of pride. Fallon understood. Rebellion had been Michael's way of handling the pain. Much like Laurie's, she realized.

"The day I turned sixteen, I hopped a bus and went to the Child Protective Services demanding some answers. They shuffled me around for a while and finally told me that my mother had died several months before. They hadn't even bothered to let me know. That did it. That night, I packed the few belongings I had and ran away."

That was something she hadn't suspected—that he'd once been a runaway, too. On closer inspection, she saw that the old wounds of that time weren't raw and bleeding, but they were far from healed. "I guess you do know how these kids feel."

Michael drained his glass, stretched out his long legs and kept her hand wrapped in his. "Yeah, all too well."

"Where did you run to? How did you survive?" Her interest had accelerated. The choices he'd faced then were the same ones Laurie had faced recently.

"I knew they'd come after me, so I hitchhiked out of Michigan. I set out for California where I'd heard the weather was great and there were plenty of opportunities for those not afraid to work hard."

"You couldn't have hitchhiked all that way. What did you use for money?" In the foster-care system, he couldn't have had much. Laurie at least had her small bank account.

He turned to face her, searching her eyes, wondering how she would feel if he told her more. In a very short time, her opinion of him had come to matter, perhaps too much. Yet lying wasn't in his nature nor was it a good way to begin a relationship. If she condemned him for the things he'd done to survive, he might as well know up front.

"Occasionally I stopped in a city long enough to work an odd job or two, lying about my age. There are still a few places that don't ask too many questions when hiring a strong back. I called myself Michael Smith—fooling no one, I'm sure, but I wanted no connection to Michigan or my past. I washed cars, worked with a construction crew and as a short-order cook. Stuff like that. And, there were times when I couldn't find work and I was hungry, so I stole. Food and things I could sell in order to eat." His gaze steady, he waited.

Fallon didn't blink. "Are you expecting me to look down on you for doing what you had to do in order to survive?" She thought of Laurie, desperately afraid she was facing the same things Michael had faced nearly two decades ago. "I've never been in a similar situation, but we have to do what we have to do." She understood better now why he'd gone to the police station to speak up on Daryl's behalf.

He could see she meant every word and was surprised how much her reaction pleased him. But he wasn't finished. He squeezed her fingers, then let go. "There's more. I finally made it to San Diego and became friends with Paul Ramirez, a kid who was also a runaway."

"You mean the doctor you use at the house?"

"Right. His parents were migrant workers with four other mouths to feed and not enough work, enough money or food, so Paul left. He was two years younger than me and I sort of looked after him." He chuckled at the memory. "I showed him how to steal without getting caught. Some friend, eh?"

"The friendship's lasted, so apparently neither of you was caught."

"Oh, but you're wrong. I got pretty good at petty thievery, then got cocky and decided to branch out. I stole a car in downtown San Diego. Stupid. I didn't even have a driver's license. I got caught before I'd gone more than a couple of miles. They put me in Juvenile. The cop who caught me was Sam Damien, the sergeant you met last night." Lord, had it been just last night?

"And now, he's turning juvenile offenders over to you." The irony was beautiful.

"That's right, but he wasn't any too happy with me back then. Especially when I escaped."

"You didn't?"

"Yeah, I did. And it turned out to be the best thing that ever happened to me. It was dusk and I was running along the shoreline next to Harbor Drive, keeping to the trees, ducking every time I heard a car. Suddenly, I heard someone shouting for help. There was this older man frantically waving his arms, yelling for someone, anyone, to help save his grandson. He ran right onto my path, grabbed me and told me the kid had slipped into the water and the poor guy couldn't swim. I told him to get out of my way, sure that if I stopped, the cops would spot me and haul me back. I left him standing there."

He saw her frown of disapproval; he'd expected it.

"You're right. Pretty selfish. However, about a block away, my conscience kicked in and I went back. I dove in and pulled the kid out. He was seven and small for his age. His lips were already blue, and he wasn't breathing. The old guy was overwrought. I'd learned CPR back when I'd been going to school. It was a requirement in swim class. The kid's name was Timmy and he finally came around. The grandfather was so grateful he started to cry. I'd done my good deed and I needed to get going, but he grabbed my arm and wouldn't let go."

"Judge Jonathan Redfield, right?"

"I thought you'd figure it out. Yeah, Jonathan. He hustled us both into his Lincoln and drove us to his estate in LaJolla. Later, he got it out of me why I hadn't stopped right away. He got the charges dismissed against me since it was my first offense. Then he took over my life."

"A lucky break."

"The best. Jonathan was a widower with no sons and only the one married daughter, Timmy's mom. He insisted I move in with him, telling me he was lonely in that big old house." Michael chuckled. "Like he didn't have loads of friends. From then on, he treated me like family, seeing to my education, paying for everything. I told him about Paul and he found a sponsor for him, one of his lawyer friends who paid for Paul's schooling and put him through med school. Now do you see why I changed my name to Redfield? He's one hell of a guy."

The same thing Daryl had said of Michael. "Certainly sounds like it."

"Jonathan wanted me to go into law, to follow in his footsteps, but I had a different leaning. I got my degree in psychology because knowing what makes people tick had always interested me, but I still didn't know what I wanted to do with my new degree. Until the day I ran across a kid who'd broken into my car looking for something to sell so he could eat. The kid was shoeless, dirty, wearing dingy clothes. I discovered he'd just turned sixteen. His folks were dead and he was living on the streets with no one to help him. He had this tough veneer, but I could see that inside, he was pretty scared. I had this rush of déjà vu and that's when I decided what I wanted to do was work with kids like him." He turned again to face her. "Sounds like the plot of a B movie, but there you have it. So now you know all about me."

Fallon doubted that that was everything. "I have a great deal of admiration for the way you turned your life around. With Jonathan's help. I'd like to be able to do that for Laurie. You ran away because you had no one you could count on. I don't know why Laurie left, but I have this gut feeling that if I can just find her, if I can talk with her, it'll be all right."

She saw that he was about to contradict her again, and raised her hand to stop him. "I know what you're going to say, and I agree that kids like Wendy who've been traumatized and Daryl who's been beaten and abandoned need more than a few kind words to straighten out their lives. But Laurie's not like that. She has people who care. Mom and me. I *will* find her and I *will* take care of her."

Michael hadn't expected to change her mind with his life story. He had hoped she would get some insight.

One of the things she couldn't know was how life on the street could change a young person. The daily struggle, the constant fear, the pervasive hopelessness. The Laurie she would find wouldn't be the same girl who had left home nearly three weeks ago. Some life experiences could bring about huge changes in a very short time. But again, he saw no reason to discourage her further by telling her that right now.

He moved closer, lightly touching the ends of her hair. "I know you'll find her, too. I'll help all I can."

Fallon hadn't expected him to be so agreeable, so she was taken aback. She studied his suddenly serious face as she felt his fingers move from her hair to curl around her neck, his thumb lightly stroking her skin. The distraction drove their discussion from her thoughts. "What are you doing?"

"Is it me or don't you like being touched?"

"Yes, to both questions. Michael, I think we should keep this on an impersonal level. You help find runaways. I need to find a runaway. That's the one and only reason we're here together." She saw his eyes darken and felt her pulse quicken.

"Is it?"

"It is on my part and ..."

Michael bent his head and took her mouth.

Chapter 6

Fallon didn't resist. She was too stunned to push him away. For several long seconds, she didn't respond. She was too shocked to fully comprehend what was happening.

Then, suddenly, her senses were flooded with feelings: a flash fire of desire, an eruption of need, a wave of wanting. She hadn't been consciously aware of this incredible craving, this raging longing, this terrifying yearning. Yet it had been there, dormant, waiting, ready to explode.

His mouth was hard, demanding, persuasive, yet his hands as he molded her to his powerful body were gentle. He made her feel soft, feminine, delicate by comparison. With a breathy moan, she wrapped her arms around him.

Michael had done something he hadn't done in ages: given in to an impulse. He'd had to know if she tasted as intoxicating as she looked, as she smelled. Just a quick taste, he'd told himself. A little kiss. No big deal.

Who was he kidding? he asked himself as his tongue entered her mouth, heating his blood, muddying his mind. She tasted sweet and guileless, yet as hot and heady as forbidden sex. She was a dichotomy of innocence and temptation.

It had been a long time since he'd kissed with such abandon; even longer since he'd wanted to. He prided himself on the fact that if he couldn't control others, he could damn well control himself. Yet with each soft murmur from her, with the scent and feel of her already driving him mad, he lost a little more control. If he didn't stop now, Michael knew he would soon be begging.

He pulled back and blinked to clear his vision, and saw the arousal in the jade green of her eyes. As his mouth slanted over hers, he knew he was lost, needing more, needing it all.

Outside the shuddering windows, a flash of lightning neither of them saw split the night sky, followed by a crash of thunder. In the grate, a log shifted, sending sparks flying upward, sizzling and spurting. The smoky scent lingered in the room, drifting to the corners. At their feet, King stirred, eyeing them restlessly, then retreated to curl up by the hearth. Michael and Fallon took no notice.

Fallon was jolted into such a sharp awareness that she was able to separate the myriad sensations buffeting her: the feel of his strong hands stroking her back through the thick robe, the touch of his lips caressing hers, the exciting male scent of him seeping into her pores. Nothing she'd ever experienced had prepared her for this onslaught, this overwhelming demand.

This time it was Fallon who pulled back, placing a hand on his bare chest to put some space between them, only to find her fingers tangling in the crisp hair. Taking a deep, hopefully calming breath, she inched back farther. She raised her eyes to his and saw the hunger he seemed unable to hide, and wondered if he could recognize the same need in her.

With a trembling hand, she drew the folds of the robe closer together, waiting for her heart rate to slow. She was shaken to her very core. Her response to Michael had been primitive, elemental and shocking. It simply wasn't like cool, controlled Fallon McKenzie to react so instantly, so completely, to what amounted to a lusty kiss.

She felt him watching her. She had to say something, to explain, not just to him, but to herself. "I honestly don't know what came over me," Fallon said, annoyed that her voice wasn't quite steady. "That...that isn't at all like me. I hardly know you. I—"

"Don't overthink it, Fallon." He was every bit as baffled as she at how fierce a reaction she evoked in him. It was the tumultuous weather stirring things up, he told himself, and the two glasses of port he'd downed and the emotional reliving of his past through the memories he'd shared with her. All of it had combined to make him vulnerable to a beautiful woman wearing only his robe and sitting very near him.

Yes, that had to be it.

"I won't deny I wanted to kiss you. And now I have, so that's that." The hell, you say, his conscience screamed. Already he'd had to turn away from her in order to keep from reaching for her again. Once, twice—not enough. Not nearly enough.

Apparently he was handling things far better than she. Fallon shifted until she was at the far end of the couch, her legs drawn up protectively under the generous folds of the robe. "Right. I won't deny that there's a certain attraction between us, but we're adults. We can ignore that and work together until we get the job done. Besides, relationships haven't exactly been my strong suit."

"Mine, either," Michael agreed. It had been his choice to keep women who might have wanted to get closer at bay. He'd told himself he was too busy, too committed to his work to have enough time and energy left over to commit to a woman, to a family. He'd managed for many years without a serious entanglement. He was a private man, one who liked his life exactly as it was. He cared about the kids under his supervision at Michael's House. That commitment occupied his time and satisfied his needs. That was enough for him.

He almost believed the lie.

Michael rose, buttoning his shirt. He ran his tongue over his lips and could still taste her. He cleared his throat. "How about that chicken now? You must be hungry."

She couldn't have swallowed a mouthful with her emotions in such turmoil. "Actually, I'm not. I had a big lunch. Anyhow, it must be late. My clothes must be dry by now." He'd thrown them in the washer when they'd first arrived, then the dryer. "Would you mind driving me back to the house?"

He glanced out at the storm still pounding at the windows. "Look, it's not necessary to go out in this. I have two spare rooms. You can use either one. In the morning, we can make a plan and start our search." He'd lost his appetite for food, too. Another, stronger hunger had chased it away.

She should probably insist on returning, but it seemed foolish and petulant, given the status of the weather. Slowly, feeling light-headed, she got to her feet. "All right, if you'll show me which room you prefer I use."

He led the way upstairs, after gathering her clothes from the dryer, and stopped at the room across from his own. "You'd best shut the door or King will come in and bother you," he told her.

Or perhaps he himself would.

Fallon's bare feet hit the damp sand, sending small clumps flying as she ran along the beach, with King racing ahead of her. The ecstatic dog stopped to pick up the stick she'd thrown and hurried back to her. Slowing, she pulled it from his mouth and threw it again. Tongue hanging out, he took off.

The thermometer gauge on Michael's patio had read sixty-five degrees at six when she'd stepped out with the eager dog, surprised that her host wasn't up yet. Instead of rushing to brew coffee, she'd decided that a run on the beach was just what she and King needed. The sun was shining and, except for some clusters of seaweed that had washed ashore, there was little evidence of last night's storm.

Fallon shook back her hair and turned her face up to the sun, wondering if Laurie was out somewhere nearby gazing up at the same bright day. Where had she been during the downpour? Where had she slept, how was she eating and getting by? Who was she with and, most important of all, was she all right?

Fallon felt a wave of guilt at having spent a cozy evening by a warm fire while her sister had been God only knew where. Laurie, after all, was the purpose for her trip, the reason for her being here. She should have looked longer yesterday, tried harder, passed out more flyers. The search, only just begun, was already taking its toll on her nerves. How long before she had Laurie safely home?

Slowing, she jogged to a halt and bent from the waist, placing her hands on her knees, breathing deeply and cooling down. She was out of shape, for she'd run scarcely a mile and was winded. Of course, she hadn't eaten dinner last night and she hadn't had her start-up cup of coffee yet this morning.

And she'd been converted into a pile of mush last evening by a couple of soul-shattering kisses.

King came charging over, the stick in his mouth, and waited.

"Aren't you tired, fella?" she asked him. He cocked his head at her expectantly. No, he didn't appear ready to end their exercise program. Gamely, she threw the stick again, this time in the direction of Michael's home.

It was beautiful here, Fallon acknowledged, gazing around at the stately homes facing the ocean, the sloping lawns, the fenced-in pools, the dazzling bougainvillea seemingly growing wild in bright splashes of red and pink. She liked her small apartment in Denver, but it would fit into one corner of Michael's place. She passed a neighbor's tennis court and another's putting green, and wondered what the owners did to be able to afford such homes.

Quite a contrast to the neighborhood where Michael's House for runaways was and the section where she'd been roaming about taping up flyers. He seemed to live in two very different worlds and handled both with ease. She

caught sight of him seated on his patio alongside the pool
and adjacent hot tub. A fascinating man.

And a dangerous man.

A man who could kiss like that, who could empty her
mind and undoubtedly fulfill her wildest dreams, was dangerous to her health and well-being. He could divert her
from her goals, weaken her resolve to stay uninvolved with
strong, controlling men and destroy her best intentions. She
would do well to remember that and to be wary in his presence.

As King came bounding over, she took the stick from
him and climbed the grassy bank one last time.

Wearing only blue cotton drawstring pants, Michael
sipped his orange juice and watched her approach. Her hair
was windblown, her cheeks ruddy, her shirt billowing in a
sea breeze and her jeans were rolled up on her slender
calves, her feet sandy. She was fresh-faced and free of
makeup, her eyes a deep sea-green. She was laughing at the
dog's antics as he danced around her in his best effort to
persuade her to resume their game.

She was a knockout and appeared not to know it.

Fallon flopped into the chair across the glass-topped
wrought-iron table and ran a hand through her hair. "It's
gorgeous out here. I don't know how you tear yourself
away every day." And part of the appeal was the man himself—everyone's idea of the all-American male with his hair
bleached blond by the sun and his eyes a vivid blue in his
tanned face. And that mouth that could turn a woman's
knees to water.

He poured orange juice from a frosty pitcher and held
the glass out to her. "It is great, isn't it?"

She'd brazenly toured the downstairs rooms before her
run and found sleek modern lines and lots of glass, yet de-
cor in warm, restful colors. A dichotomy, like the man
himself. "Did you have the house built?"

"Yes. Jonathan had owned the lot forever. I worked with
one of his architect friends, trying to come up with a design I could live with." The need for roots, for a solid home
was a big part of him. "Plenty of windows and open space.

I can't stand small places that make me feel closed in." He bent to acknowledge King who'd come to him after giving up on Fallon. "I'm like King about freedom. He's a stray I ran across a couple of years ago. He'd been free too long to be penned up, so I had that dog door built in for him so he can come and go as he pleases. He can jump any fence I'd put up, but he always comes back because he knows I won't keep him confined."

Yes, just like his owner, Fallon couldn't help thinking. She drank the juice thirstily, recognizing it as freshly squeezed. His housekeeper must be in the kitchen.

Michael loosened the top on the carafe and reached for two cups stacked on a wooden tray. "Would you like some hot coffee? I'm surprised you were able to run without a jump start."

She smiled. "It wasn't easy." Gratefully, she took the cup and inhaled the wonderful aroma before tasting the rich brew.

Overhead, the flapping of wings had them both looking out to sea where a group of pelicans was flying north. Fallon studied the birds for long minutes. "They fly in formation," she commented. "I didn't know that."

"Yeah. A lot of birds do."

Sort of like me, Fallon thought. Always in formation. Regimented, unwavering, steadfast, conventional. And another word came to mind: *boring.*

She turned to Michael. "What's it like to be free, to answer to no one?" She'd never asked anyone that before, but then, she'd never known anyone independent and confident enough, financially and otherwise, to be able to exercise true freedom in their daily life. That description fit Michael.

The question surprised him; he wondered if she realized how much it revealed about her. "It's a good feeling. Why don't you try it?"

She sipped her coffee thoughtfully, wanting to give him an honest answer. "To live exactly as you want takes two things I don't have in abundance: money and courage."

Michael poured himself more coffee. "I agree that it takes courage. Hell, living takes courage. But not money." He leaned forward, elbows on the table, the cup cradled in both hands. "I've met men, and women, in all walks of life who live exactly as they choose without much funds. There's this homeless fellow who lives around Balboa Park. Matter of fact, I think we need to talk with him because he knows literally everyone who's out on the street these days. He calls himself Sherlock, though it's probably not his real name. He used to be a well-paid executive with a big house in the suburbs, cars, boats, the whole nine yards. But he wasn't happy so he walked away from that life and now, he's much happier, though he lives very unconventionally."

Fallon wrinkled her forehead. "I've heard that there are some people who don't have a regular address, yet aren't on the streets because of financial problems but because they actually *choose* to be. I find that difficult to believe."

"Believe it. Sherlock's educated, bright, even well traveled. But he hates rules, confinement, monotony. Corporate life was killing him, or so he told me."

"Did he walk away from a family?"

"Yes, but he left all his assets behind and told his wife to divorce him, which I believe she did. He never mentioned children."

Fallon shook her head. "I still don't get it. There's no security, no safety, no future."

"Jonathan taught me that security is within a person, not what you own."

"Easy for him to say since he's got plenty of everything. I notice it's always the wealthy who make those kinds of comments."

He could tell she was remembering the lean days when her real father was alive. That time seemed to have influenced Fallon nearly as much as her mother. "Maybe. But there's a lot to be said for being confident in your own mind, controlling your own destiny."

Fallon sighed, thinking of her manager, Craig Miller, and wondering if she would have a job when she returned.

Everyone had someone they had to answer to, didn't they? "That's not as easy to achieve as you make it sound. Oh, I suppose I could quit my job and live on the streets, but I doubt that would make me happy, even though I'd be living without rules, so to speak."

"There are always rules, even on the street. Kids and adults who are there learn them fast in order to survive. I don't want you to think I agree with Sherlock's choices or his way of life. But it suits him, makes him happy." He reached across the table and touched her chin, forcing her to meet his eyes. "Are you happy?"

She felt boxed in and didn't like it. She angled her face away from his hand. "Much of the time, but not always. No one is. Are you?"

Michael frowned, considering. "Basically, I am."

"Then we're back to square one. You're happy because you can live as you please. Some of us don't have that luxury. We have to work to eat, to put a roof over our heads, to—"

"I've met a lot of unhappy successful people, Fallon. I give dozens of speeches to all sorts of business people in the private sector when I'm fund-raising for my runaways. Some people are so busy playing one-upmanship or trying to get to the top, to marry well, live in the right neighborhood, belong to the right club, and so on, that I don't even think they stop to ask themselves if they're happy."

She was growing weary of the topic, especially since she was certain they would never agree. "Right now, I'd be happy if we could get going on our search."

She did that often, changed the subject when their conversation hit too close to home. "I've already started. I called Donovan and had him get the flyers from your car. He's faxing a copy to all the runaway hotline numbers we have in the entire Southwest."

Impressed, she sat back. "Well, I guess you weren't just sleeping in. Okay, what's next?"

"Breakfast. Eldora's in there rattling the old pots and pans even as we speak. Things are quiet at the house, according to Opal, so I've got time. I would like to stop at the hospital to make sure Wendy's okay.''

Fallon's heart went out to the young girl who'd lost her baby. ''I'd like to go with you, if you think she wouldn't mind.''

''Fine. She might open up more to a woman. I've set her up to talk with the rape counselor later, when she recovers. I tried a while back to get her to go, but she wouldn't. Maybe now she will. She really wanted this baby. Not that she had any means to support the child. She's still a kid herself, at fifteen. It's just that she wants someone of her own to love.''

Was that what Laurie wanted? Fallon asked herself. Had she left because Roy loved only Danny and Mom didn't seem to care and, of course, she herself had brushed her off? Guilt settled on her shoulders like a heavy woolen blanket.

''Don't, Fallon,'' Michael said. He'd been watching her face and could guess what she'd been thinking. ''Laurie isn't Wendy. We'll find your sister. I think we should talk with Sherlock. It shouldn't be too hard to locate him.''

Fallon shifted in her chair, blinking to hold back the tears. Crying wouldn't help find Laurie. She would have to set aside her own emotions for now.

He noticed and wanted to reassure her. ''Fallon, why do you blame yourself for your sister's disappearance? You're not the problem and you're not the solution. Don't add unnecessary guilt to the heavy load you're already carrying. Give it some time.''

''I know.'' Her gaze landed on a large piece of sculpture at the far end of the red-tiled patio, and she zeroed in, needing a diversion. ''Venus. I've always liked that piece.'' Rising, she walked over for a closer look, buying a little time to compose herself.

Michael followed. ''Jonathan coaxed me to this art auction one day at a gallery owned by one of his friends.'' He reached around her to point out a hairline crack. ''She wouldn't have sold to a serious collector, but I like her better this way. Flawed, like all of us.''

She swung about to study him instead. "We are, aren't we?" she asked softly.

He gave in to the urge to touch her, trailing the backs of his fingers along one satiny cheek. "Yeah, we are. We all make mistakes. That's why they put erasers on the ends of pencils."

Fallon felt a rush of awareness at his touch, a reaction that both warmed and annoyed her. She needed to keep her distance from this man, she reminded herself. Sidestepping him, she headed for the door. "I don't know about you, but I'm starved. Let's go have breakfast."

Smiling, Michael followed her. She wasn't fooling him for a minute. It hadn't been breakfast on her mind when he'd touched her just now.

Sherlock had gray hair and a full beard, a weighty paunch and resembled Jerry Garcia, right down to the baggy jeans and the tie-dyed shirt. He smiled in the same friendly manner as Michael introduced Fallon.

"Step over to my office," Sherlock said, indicating a somewhat secluded picnic table nestled among several thick shrubs in Balboa Park. At ten in the morning under a cloudless sky, there were few people around. A couple of mothers with children around the swings and slides, a vagrant asleep on the grass under a shady tree and some bicyclers trailing along the paths.

"Fallon has a picture she wants to show you, to see if you recognize the girl. Her sister, Laurie, has been on the run for about three weeks." Michael sat down on the bench opposite Sherlock.

Fallon settled herself next to Michael and handed Sherlock one of the flyers. "She's only sixteen," she added.

Sherlock shoved his tinted wire-rimmed glasses higher on his nose, tilted his head back and studied the flyer but a moment before laying it down on the table. "She's from Colorado, right?"

Fallon's eyes widened. "Yes. You've seen her?"

The burly man rubbed his shaggy beard and nodded. "It was a week ago, maybe less. She was with this redheaded kid they call T.J."

Aware of Fallon's excitement, Michael placed a calming hand on her arm. "Do you have any idea where T.J. hangs out?"

Sherlock shrugged, then narrowed his eyes as he studied Fallon, his friendly manner no longer apparent. "You planning to take your sister back?"

She felt Michael's fingers tighten on her wrist before she could answer.

"She just wants to talk with Laurie, make sure she's all right. Fallon doesn't live with the parents. If there's a problem back there, maybe she can help." He gave Sherlock a reassuring smile. "She's not going to drag her back if she doesn't want to return."

Sherlock stuck a toothpick in his mouth and chewed on it as he considered the situation. "A lot of these kids are better off here than back home, if you get my drift." His gaze slid to Michael. "You know that. You work with 'em."

"I do know that," Michael said. "And I've never forced anyone to return if they didn't want to. But we feel that something might have happened that caused Laurie to leave home. We don't know what. Fallon's willing to work with her."

Fallon was getting awfully annoyed at having Michael speak for her. "I love my sister. I want only to find her, to talk with her and help her if I can. And I'm sure I can."

The blue eyes magnified by the glasses shifted to her. "A lot of kids get hurt in the name of love."

She didn't want to debate the issue with this man, but she had a feeling he knew something and didn't trust them enough to reveal it. "I swear, I don't intend to force Laurie to return."

Sherlock was silent for several moments before finally coming to a decision. "T.J. drops in at the Rodeo Bar most evenings."

"I know the bartender there," Michael added. "Rollie."

"Yeah, that's right. There's also a beach house up around Newport where a bunch of the young people hang out. Guy by the name of Alex seems to be the head man there."

"I've met Alex, too," Michael said. "What's T.J.'s story, do you know?"

Another shrug. "He's sixteen or seventeen. Been on the streets a couple of years. His mother died and his father remarried. The stepmother's a bitch, to hear him tell it. So he took off."

That would give Laurie and this boy something in common, Fallon thought immediately. Then another fear surfaced. "Are they . . . involved?"

Sherlock smiled. "I don't keep track of that kind of thing. Live and let live, that's my motto."

Fallon was grateful for the leads, slim as they were, and she told him so.

"Sure." He glanced down at the flyer on the table. "Funny thing, you're the second person who's come around asking about that girl."

Fallon was stunned. "Who was the other one?"

"A big guy, probably in his forties, with a dark beard."

"When was he here?" Michael asked.

"Just yesterday, before the rain. It wasn't that flyer. He showed me two snapshots. But it was her, all right."

"Did you ever see him before?" Michael wanted to know.

Sherlock shook his head. "Drove up in a big old Cadillac. He's a dick. I can spot John Law clear across the park."

"A regular cop or a P.I.?" Michael persisted.

"P.I." Sherlock frowned. "Wait a second." He reached under the table and brought out a cigar box, then rummaged around in it until he found what he was looking for. "He gave me this. Told me to call him if I ran across her. Offered me fifty bucks if I could tell him where she was."

"What'd you tell him?" Michael asked.

Sherlock shifted the toothpick to the other side of his mouth. "Nothin', man. I hate those guys. Always nosin' around."

Fallon studied the card. Raymond T. Tompkins, Private Investigator. Colorado Springs. "He wanted you to call him in Colorado?"

Again, Sherlock shook his head. "He wrote a local number on the back. Motel 6 or something like that."

She turned it over and read the phone number. "Mind if I keep this?"

Sherlock put his box back. "I have no use for it."

Michael's hand reached to grasp Fallon's as he got up. "Thanks, man. I appreciate your help." His other hand slipped into his pocket and curled around a folded bill before he stretched to shake Sherlock's hand.

The meeting over, the older man rose and pocketed the money. "See you around, Michael." He sauntered off toward the paved pathway.

"You paid him for information?" Fallon asked as they headed back to the van.

"The man's got to eat, Fallon. He had something we needed. We paid him for it. Do you have a problem with that?"

"I guess not. Sorry. I'm a little on edge." She studied the card as they walked. "I never heard of this guy, but I think I know who hired him. And I must say I'm surprised."

At the van, Michael unlocked the door. "Your mom?"

"Mom doesn't have money of her own and she wouldn't risk upsetting Roy if she did." She climbed up. "It had to be Roy. But why when he was so against me looking for Laurie?"

Michael got behind the wheel. "Maybe he had a change of heart."

"Roy? The day pigs fly." She slipped the card into her pocket. "There's something funny here. I need to talk with him."

Michael headed for the house. "You can call from my office. Less static than on the car phone, especially on long distance."

* * *

It was Sunday so Fallon knew Roy would probably be home. But Jane Gifford answered the phone. She heard the anxious tone and knew that her mother wasn't any calmer than when she'd left. Fallon took a few minutes to update her, then mentioned that she'd discovered that a private investigator was also in San Diego making inquiries about Laurie. "What's going on, Mom?"

"Why, I don't know." Jane sounded flustered. "What's his name?" She listened while her daughter told her, then called out to her husband. "Roy, do you know anything about a man named Raymond Hopkins, an investigator?"

Fallon heard a cough and the scrape of a chair, then her stepfather's voice. "Fallon, is that you?"

"Yes, I'm here. Did you hire a P.I. to track down Laurie?"

"Yes, I hired him. I know how worried your mother is and I wanted to put her mind at ease. So I sent a professional to look for your sister. Hopkins is very good. Comes highly recommended. So you can come on home and get back to your job where you belong. Leave the detecting to the trained investigator."

Fallon struggled with her temper, hoping for her mother's sake to keep from irritating her stepfather, knowing he would take it out on Jane after they hung up. "I thought you were against finding Laurie, that you said she'd come home on her own."

"I don't believe I said that in so many words. At any rate, this has gone on long enough. Your mother's a nervous wreck and I just want to end it. So I hired Hopkins. You needn't worry. He'll get the job done. Just catch the next plane back to Denver and I'll handle your sister." His voice, as always, was curt and commanding, as if expecting her to leap to his bidding.

Fallon noticed that she was gripping the phone so hard, her knuckles had turned white. She forced herself to relax.

"Have you heard from Mr. Hopkins? Has he found any traces of Laurie?" Odd that the man hadn't stopped in at

Michael's House, even though Roy knew that Laurie had been headed there.

"He reports to me daily, at the office. He hasn't actually seen Laurie, but he has several good leads he's following up on." His tone sharpened as his aggravation increased. Roy Gifford wasn't used to explaining himself to people, especially to his stepdaughter. "Enough of this, Fallon. You get on the next plane, you hear? Need I remind you that you have obligations to the people who sign your checks? Good jobs don't grow on trees, you know, and the rent comes due every month."

In his office sitting across the desk from Fallon, Michael watched her green eyes blaze and her face flush. Seeing her determination, he almost felt sorry for Roy Gifford.

"Need I remind *you* that you have nothing to say about my checks nor have you ever paid my rent? And, for your information, I'll leave here when I'm good and ready." She slammed the receiver down, so furious she was shaking.

"Got your Irish up, did he?" Michael dared ask.

"Yes, he did, damn him." Jumping up from Michael's desk chair, she began to pace the room, needing to walk off her anger. "Who in hell does he think he is, hiring people behind my back, then ordering me to get myself back home? The nerve of him. The colossal nerve!"

Michael had overheard her end and guessed the other. "You still think Roy's not trying to cover up something?"

"Actually, I'm beginning to think you're right. But don't think it's because he came on to her." She stopped pacing, sat back down. "Maybe Laurie's got something on him and she threatened to tell Mom. Maybe the whole thing's a setup and Roy gave Laurie money to run away. I wouldn't put it past him."

"Something on him like an affair she learned about, you mean?"

Fallon shuddered visibly. "Personally, I can't imagine another woman wanting him, but I guess anything's possible."

"Or embezzlement?"

"Doubtful. He works for the IRS. He wouldn't risk a federal prison term. Besides, how would Laurie ever discover such a thing, at her age?"

"Yeah, I guess you're right. Back to sex."

"No, that's not it. If I just knew what it was."

"How about Danny? Maybe he overheard something. Why don't you call him at the academy?"

Fallon thought that over. "I could, I suppose. Only Danny's very smart and he damn well knows what side his bread is buttered on. He wouldn't say a word against his father, not even if Roy murdered someone in front of his face."

"Dead end then, I guess." He saw she'd calmed considerably and become thoughtful. "I take it you're not giving up just because Roy suggested it." He didn't want her to leave. He acknowledged that fact to himself, although he didn't want to question why, exactly, he felt that way. Not at the moment.

"Suggested? He didn't suggest, he demanded. No, I'm certainly *not* going back to please him. I hadn't intended to, anyway, but this call really did it. I'm not quitting until I find my sister, period. I rarely do things in half measure."

He had rather guessed that about her. "All right, then. How would you like to take a drive up to Newport Beach? We could check out this house where kids hang out with someone named Alex. The Rodeo Bar's closed on Sunday so we can try that tomorrow, if this doesn't pan out. I think I'll call Rollie and tell him we'll be by and why. It can't hurt to alert him in case we get delayed."

Fallon nodded. "Sounds like a plan. How far is it to Newport?"

"Forty, fifty miles. Won't take that long. It's straight north on Interstate 5." He rose and dug his keys from his pocket.

She put Roy's obnoxious demands out of her mind, walked around the desk and smiled at Michael, pleased he was able to help her. They were making some small progress. "Are you sure I'm not dragging you away from something you have to do?"

"All's quiet on the western front, according to Opal and Donovan. Listen, did you pack a bathing suit? We could duck into the surf for a swim, maybe."

She sobered quickly. "Michael, I didn't come here to have fun. I have to find Laurie."

"I know and we will. All I suggested was a possible dip in the ocean." He touched the ends of her hair, then pulled back because he wanted to touch much more. "Don't you ever do anything spontaneous or impulsive?"

With a groan, Fallon leaned against the desk. "I'm not in the least impulsive. Actually, 'impulsive' scares me."

"Really? Why?"

"Let me tell you a story about impulsive. I have a friend at the store, Tanya Williams. She told me she met a man in a hotel elevator one evening, and their eyes connected, just like in the movies. Silent communication, you know. They rode to the top floor together, got out and all he said to her was, 'Your room or mine?' She went with him and had the most incredible night of her life. Her words, not mine. Now, *that's* impulsive, and dangerous."

"And you'd never do that, would you?"

"No, I wouldn't. He could turn out to be some deviate or a serial killer or have some disease. I'm much too practical." She sighed. "Tanya says I miss out on a lot of fun, but I like to think I avoid a lot of trouble."

Michael slipped his arm around her slender shoulders. "Come with me, lady. I think your malady's curable."

Chapter 7

Fallon sat back in the passenger seat of the van as they drove north, passing through San Clemente on Highway 1. "You mentioned that you've met this Alex, so you know where he lives?"

"Sort of. I know the area. There's a group of rentals right on the beach, all owned by the same guy. They're popular with the Zonies, residents of Arizona who want to escape their sizzling summer weather by staying on the water. College kids hang out there on their breaks. Alex rents one."

"But T.J. and Laurie don't fall into either group."

"No, but Alex's place is popular with all kinds of kids." Michael slipped his sunglasses on against the afternoon rays that poured through even his tinted windshield. "He's a veteran, about forty, walks with a limp and gets a disability check each month. He attracts all sorts."

"You mean runaways that he tries to help, like you do?"

He passed a slow-moving Chrysler filled to the brim with tourists before answering. "I doubt that. Alex just sort of drifts through life—no job, no ambition. He had a few rough breaks after his discharge and decided not to fight the system so he became a beach bum instead. How could he help anyone if he can't help himself?''

Wonderful. And this was where Laurie was staying, with someone like that? Fallon felt more uneasy than when they'd set out. "I don't get it. What's the appeal for these kids, hanging around guys like Alex?"

Michael shrugged. "He leaves them alone, lets them crash at his pad, doesn't criticize. That might sound appealing to kids running from parents with a heavy list of rules. Alex isn't a bad guy and he's generous. He shares what little he has until the money runs out.''

"How'd you come to know him?"

"I don't really *know* him, but we've talked. I traced another runaway up here a while back.''

"And did you find the person?"

"Yeah, but he refused to come back with me. The kid's father was with me. The guy cried all the way back to San Diego. The boy was nineteen and legally couldn't be forced to return.''

"I'm having a hard time believing Laurie would want to be with people like Alex—drifters and misfits. She's always been wholesome and ambitious. She told me she wants to be a CPA. She's terrific with numbers, always has been. But now, if we don't find her soon, she'll get behind in school.'' Fallon ran a hand across her face. "What a mess." Something else was bothering her. "I wonder just how attached she is to this kid, T.J., and just who he is.''

"I called Sergeant Damien before we left. He wasn't in, but I left word to have him check out the kid.''

"With just those initials, no last name?"

"Sam's worked Juvenile a long time. He's got a lot of sources. If T.J.'s been around awhile, Sam'll have something on him. And I described both of them to Rollie on the Rodeo Bar's answering machine and asked him to call me at the house if either one comes in. I've done a few good turns for Rollie so he'll keep a lookout. We'll drop in tomorrow and take him a couple of flyers, see if he knows anything.''

Fallon was quiet and thoughtful for several miles, then turned to him. "Tell me the truth, Michael. You work with runaways, so you must know. Is there a lot of, you know, sleeping around? Drinking? Drugs?"

He'd been wondering when she would get around to asking. "I'm sure not going to tell you that none of that happens. I can guarantee it doesn't at my house. As I've already told you, we have rules and those who stay have to follow them. It's been my experience that most of the kids I run across are too troubled for involvements. And the real drinkers and druggies stay away from my place. Still, on the street, anything's possible. That's the best answer I can give you."

Which was barely an answer at all. She had a feeling he was protecting her from a more harsh truth. She sent up a silent prayer that they would find Laurie before she got involved with someone or tried drugs.

Michael glanced at her, noticing that she'd changed into white shorts and a loose yellow top. He thought she looked terrific. "You have great legs. You shouldn't cover them up all the time."

She sent him a look of dismay. "Will you keep your mind on the reason for our trip and leave my legs out of this?"

He gave her a sassy grin. "That's a pretty tall order. I'm not sure I can handle it."

"Well, try." Fallon spotted a roadside sign and sighed. "Laguna Beach. I've wanted to come here for ages. I hear it's really lovely."

"We can stop, if you like. It's past noon and we haven't had lunch."

"No, I really want to keep going. I want to talk with this Alex person."

Michael had suspected she would say that. He also suspected she wasn't going to be thrilled when she spoke to the man.

Alex's thinning hair was bleached almost white by his constant exposure to the sun, and his skin was deeply tanned and wrinkled, making him look older than his forty-

odd years. His blue eyes were deep-set and he had a six-inch
scar along one cheek that looked as if it had been made by
a jagged knife and left to heal without much medical assistance. He was shirtless, wearing faded cutoffs, and his left
leg was badly scarred.

On the weathered wood porch with the bright blue sea as
a backdrop, Fallon stood several steps behind Michael, not
because she was afraid of Alex but because the man smelled
as if he hadn't bathed in at least a week. His body odor
mingled with heavy cigarette smoke wafting through the
screen door that led into a dim room where she could make
out several people lounging around. k. d. lang was strum-
ming on the stereo.

Squinting at the picture Michael held out, Alex gripped
the wooden porch railing, a bit wobbly in his bare feet. Finally, he nodded. "Yeah, she was here. Coupla' days ago,
I think." He grinned and showed a missing front tooth.
"You kind of lose track of time out here, you know."

"Uh-huh." Michael took his measure and decided the
man was sober enough today to answer more questions. He
knew that Alex drank fairly heavily around the first of the
month when his check came in, but he'd decided not to tell
Fallon. "Was she with anyone?"

Alex rubbed his stubbly chin. "A skinny kid with red
hair. Let's see, what was his name? Oh, yeah. Called himself T.J. He's got shifty eyes. I didn't much like him."

Oh, swell. This beach bum didn't like the other one.
Fallon felt like weeping. "Did they stay here with you?" she
asked, not bothering to hide how much even the thought of
that upset her.

"Naw. They slept on the beach."

Her brows shot up. "Together?"

Alex winked and grinned again. "Probably. She's a cute
kid. Why not?"

Fallon angrily took a step forward, but Michael's outstretched arm held her back. "The girl's her sister."

"Oh," Alex muttered, as if that really made a big difference. "Sorry."

"How long did they stay?" Michael asked.

Scratching his bare chest, Alex shrugged. "Day or two. I don't remember."

The man was too vague to be of much help. Michael decided to try one more question. "Do you have any idea where they were headed when they left here?"

Alex's small eyes narrowed shrewdly. "Yeah, I do. What's it worth to you?"

"He doesn't know anything," Fallon told Michael disgustedly. "Let's just go."

But Michael didn't want to miss a chance. He passed a folded bill to Alex.

The money was swallowed by a grubby hand. "Thanks, man. T.J. made a call and they left real quick to hitch a ride to San Diego. He was real happy. They were meeting some guy at the Rodeo Bar who owed them money."

"This man owed money to T.J.?" Michael asked.

"Naw. The girl. She had some money comin' from this dude, or so T.J. told us. See, he owes me fifty bucks and he said he'd have it in a week or so and he'd drop it off on his way."

"On his way where?"

"He didn't say." Alex turned aside and opened the screen door. "That's all I know."

Frowning, Fallon watched him go inside, then shook her head. "That's ridiculous. Who would be giving Laurie money? She doesn't know anyone in California."

Michael ushered her down the stairs and along the sand, his mind searching for possibilities. "She could have worked for somebody for a few days and the guy hadn't been able to pay her right away. As I said before, I did a lot of odd jobs when I lived on my own. No one ever paid ahead. And a couple of times, they didn't pay at all, leaving me no recourse. Everyone knows that street kids won't call the cops on them."

"A job! What's Laurie qualified to do? She's worked a couple of months behind the counter at a drugstore. She's just a kid." Fallon's sandals kicked up sand as she walked.

"She could always wait tables."

"I don't know why we'd believe that smelly creep back there. Did he honestly recognize Laurie's picture, or did he make all that up to get some money from you? Even if they were here, he was probably drunk or stoned, whatever. For that matter, why'd we listen to Sherlock? He's nothing but a middle-aged hippie living in a park under a pretentiously false name, making believe he's some sort of guru to those poor lost kids. He left his home and family to be free and I find that pretty pitiful. And he takes money for information when he could be out *earning* a salary."

Michael could feel her disappointment, yet not agree with her logic. "Don't look now, but you're being a little judgmental, here. How do you know what sent Sherlock and Alex away from their families? I told you Sherlock just couldn't handle his former life. And do we know what kind of action Alex saw in the service that made him give up? Not everyone who doesn't live as you do is a derelict or mentally deficient or just plain lazy, you know. Ever hear the one about not judging a man until you've walked in his moccasins?"

Fallon heard his defensive tone and felt chagrined. "You're right, and I'm sorry. You were on the street and you're certainly none of those things. But Michael, I feel so damn frustrated and at the mercy of these two men who won't tell you anything unless you give them money. How trustworthy is that?"

He shrugged. "Maybe not at all. You come up with a better way and we'll try it."

"That's just it, I can't." She slipped off her shoes and walked toward the sea where the frothy waves were gliding in. "I don't know what to do next—whether to follow that clown's suggestion and visit the Rodeo Bar, or slap Laurie's picture on a dozen billboards along the interstate." She turned to watch him remove his shoes and follow her into the cooling water. "Do you *honestly* ever get anywhere following these haphazard methods, going from one slim lead to another?"

Michael heard the impatience and the anger behind it and understood. Telling her to be patient wasn't going to mag-

ically make her feel better. "I think you've got a case of
nerves, here."

Fallon swung back to face him, giving in to her temper.
It felt much better than giving in to despair. "You're right,
I do. I've got a mother back in Colorado who's undoubtedly crying her eyes out every night over this, a stepfather
who's furious at me for daring to defy him, a sister who is
wandering around God-only-knows-where with losers like
Sherlock and T.J. and Alex, and a job that is quite likely in
jeopardy the longer I'm away. Don't you think all that
qualifies me for just a small case of nerves now and again?"

Her speech, delivered with both fists planted on her slim
hips and her green eyes fiery, had him fighting a smile.
"Did anyone ever tell you you're beautiful when you're
angry?"

"Oh! Did anyone ever tell you that you're an infuriating pinhead?"

He gave her a guileless look. "No, not in those exact
words." He stepped closer to her. "Come on, Fallon.
Lighten up. This isn't helping anything. We'll find her, by
taking one step at a time." He reached to put his arms
around her, but she turned from him.

"Leave me alone. Just let me be." She took off, march-
ing away in the wet sand, her bare feet sinking and sliding
in her rush to be free of him.

She needed cooling off, Michael decided. And he was
just the man to do it. It took him only half a dozen long
strides and he was beside her. With no warning, he scooped
her into his arms, changed direction and headed out to
deeper water.

"Hey! What are you doing?" Fallon began to pummel
him, to kick her legs, trying to get free of his hold. But his
arms were like steel belts and his big hands only tightened
on her. "Put me down this instant."

The water was swirling around his waist. He stopped
abruptly. "Your every wish is my command." He dropped
her unceremoniously into the next rushing wave. "I hope
you can swim."

Fallon jackknifed, sinking to the sandy bottom, then came up sputtering mad as her body was hurled toward shore with the force of the tide. Moments later, she was sucked under, whirling back in Michael's direction before she could regain her footing. She broke the surface out a ways and kept herself afloat with her arms as she looked into his grinning face.

"You want to play dirty, do you?" she asked. Quickly, she dove under and went with the wave, her arms locking around his knees and pulling him down to join her. Abruptly letting go, she kicked upward and came up, tossing her wet hair out of her eyes before looking around for him.

Michael was nowhere in sight.

Swiveling, she scanned the shoreline, then looked out to sea. She knew he could swim because he'd told her he'd rescued Jonathan's grandson. Where was he?

Stealthily, he came skimming toward her underwater, his hands first yanking her down, then hard up against his body. He grabbed her wrists to stop her struggles, then took her mouth. He kept her there for a long moment before planting his feet in the shifting sand and finally pulling her up, his lips still locked on hers.

Desire consumed him like a tidal wave with the force of the relentless sea. His blood roared through his veins, heated, insistent. His mouth moved over hers, trying for control, for patience. This time she'd responded instantly, her tongue seeking his, her arms snaking around him and holding on.

Michael pulled back, for air, for balance. Her hair was plastered to her head, her eyes blinking away moisture, registering the hazy confusion of passion. His gaze dropped to where her pale yellow knit shirt clung to her breasts, the points dark and rigid under the sheer material of her bra. He bent his knees and, aided by the buoyancy of the water, lifted her, then guided her legs to fasten around his waist. He settled his mouth on one breast and heard her soft moan as her head dropped back.

Fallon felt the tug deep inside, felt her bones turn to water as her hands settled in the thickness of his hair. This was what she'd wanted, needed; this mindless oblivion. No time to think, to worry, to cast blame. Time only to feel.

And oh, he felt glorious, his mouth moving to make love to her other breast with teeth and tongue, causing ripples of desire to surge through her. His large hands on her bottom were hard and possessive. His eyes as he lifted his head and gazed at her were burning with a fierce need she understood all too well.

"I want you, *now*," Michael said, his voice husky.

"No, I— This is a public beach." Suddenly remembering that, she looked around but saw no one. Nevertheless, she couldn't. "Not here."

He cursed the wait, but understood. He let her slide down his body and saw her eyes widen when she realized how aroused he was. "Come on." He took her hand and walked her out of the sea, hoping the breeze would cool his blatant need temporarily. At the van, he unlocked the door, reached for the towels he always kept there, and handed her one. He had the engine going before she managed to fasten her seat belt with wet, shaky fingers.

The first motel was a mere five miles away, tucked in a grove of trees off the highway, a series of small cabins. Without a word, Michael jumped out and hurried to the office.

On the short ride over, Fallon hadn't let herself think about anything except Michael. Michael and the incredible way he made her feel—elemental and needy and wonderfully female. She'd never been impetuous or rash or even terribly spontaneous, as she'd explained to him. Until now. Until Michael.

He made her aware of herself as a woman, a very desirable woman—something no one else had ever quite managed to do. He made her want things she hadn't known she wanted. This was all happening too soon and yet, she'd lived twenty-six years without ever reaching for the brass ring, without ever following her heart or acting on impulse. This time she would. This time was just for her, and the timing be damned.

She saw him leave the office and rush to open her door, then pause, in his eyes a question. She knew he was giving her one last chance to back out. She studied him for several seconds, then made up her mind. Trembling, she placed her hand in his.

The small cabin was shadowy. Michael locked the door and closed the drapes, then turned on the bedside lamp. It glowed softly, revealing a king-size bed. He yanked down the spread and light blanket, exposing pale blue sheets.

Then she saw nothing else except Michael in front of her, Michael looming large and very male, Michael with his damp hair that fell forward onto his handsome face. He slipped off his shoes and whipped off his shirt, tossing both aside.

The air conditioner clicked on noisily in the background. The lamplight dimmed with the power surge, then settled. He took in the wet T-shirt that outlined her soft curves. "Let's take that off. I don't want you to catch cold."

Tentatively, her hands went to the hem of her shirt, then hesitated. "This probably isn't the wisest thing I've ever done."

"Wisdom is overrated, don't you think?" He bent to rain kisses on her face and smelled sunshine and sea on her skin.

"You always smell so good. How do you manage that?"

Her breath hitched in her throat as she reached to touch his chest, feeling the strong muscles, the springy blond hair. "You have a beautiful body, did you know that?"

"You think so?" He grinned down at her. "You show me yours and I'll show you mine." He decided to hurry her along and tugged the shirt off over her head. Her hair, already dry, settled as she squared her shoulders, as if for battle. He would give her one. Her bra was a wisp of satin, the peaks of her breasts already swelling. He gave in to a rush of yearning and put his mouth over her.

Fallon groaned at the contact, wanting to be flesh to flesh with him, her hands reaching behind her back to unfasten the obstacle. She yanked her bra off and when his lips touched her finally, she closed her eyes as the heat built and spread.

He could no longer wait, no longer be patient. He crushed his mouth to hers and tumbled with her onto the blue sheets. His hands shoved at her shorts, struggling to slide the wet material from her while her fingers fumbled with the snap of his jeans. Half-mad with a raging need he hadn't felt in years, Michael ripped off the last remnants of her clothing, breathing hard as his eyes caressed her secrets.

"I've never been like this, never wanted anyone like this," Fallon murmured in breathy gasps as she insinuated her hand inside the jeans she couldn't seem to remove fast enough. Hungry and seeking, her mouth returned to his as her fingers finally closed around him.

He bucked at the contact, then swore under his breath as he wrestled with his pants. Her ministrations tormented him, driving him on to free himself completely. They rolled and thrashed over the cool sheets, desperation driving them. Michael paused only long enough to reach into his damp back pocket for his wallet to yank out the foil packets he was never without.

Then there was no thought to go slowly, to be gentle or tender. Not now, not this time. This was all flash and fire and feeling, racing through him, not unlike the thunderous waves they'd left minutes ago. Gone was the hesitant, almost-shy woman he'd glimpsed from time to time. Her mouth and hands roamed his body with the same sense of urgency, the same delighted curiosity that had him seeking and finding her most vulnerable spots.

Fallon gloried in the wonder of having him here all to herself, to do with as she pleased. His hard, muscled body trembled as her lips moved to taste his sleek male flavors, to nip and nibble at his flesh. She heard him draw in a deep, shaky breath as her clever fingers worked their own brand of magic on him.

Then it was her turn to gasp as his mouth returned to devour hers and his hands went searching. She arched when he sent her over the first wild peak, then trembled as he drove her up again. Just when she thought she couldn't handle another onslaught, he slipped inside her and promised her more.

Michael gazed down at her as he began the rhythm. Her hair tumbled about her flushed face, her lips parted slightly and her green eyes grew smoky with passion. He'd never wanted a woman as much in his life. He closed his eyes then, and saw her still. She filled his vision, his mind, his memory. He felt her clench around him and heard her cry out.

And then he let the flames consume them both.

He didn't want to move, wasn't sure he could. His head lay on her breast as he listened to her heart trying to return to normal. He wasn't certain his ever would.

"I'm not usually like that," Fallon finally said, disliking the apology in her voice, yet finding herself unable to disguise it.

Michael angled around so he could see her face. She wouldn't meet his eyes. "Is that a fact? What are you usually like?"

That caught her off guard. "Uh, well, you know. Not quite so aggressive or in such a hurry." Raising a hand now that she finally felt able to move again, she finger-combed her hair back from her face. "I don't know exactly what happened."

Bracing himself on his elbows, he rose above her. "Whatever it was, I like it. No, I love it." He dipped to kiss her, slowly, lingeringly. Now that the first passionate flare-up had ebbed, he could afford to be tender. And he felt a bit chagrined himself. "I didn't mean to be so rough. I hope I didn't hurt you."

Lazily, she smiled up at him, deciding that they'd been well matched after all. "You weren't rough, and I'm not hurt. I guess we were both a little . . . anxious."

He kissed the tip of her nose. "You could say that." He became aware of their positions and decided he was probably crushing her. He rolled onto his back, taking her with him so that she was sprawled atop him. "You're full of surprises, Fallon," he said, his hand stroking her cheek, her silken throat, her satiny shoulders, realizing that although he'd just had her, he wanted her again.

"In what way?" she asked, curling into his touch.

"You have this cool, almost-unapproachable way about you at first. You keep people at a distance with just a look." His hands tightened their hold on her and his eyes warmed. "But when I touch you, something happens and you change."

Exactly what she'd been thinking—and it worried her.

Frowning, she eased away from him.

"Wait. Where are you going?"

"I'm trying to figure out just what there is about you that does that to me, that makes me behave out of character." She'd enjoyed making love with him, but it had also frightened her. Her reaction to him made her vulnerable, and that worried her.

Shifting onto her back, Fallon pulled the sheet up, needing the small protection it offered. "As terrific as this was, we have nowhere to go, Michael."

He'd been watching her, realizing that her thoughts had turned inward and her protective armor had slipped back into place. He rolled toward her, placing a finger on her chin and forcing her to look at him. "Do we have to be going somewhere? Can't we just enjoy this, what we've discovered? I'm not making any demands here. Are you?"

"Certainly not. It's just that... that feeling this way is unnerving. Losing control like that, it's upsetting." She stared up at the beamed ceiling as if answers could be found there.

"Not if the other person feels that way, too."

Surprised, she turned her head. "Do you?"

He raised an eyebrow. "Weren't you here in this bed with me? Didn't you notice my wholehearted participation? In case you're wondering, that wasn't a performance. And, for your information, I don't like losing control any more than you do." Which was certainly the truth. But he could handle this, of that he was certain. He could enjoy without

giving away parts of himself. He'd been doing it for years.
"Let's not overthink it, Fallon." His hand pulled down the
sheet, skimmed along the underside of her breast and he
saw her flesh react instantly to his touch. "Let's enjoy what
we have."

Her breath caught in her throat. How could this happen
again—so soon, so swiftly? She placed her hand atop his.
"We can't. It must be late. We have to get back and..."

"Why? What are we rushing back for? We can't go to the
Rodeo Bar till tomorrow." He leaned down and kissed her,
tenderly at first, then more deeply. Lifting back, he looked
into her eyes. "Unless, of course, you don't want me as
much as I want you?"

How could she fight this? Slowly, she wound her arms
around him. "Shut up and kiss me again."

They were sitting cross-legged on the bed eating chicken
lo mein, sweet-and-sour pork and shrimp-fried rice from
cardboard containers with chopsticks. Fallon wore a towel
wrapped around her while Michael had on only his jeans,
still not quite dry. After round two, they'd napped a bit,
then awakened starved. Not wanting to dress and go to a
restaurant, Michael had checked the Yellow Pages and
found a Chinese restaurant not far away that would deliver.

"Mmm," Fallon all but purred. "This was a *good* idea."

Michael swallowed a tasty mouthful. "Yeah, I have one
every once in a while."

Fallon's eyes smiled into his. "More than one lately." She
didn't even blush when she said it. How far she'd come in
a few short days, she couldn't help thinking.

He grinned back at her. "Hold that thought. The night
is young." It amazed him, absolutely amazed him, but he
felt tireless, indefatigable. He went back to eating before he
threw the cartons aside and ravished her again without allowing her to finish her dinner.

Afterward, as she sipped tea from a cup, Fallon grew
thoughtful.

It was only seven according to the bedside clock that was bolted to the nightstand. "You're sure that the Rodeo Bar is closed tonight?" They could still make it back to San Diego before the usual evening crowd descended. For a short time, she'd almost forgotten her reason for being here.

Michael nodded as he finished the fried rice. "Always on Sunday." He dropped his chopsticks into the carton and set both on the floor, then took a sip of tea. "But I think I'll call the house and talk with Opal. See what's happening, if anything."

He swung about, placing his bare feet on the floor, and reached for the phone.

"I'm going to take a quick shower while you make your call," Fallon told him as she stuffed cartons into a brown paper bag. She tossed the trash and went into the bathroom.

Humming to herself, she turned on the shower and stuck her hand in, waiting for the water to warm. She should be tired, she knew. She hadn't slept really well in over a week. And this afternoon, when she could have been resting, she'd put her body through the most vigorous workout it had ever known, one that might exhaust an Olympic trainee. She felt a smile form.

And she'd loved every moment of it.

Amazing what a spirited round or two of earth-shattering sex could do for the body and soul. Even the mind. She felt refreshed, eager to get moving, energetic. Like nothing she'd ever known before. But then, never had she experienced anything close to what she and Michael had shared in that small, dim room.

Grabbing the nearly threadbare washcloth, she stepped under the spray and gazed at the pitiful cube of soap. Oh, well, even these small inconveniences couldn't dampen her spirits right now. As much as possible, she worked up a lather.

Of course, she knew it would be foolish to make too much of what had happened. They were two healthy people who'd each met their match physically, that was all.

Aside from that, they had little in common. They had separate lives, different commitments, distinct and unrelated goals. Just because they were simpatico in the bedroom certainly didn't mean they would be a good match in other areas of their lives.

Michael was too focused, too dominating, too controlling for the long haul. And she was too independent for him, too challenging, too different. She needed someone who treated her more like an equal. He needed someone who wouldn't mind a man making all the decisions.

They were definitely incompatible.

She turned off the water and stepped out of the shower in a cloud of steam. The towel wasn't very much larger than the washcloth, but she managed to dry herself anyway. She wiped off the mirror and wished she had a toothbrush.

The woman who gazed back at her looked contented, satisfied, almost mellow. "Good grief!" Fallon said aloud, then laughed as she wound another towel around herself and opened the bathroom door.

The first thing she saw was that Michael was dressed and pulling on his shoes. Her heart began to hammer. "Something's happened. What is it?"

"Opal said that Rollie called and left me a message. It seems that Laurie and T.J. were in the Rodeo Bar last night."

I have not written for nearly two weeks now. We've run into one problem after another. Only our fierce determination keeps both Sloan and me going.

First, there was the rain—three days and four nights. Drenching, unrelenting, devastating rain. We were soaked to the skin with no dry clothes left. We nibbled on dried fruit and beef jerky and drank rainwater, our appetites almost nonexistent. Then Sloan came down with a sickness.

We were high in the mountains, miles from anywhere. The few cabins we'd passed on the way up were inhabited by people dirt-poor and unable to help, I know. He must have picked up a bug, perhaps from food he wasn't used to eating, or a chill from being wet for so long. Funny, he'd

*been worried that I would be the one to come down with
something with my frail health. Yet somehow, perhaps because Sloan needs me, I am the strong one.*

I had no choice but to scout out a cave that at least would
keep him dry. I kept a fire going and made soup from the
provisions we'd taken along. Then something odd happened. An old woman came along riding on a skinny mule.
She stepped in out of the rain and saw how the fever raged
through Sloan. She opened her saddlebag and took out
some herbs, then had me brew a pot of strong tea. She put
the herb mixture into the tea and forced Sloan to drink
some. At first, I was hesitant to let her, but he'd been ill for
days and only grew worse. The old woman stayed with us
and by morning, Sloan's fever broke. In another day, he
was able to eat solids and to get up, although he was weak.
That evening, we lay down on our bedrolls and sometime
during the night, the old woman left us.

I wonder if God sent her to us, for we badly needed a
miracle.

Now, we trudge on. Twice we've run into roaming gangs,
bandidos, men with little regard for the law or for human
life. We hide and wait and, so far, we've been lucky, for we
haven't been hurt. Yesterday we met a young soldier home
on leave and I asked him about the cabin we seek, about
Monica and Christopher, and Al Torres. He told me we
were on the right path to the Torres house. It is another
thirty miles away, he estimated, along a twisting, torturous
mountain road.

It might as well be a thousand miles.

I am so weary and often frightened. I would cry except I
have no tears left. And I must keep up my spirits for Sloan's
sake. He is such a good man, such a dear friend. Sometimes we just hold each other, our fearful thoughts on our
children who are not with us.

I pray that one day Sloan's Christopher and my three
beautiful children will all be reunited, God willing.

Chapter 8

Michael was lucky. Sergeant Sam Damien was in his office even though it was Sunday night because a teenage girl had been attacked and left bleeding in an alleyway in his district. Sam's voice was clipped and angry. The creep who'd slashed the fifteen-year-old on her way home from the movies was the same age, but with a rap sheet longer than a dead snake. Another half an inch and he'd have punctured her carotid artery. Sam's large hand was balled into a fist as his other gripped the phone.

"Yeah, I remember, Michael. You wanted me to check on a kid called T.J." Sam unclenched his fingers and rifled through a stack of folders until he found the one he wanted. "Here it is."

In his office at Michael's House, Michael didn't know whether to be pleased or worried. Pleased because maybe Sam's file would reveal something about the kid that Laurie McKenzie had apparently been hanging out with—or worried that if T.J. had a file in Sam's office, it probably meant he'd had some brushes with the law. Maybe even a record.

Sam opened the file and quickly scanned the first page. "Thomas Jefferson Owens the second, seventeen, five foot ten, 145 pounds, red hair, blue eyes. Birth mother dead, father's got the same name and his stepmother's Alice. They claim they can't handle T.J., that he dropped out of school, won't go back, smokes pot and steals." The sergeant flipped to page two. "He's been arrested twice for petty larceny, put on probation due to his age."

"That's it?" He could only hope. The kid's record sounded a lot like his own had. Most runaways ran into some trouble with the law.

"Until last spring. Got busted for possession. Cocaine. Ordered into a rehab center. Walked away after two days."

"Damn," Michael muttered. A kid with a habit was bad news.

Sam shifted the toothpick he was chewing to the other side of his mouth as he read on. "He's a slippery one. He roams up and down the coast and you know the code. His friends won't rat on him—and he seems to have plenty of friends."

Terrific. Just the sort of clean-cut boy Fallon would want her sister traveling around with. "Thanks, Sam. Is there a warrant out on him?"

"Not really. But if he's picked up for something, even a traffic violation, he'd be brought in. His father paid for his rehab treatment in that new center downtown. Costs around seven grand for thirty days. You can imagine, the old man's not happy and wants to be notified if we pick up his son." Sam closed the file and stuck it on top of his never-ending pile. "You got a line on where T.J. is?"

"I wish. I'm trying to track him. If your guys find him first, would you call me?"

"Sure. I wish you luck. These kids can disappear into the woodwork if they want to. They've got a network the CIA could use."

Michael had to agree. "I'll be in touch." He hung up and swiveled his chair around to look at Fallon. She wasn't going to like the news. He told her anyhow, because she had a right to know.

"Cocaine? Oh, no." Fallon felt impotent anger rise to the surface. Had she been naive in thinking that her sister would live on the street with all manner of runaways and not get involved with them, with drugs, possibly even sex? Yes, probably she had. She felt like crying for Laurie's lost innocence.

"That doesn't mean that Laurie's using. Let's try to stay optimistic."

Fallon rose to walk to the window and stared out unseeingly, her thoughts in a jumble. They'd driven back to San Diego only to find that Rollie had his answering machine on and wouldn't be available till tomorrow. It was nearly ten and she should be tired, but she was too revved up to sleep. "I don't feel too optimistic."

Michael got up and went to her, sliding his hands along her folded arms, burying his nose in her hair. "We're closer than we've been. That's something."

She was in no mood to be cajoled. "I don't know why this Rollie person couldn't have told Opal more, like, did Laurie and T.J. meet someone at his bar or were they alone, how long did they stay, where were they headed, did they seem all right. That kind of thing."

"That's expecting a lot of a bartender, don't you think?"

Fallon knew he was right. She refocused her anger, turning it onto Laurie. "Just wait until I get a hold of that girl. Does she have even a small idea of what she's put us all through? I'm going to drag her back to Denver if I have to take her kicking and screaming. And I'm going to enroll her in a convent school where a group of strong nuns with baseball bats and sturdy locked doors watch over her every move until she's at least thirty."

He knew he shouldn't smile, for her anger was real, but he couldn't help it. "Sounds good. I know she'll go for it."

"I don't give a damn whether or not she does. She needs to have a few things pointed out to her. She has to realize that she can't keep worrying people who love her with her immature behavior."

Michael decided enough was enough. Gently, he turned her around to face him. "Fallon, I know you're hurt and worried. But getting angry at Laurie isn't going to fix the situation. She doesn't need someone to lock her up or to point out the error of her ways just now. I know. I've been where she is."

She was listening, but he wondered if she was hearing. "If I'd had someone who cared about me and who'd come after me, I'd have listened like a good boy to their scolding, and then I'd have run away all over again. You've got to realize that the running away isn't the problem. It's the symptom. You have to discover what made Laurie leave, what problem prompted her to walk away from everyone and everything familiar. Then, and only then, can you begin to help her."

Fallon let out an exasperated sigh. "Michael, I know you mean well. And I'm sure you've helped a great many runaways. But my sister isn't like T.J. with his cocaine addiction, or Wendy dealing with both a rape and the loss of her baby, or lost souls like Alex and Sherlock. She comes from a good, solid home in the suburbs—not wealthy but comfortably middle-class. A little strict maybe, but tolerable. She has no addictions, no police record, no boyfriends, even."

"That you know of," he said quietly.

Her green eyes blazed back at him. "What do you mean?"

"Oh, Fallon, listen to yourself. Do you think that Laurie's lived on the streets with all these people and remained totally untouched?"

Hadn't she just berated herself for her own naiveté? Yet, coming from him, it sounded worse. "You did."

"To some degree. I didn't do drugs because I saw what people with fried brains became. But I stole, I smoked, I drank, I experimented with sex. I was a wild kid for over four years. That sort of thing leaves marks on you. I got lucky. Jonathan got help for me. I didn't mention this earlier, but I was in counseling for another four years, trying to deal with the death of my parents, which I'd never addressed, and the anger I felt for the hand I'd been dealt. You don't get over that in a day or two, nor will a couple of

well-meaning conversations bring you around. On th
street, you're filled with pain and anger and fear. That'
why so many turn to alcohol or drugs—to escape.''

Fallon forced herself to relax, to try to understand wha
he was saying, if not to totally agree with his opinion. ''
know it isn't going to be easy for her. Or me. But I still re
turn to the same thought, and that is that you didn't hav
a parent left who loved you or a sister who took a hiatu
from her life to find you so she could help you. Laurie wi
be all right if I can just get her back home, away from th
street people and the life she's in now. I know it.''

A brick wall. He was talking to a brick wall. There wa
no point in continuing. Michael was certain he was righ
He'd spent half his life learning his hard lessons. Fallo
would have to learn, but apparently not from him. ''A
right, let's not argue about this.'' He turned her aroun
again and placed his hands on her shoulders, hoping t
massage away the tension. ''Let's concentrate on findin
her. I'm sure when that happens, you'll know what to do.
At least, he hoped so; for both Laurie's sake and Fallon's
he thought as he dug his fingers into her taut muscles.

A knock on the open door had them both turning. Dary
stood in the doorway, looking nervous and hesitant.

''Come in, Daryl.'' Michael walked toward the boy
''How are things going?''

Daryl glanced at Fallon, then back to Michael, obv
ously reluctant to talk in front of her.

She smiled at the thin boy who was still wearing the ver
white, still-like-new running shoes Michael had paid for. ''
think I'll go up to my room. See you both later.'' Fallo
grabbed her purse and walked out into the hallway. She'
taken only two steps when the large shoulder bag slippe
out of her hands and fell to the floor, spilling its contents
Annoyed, Fallon bent to pick up her things.

''I've been having bad nightmares,'' she heard Daryl sa
from behind the office door she'd left ajar.

''What kind of nightmares?'' Michael's low voice asked

"You know, about the beatings, my folks passed out on the floor, the awful smells. I wake up sweating. It hurts to remember."

"A lot of things hurt, Daryl. You have to face your fears and pretty soon, they get easier, then finally go away."

"I try, but it's hard. I don't know if things will ever be different. I don't think so."

Finished gathering her things, Fallon straightened, but didn't leave. She felt embarrassed eavesdropping, yet she badly wanted to know what Michael would say to this poor sad young boy.

"Yes, they will. You have to believe that, Daryl, because only you can make them better."

"Don't!" Daryl said, his voice suddenly stronger, louder.

"Don't what?" Michael asked, sounding honestly baffled.

"Don't make me want things I can't have." The boy's voice was once more timid. "When I was nine or ten, I figured out there's a whole lot I can't have. So I made myself stop wanting them. Now, you make me think I can." His voice cracked, quivered. "Michael, I'm scared."

"I know. It's all right to be scared, Daryl. We all get scared sometime."

"Even you?"

"Oh, yeah. But there's an old saying I really like. 'What the mind can conceive and believe, it can achieve.' You *can* do it, Daryl. You can be anything you choose. Just believe it and go for it."

"You really think so?"

"Absolutely. Focus on that and I guarantee you, your nightmares will disappear." His voice lowered, as if he was leaning closer to the boy. "I know, because it happened to me, just like it's happening to you now. I concentrated on what I wanted. I actually pictured it every night before I went to sleep. Pretty soon, I began to believe it would happen. And in time, with lots of hard work, it did." Michael cleared his throat. "Tell me, are you reading the books I gave you? School starts next week, you know."

"Yeah, but I'm worried about that, too." He paused, as if reluctant to reveal even more weaknesses. "I'm small for my age and I'm already a grade behind in school. The kids, some even from here, make fun of me. My voice cracks. Girls won't even look at me. I . . . I hate it."

Michael's voice was deep, reassuring. "Daryl, the true measure of a man isn't how deep his voice is or how many girls notice him. It's how he sees himself and how he views the world. Picture yourself as strong, smart, good. And that's how others will see you, too. Those kids who make fun of you now, those blowhards, they're scared deep down inside, too. They're whistling in the dark, afraid to face their fears. You can be better than that. You can walk tall and be proud. Think you can do that?"

"Do *you* think I can do all that?"

"You bet I do."

Walking quietly away, Fallon left the hall and went into the rec room where the television set was on low. Her mind was still on the conversation she'd overheard. She didn't always agree with Michael, but she had to admit he had a knack for talking with these kids, for inspiring them.

She heard a sound behind her and turned to find a young girl in her early teens huddled in a corner of the couch along the sidewall. She was crying softly into a soggy tissue. Fallon walked over. "Are you all right?"

The girl looked up and gave her a teary smile. "Oh, sure. I just watched this really sad movie. It's called *Ghost*. Did you ever see it?"

"Yes, a while ago."

The girl sat up taller and dabbed at her eyes. "I don't really believe in ghosts, but it's such a beautiful love story. He dies but he won't let them take him to heaven until he makes sure the woman he loves is all right. And she can feel him in the room with her, even though he's a ghost. Isn't that something?"

Fallon couldn't help smiling. "Yes, that's something." On closer examination, she guessed the girl to be about fourteen, younger than Laurie. She was considerably heavier, though, and her black hair was worn in a long braid that hung down her back. "What's your name?"

"I'm Roxie. Who are you?"

"Fallon, a friend of Michael's. Do you live here, Roxie?"

"Yeah. I've been here the longest. Nearly two years, since I was twelve."

Curiosity had Fallon sitting down on the opposite end of the couch. "Do you go to school?"

"Oh, sure. Michael makes all of us go to school. I'll be a freshman in high school, starting next week."

Fallon hesitated, but decided to plunge in. "Where are you from? Where's your family?"

Roxie's expression didn't change. "From Manzanita, the Indian reservation near the border. I don't see my family. My dad was injured and can't work anymore. My mom can't afford to buy me clothes or send me to school, so I ran away. My brothers and sisters stayed, but there's no future without school. Lucky for me I met Michael in the park one day. He says education's really important."

"I agree. Are your grades good?"

"All A's except math. I've got to take algebra this year." She wrinkled up her nose.

Fallon just had to ask. "Do you miss your home, your family?"

Roxie waved her hand at the room. "Not anymore. This is my home and the kids here are my family. And Opal and Sukey and Michael."

Fallon didn't know what to say to that, so she rose. "I'll leave you to your television watching."

"I'd like to see *Ghost* again. Do you ever wish when you watch a movie that you could change the ending? I wish the man hadn't died. She loved him so much." Looking very young and innocent, Roxie looked up at Fallon. "Do you believe you can have a love so strong that you can feel that person's presence even if they're not with you?"

Did she? "I'm not sure that I do. But it's a lovely thought. See you later, Roxie." Feeling pensive, Fallon climbed the stairs to her room.

* * *

The Rodeo Bar, as Fallon had imagined, had a Western motif and was frequented by cowboys, both real and pseudo. The plank floor was covered with sawdust, the split-pine bar ran the entire width of the large main room and the music was loud enough to turn normal conversation into a shouting match.

At nine on Monday night, Rollie came out from behind the bar carrying three steins of beer, leaving his two assistants in charge as he joined Michael and Fallon at one of the tables toward the back. Thankfully, the enthusiastic band had just finished a set and gone outside to take a break.

Rollie offered a beefy hand to Michael and nodded to acknowledge his introduction to Fallon. He was a barrel-chested man with tattoos along both arms, a black handlebar mustache and not a hair on his shiny head. He waited until they'd taken the first swallow of the ice-cold beer before speaking.

"Like I told Opal, the two kids you described on my machine were in on Saturday night." He jerked his head in the direction of the next table under the side window. "Sat right over there." He wiped foam from his mustache. "That damn T.J. knows I got his number, but he keeps on trying."

"What do you mean?" Michael asked.

"He's underage, yet he orders a beer every time. I just laugh and hand him a root beer. He gets real red in the face. The kid's got a temper."

That wasn't what Fallon wanted to hear. She removed a folded flyer from her shoulder bag and placed it in front of Rollie. "Is this the girl who was with T.J.?"

The light wasn't all that bright. Rollie squinted as he studied the photo. "Yeah, that's her. Skinny little thing. Had on jeans and a big, floppy shirt. Her hair was tied up with a piece of yarn. She sure as hell wasn't even old enough to be in a bar."

"She's my sister and she's only sixteen," Fallon told him

"I knew she was young. T.J. acted real self-important, like he usually does, but the guy who was waiting for them wanted to talk to your sister, not him." Rollie took a long swig of beer and propped one bent leg over the other as he regarded them both.

Michael felt Fallon tense and put his hand on hers. "What did the man look like?"

"A big guy with a dark beard, maybe forty-five. Losing his hair on top so he grows it on his face." Rollie ran a hand over his own bald pate and laughed. "Like me. Anyhow, he gave me his card, but I don't know what I did with it. He'd been in here before, asking about the girl and T.J. I told him he'd just have to hang around and wait till they came in, 'cause I don't keep track of nobody."

"Would you remember his name if you heard it?" Fallon asked.

Rollie shrugged. "Probably. I'm pretty good with names."

"Does Raymond Tompkins sound right?"

"Yeah, that's it. A P.I. from Colorado. Wore boots and a bolo tie with his shirt, brand-new jeans. A restless dude. Kept going to the phone and making calls."

"Saturday night, when he met with T.J. and Laurie, did you happen to hear anything that was said or did you notice anything that might help us find the two kids?"

Rollie frowned. "See that bar way over there? That's where I was standing. In this place, no way you're going to overhear something unless you're damn near sitting on the guy's lap. I did notice one thing, though."

Fallon's hand under Michael's tightened into a fist. "What was that?"

"The P.I. handed the girl an envelope. Don't know what was in it, but I can guess."

"All right," Michael said pleasantly, "guess."

"Had to be money. She opened it and her fingers moved inside like she was counting. Then she smiled at the dude." Rollie snorted. "I could see that T.J. wasn't happy, because he held out his hand for the envelope, but she shook her head and slipped it inside her shirt. Smart girl. Money slips through that kid's hands."

"What do you know about T.J.?" Michael asked.

"Not much. Like I said, he comes in mostly to hang around, shoot some pool. I catch some guys sneaking him a beer now and then and toss them all out."

Fallon's lips were a thin line. Not only did T.J. use cocaine but he drank. What in the world had Laurie gotten into? "Did they stay long? Did they leave together?"

"The P.I. had the girl sign something, then he took off. The kids put their heads together, whispering and arguing. Then T.J. came over to the bar and asked me if my friend, Niko, still had a place up near Lake Elsinore. I told him, sure. He asked me to write out directions to Niko's. Then they left. Ain't seen them since."

"Who is this Niko?" Michael wanted to know.

Rollie drained his mug before answering. "A lucky stiff is what Niko is. Some uncle died and left him a pile of dough. Niko owns a motel on the lake, a restaurant and bar, a big house and a refurbished Bentley he bought from some movie star. But he's good people, you know."

"Why would T.J. want to go visit Niko?" Michael asked, truly puzzled at this new development.

"Probably because Niko used to be on the streets until his ship came in. He's got a soft spot for kids like he used to be. He rents cheap to them, gives them a job when they need one, stuff like that. You ask around L.A. Everybody knows Niko."

Michael turned to Fallon. "Feel like another trip?"

"What choice do we have?"

"Will you draw us a map to Niko's?" he asked Rollie.

"Sure. Wait here." Rollie grabbed his empty mug and made his way back to the bar.

"What do you think?" Michael asked, looking at Fallon's strained face, wishing he could remove the worry from her.

"I don't know what to think. Why would the private investigator Roy hired give an envelope of money to Laurie? I don't get it." She sighed, feeling weary and confused.

"Do you want to give Roy and your mom a call and see if you can learn anything?"

"No. I'll only get into another yelling match with Roy, and I doubt if my mother knows what's going on since she wasn't aware that he'd hired this Hopkins in the first place." Thoughtfully, she narrowed her eyes. "I wish I knew what that worm was up to."

Michael caught Rollie's eye as he signaled from the bar and rose. "I'll meet you at the door." He threaded his way through the tables and took the makeshift map from the bartender. "Thanks." Turning, Michael pocketed the folded paper.

"No problem. Say, I almost forgot to tell you. That bearded guy who met with the kids? He asked about you, too."

Michael returned his attention to Rollie. "Oh, yeah? What'd he want to know?"

"About the house for runaways you operate, where it's located, if you ever came in here, what kind of car you drive, that sort of thing."

What kind of car he drove? "What'd you tell him?"

Rollie shrugged. "Not much. Told him your place was called Michael's House, but I didn't know the address and I didn't know what you drove. You seen him around?"

"No, I haven't." But then, he hadn't really been watching, either. "If he comes back, tell him nothing, okay?"

"Sure, man. See you." Rollie turned to wait on a customer.

Michael saw Fallon waiting for him at the front door. He decided not to tell her what he'd just learned. It would only alarm her further.

As soon as Michael's van turned the corner, he saw the familiar pale gray Lincoln parked in the driveway of Michael's House. "Well, you're in for a treat," he told Fallon. "Jonathan's here."

She cast a nervous glance at the big, expensive car, thinking about all it represented. "I don't think I'm very good company tonight, Michael. Maybe some other time."

He pulled up in front of the house and turned off the engine. "Oh, come on. Just say hello, won't you, please? I mentioned you to Jonathan on the phone last night. You'll like him."

With a sigh of resignation, she got out and followed him inside.

Jonathan Redfield was seated at the scarred oak table in the dining room drinking a cup of coffee with Opal. He rose as they came striding in.

"I was hoping you'd get back before I had to leave," Jonathan said, reaching to clasp Michael's hand, then grasp his shoulder for a minihug.

"I'm glad you dropped in." Michael drew Fallon in closer. "Jonathan, this is Fallon McKenzie. We've just been running down a lead on her sister."

Jonathan's slim manicured hand shook Fallon's while his gray eyes looked her over thoroughly. "A pleasure meeting you. I hope you were successful this evening."

"Somewhat," Michael told him, pulling out a chair for Fallon while Opal rose to pour coffee into two more cups before excusing herself to go to her room and watch her favorite quiz show.

Seating himself, Michael told Jonathan about their visit to the Rodeo Bar and their conversation with Rollie—all but the last part.

While Michael explained, Fallon had a chance to study his benefactor. Tall and quite slim, Judge Redfield gave the impression of being formidable. He had thick white hair and a trim mustache beneath a patrician nose. His suit was lightweight, pale gray and beautifully made, the creases in his trousers razor sharp. On his right wrist was a gold Piaget and he wore a pinkie ring on his left hand.

But it was his eyes that impressed her. They were the kindest eyes she'd ever seen. Fallon decided that if she ever had to appear in front of a judge, this man would be her first choice.

Jonathan turned his attention to Fallon. "I'm sorry to hear you're having such a difficult time tracking down your sister. However, if anyone can find her, Michael can."

Loyalty and pride and love. Who could ask for more? Small wonder that Michael thought the man walked on water. "Thank you, Judge. I'm sure you're right."

"You're in retail, Michael tells me. A buyer." His gaze skimmed over her green linen slacks and silk blouse. "I thought you might be a model. You have the look. Lovely."

She smiled at his flattery and noticed that Michael was watching the two of them closely. Sipping her coffee, she wondered why.

Jonathan turned to Michael. "I came by to tell you that Tim's announced his engagement and he's going to ask you to be his best man."

Michael frowned. "That's flattering, but he's too young to get married. He just finished college in May. Can't you talk them into waiting awhile? He's got four years of law school ahead."

Jonathan shook his impeccably groomed head and smiled. "Have you ever tried to talk a young man in love into waiting?" He included Fallon. "Tim's my grandson. Michael saved his life when he was seven and he acts more like his father than my son-in-law does."

"I can't believe that Cynthia and Tom are for this marriage," Michael went on. "Tim should be thinking about Stanford Law School, not marriage. Did you tell him what a demanding mistress the law is?"

"Of course I did, but he's in no mood to listen."

Fallon had never heard Michael so vehement on a subject, not even on his runaways. And she'd never realized he was such a cynic. She decided it would be best if she kept her opinions to herself. Matter of fact, she decided she would let the two men hash out Tim's future without her.

Rising, she smiled at the judge. "It was good meeting you, but I think I'll turn in. We're leaving for L.A. in the morning and I'm rather tired."

"You can use my Lincoln if you like, Michael. That van's not terribly reliable, is it?"

Fallon didn't think it was, either. "Or we can take my Mustang."

Michael only looked annoyed. "The van's fine. It runs beautifully. You know I always keep up my vehicles."

Like the courtly gentleman he was, Jonathan conceded, then rose and took Fallon's hand in both of his. "I hope we'll see more of one another when you return."

"Thank you." She tried to catch Michael's eye, but he was staring off into space. "What time do you want to get started?"

"Is seven, seven-thirty, all right with you?"

"Fine. Good night."

She left the room and was halfway up the stairs when she realized she'd left her shoulder bag on the table. Walking back, she stopped outside the dining room when she heard Jonathan mention her name.

"Fallon's lovely. She looks familiar. Too familiar." The judge's voice lowered. "Michael, she resembles Paige a great deal. I realized it the moment she walked in."

"Fallon's not Paige Hanley. She's not anything like Paige." His tone was sharp, irritated. His chair scraped on the tile floor as he shoved it back and walked into the kitchen.

"I'm having another cup of coffee. Want one?"

"No," Jonathan said softly. "I've had enough."

Fallon backed off and retraced her steps. She could get her bag later.

Who, she wondered, was this Paige Hanley that Jonathan thought she resembled, and what was she to Michael that the mere mention of her name could upset him so?

The morning was dreary with rain clouds hovering above as Michael drove north on Interstate 5, the same route he'd taken two days ago. Only this journey would take them inland and, hopefully, turn out to be more fruitful.

He glanced over at Fallon. She had on tennis shoes, white slacks and a red top, and her eyes were hidden behind huge sunglasses when there was no sun. Interesting. Was she trying to hide the ravages of a sleepless night or was she trying to avoid him?

It seemed as if ever since they'd left that seedy motel and rushed back to San Diego, they hadn't had a shared minute when they weren't worrying about Laurie, questioning Rollie or talking with Jonathan. He wanted some quiet time when they could concentrate just on each other. His thoughts about Fallon were confused, his feelings jumbled. She touched something inside him no woman had touched before.

And it scared the hell out of him.

Undoubtedly that was one reason he wasn't sleeping well. Last night, Jonathan had been in one of his chatty moods, staying until nearly midnight. Afterward, Michael had tossed and turned for hours, finally falling into an exhausted sleep so that in the morning, he'd had to force himself to get up. He hadn't gone downstairs until seven when he'd grabbed a quick cup of coffee before taking off, knowing Fallon was anxious to get going.

He wondered if she'd fared any better. "Did you sleep well last night?"

Her head tipped back on the seat, Fallon stared at the pink and white oleander bushes decorating the median strip. "Fine, and you?"

"Me, too," he lied. She'd had her door closed with the lights out when he'd finally made it up to his room across the hall from hers. Not that he'd have gone in, anyway— not in the house that he felt belonged to the kids. He had an image to maintain, and emergencies popped up frequently, requiring his immediate attention. Yet he knew he would have slept better if she had shared his bed. One night of making love with her hadn't been nearly enough. "Have you thought any more about why Laurie would accept money from that investigator?"

Fallon brushed back her hair although the breeze coming in through the open window rearranged it again. "I've thought of very little else. I keep talking myself out of all my theories. For instance, maybe Roy intended that she buy an airline ticket and fly back home. But knowing him, if that was his intention, he wouldn't have left anything to chance. He'd have had Tompkins deliver the ticket to her, not cash.''

"Maybe Rollie couldn't see all that well. Maybe it wasn't cash, after all."

"Then what was it? And why did T.J. get a detailed map to this Niko's place if Laurie had the envelope and intended to fly back to Colorado? No, I think it was money."

Michael redirected the van's air vents. The humidity was heavy in the sea air and it had begun to drizzle. "All right, then, my best guess is that Roy sent the P.I. to find her and pay her hush money."

Fallon shook her head. "I think you've been reading too many detective novels, although I have to admit, I've considered the possibility myself. Hush money for what? And don't give me the same theory about a sexual thing between the two of them. I simply can't buy that."

A white Cadillac driven by a bearded man passed them doing well over the speed limit. Fool, Michael thought, then brought his attention back to the discussion. "Okay, then, theory number two. You said that Roy and your sister didn't get along, almost from the day he married your mother. Maybe he offered Laurie money to go away, so his life would be easier." He glanced over and saw she was thinking that over.

"I could almost believe he'd do something despicable like that. But why would Laurie go for it? It would take a hell of a lot of money to coax her away from the education she's always wanted and all her plans for the future, and Roy's basically very cheap. Besides, there couldn't be very much money involved if she's living on the street with some cocaine addict."

Michael wasn't one to give up easily. "Then how about this? She could be giving T.J. money for his drugs, if she cares about him." He noticed her shocked look. "People in love do stupid things."

Laurie in love? Fallon couldn't buy that. She'd just met the guy a couple of weeks ago. That thought stopped her short. She'd just met Michael a week ago and she'd already been in bed with him. Who was she to judge her sister?

But, dammit, Laurie was sixteen, not twenty-six, she reminded herself. And a virgin, as far as Fallon knew, at least when she'd left Colorado. Of course Laurie could believe she was in love. Teenage girls often built romantic fantasies around guys. T.J. might appear mysterious and appealing to an inexperienced girl. And Laurie was a dreamer, building castles in the air. "I suppose it's possible," Fallon reluctantly admitted.

"I hope that's not the case," Michael went on. "But I've known people who imagined themselves in love, especially at a young age, and they acted on it, messing up their lives. Then they've had to live with that regret."

Fallon heard the bitterness in his tone and decided he was no longer speaking hypothetically but drawing on his observations. Or maybe personal experience. She remembered his adamant disapproval of Jonathan's grandson, Tim, who'd decided to marry before completing his education. Was that at the root of Michael's cynical outlook on young love, or was it something that ran much deeper?

"You're thinking of Tim, I imagine," she said, deciding to open this can of worms carefully. "Do you really think that twenty-two is too young to marry?"

The look he threw her was sharp. "Don't you?"

Fallon shrugged. "It depends a great deal on the people involved. Some men—and women, too—are very mature at that age, while others aren't capable of making good decisions at thirty-five. I don't know Tim...."

"I do." Michael turned right off Interstate 5 onto Highway 174, which was a two-lane trailing through several towns around Lake Elsinore. "In many ways," he continued, "he's mature, mostly because he's the only child of wealthy parents who've traveled the world with him and exposed him to all kinds of situations. But he's also inherited Jonathan's work ethic, which is dedication in the extreme. Tim's following in his grandfather's footsteps and the law is terribly demanding. In order to succeed as Jonathan has—to head your own firm and then be elected as a judge, which is what Tim's told me he wants—his private life will suffer.''

"Did Jonathan's?"

Michael flipped on the windshield wipers. The drizzle had turned into a mild rainfall. "His situation was different. He had almost an arranged marriage. His wife's parents were lifelong friends with Jonathan's family. The two grew up together and always knew they'd marry. Still, they waited until Jonathan had passed the bar and joined his father's firm. Unfortunately, his wife died two days after giving birth to their only child.''

"Oh, how sad. And he's never remarried."

"No. His way of handling his grief was to throw himself into his work. It made him forget and also made him a very rich man."

"And a very lonely one."

Michael set the cruise control on the van and relaxed in the light traffic. "To some extent, but he has Cynthia and her husband, Tom, and Tim, of course. And many friends.''

"And you—he has you." But did family and friends make up for the absence of a loving mate? "I can see that with no wife requiring attention and with his daughter probably being raised by hired help, he had all the time in the world to devote to furthering his career. But he had no personal life, to speak of. Who would choose to live like that?''

A muscle in Michael's jaw clenched. "We live the hand we're dealt, Fallon, not necessarily the one we'd choose.''

Was he speaking of himself now? she wondered. "So you feel that with a wife, Tim would be distracted in his study of the law and wouldn't be a success. Is that it?" She was honestly trying to understand.

"Partly. It's also the woman he's chosen to marry."

Ah, now we're getting somewhere. "You don't care for her?''

Michael's hands tightened on the wheel ever so slightly, but Fallon noticed nonetheless. "Let's just say that I think Karen has a hidden agenda.''

He was being deliberately evasive. Fallon's curiosity was aroused even though she knew this was none of her business. Yet she felt that Michael's view of Tim's situation revealed a great deal about himself. "Would I be out of line if I asked what you thought that was?"

Michael let out a huff of air. He hadn't planned on getting into this, yet maybe it was a good thing. Fallon would undoubtedly get the message, no matter how subtle. "Karen's father is a small-town justice of the peace. They have seven children in the family, Karen being the oldest. She attends a community college, but when you ask her what her goals are, she smiles, takes Tim's hand and says that all she wants is to make Tim happy."

As an independent woman, Fallon had a lot of trouble with women who saw themselves as mere reflections of a man. Yet many did and they had a right to their opinion. However, she thought that Michael's problem with Karen ran a bit deeper. "You think she's a gold digger after Tim for his family money?"

"I think it's as plain as the nose on her face. But I've mentioned the possibility to Jonathan and to Tom, as well. Neither agrees with me. So I say, let's wait and see. If Karen really cares for Tim, she'll wait until he finishes law school."

"Test her, you mean?"

He frowned, not pleased with the sound of that. "I wouldn't call it a test, exactly, unless it's a test of time. Tim's known Karen less than a year. Frankly, for most young men, their judgment is often clouded by their hormones and what they label love often turns out to be a trap." And therein was his real fear. "I just hope he's smart enough to be careful."

"You're thinking of an early pregnancy." She was watching his face when a thought occurred to her. "Are you thinking Karen might try to trap him?"

The muscle in Michael's jaw tightened again. "It's been known to happen."

Fallon stopped herself from asking who he meant, although she badly wanted to know. This reaction had to come from personal experience. Had someone tried to trap Michael when he was young? Maybe she was jumping to conclusions. Perhaps he was just very protective of Tim, who must seem almost like a relative to Michael after having saved his life when the boy was only seven and then having lived so closely with the entire family.

She decided to try to defuse the obvious tension she'd unwittingly created. "Well, Tim's quite worldly, as you mentioned. Surely he knows all about birth control."

Michael made a sound that resembled a bitter laugh. "Sometimes knowing isn't enough." The rain had picked up. He tapped the brakes as they cleared the top of a rise.

Fallon didn't know how to answer that so she turned to gaze out the side window. "You know, it rains more here in southern California than it does in Colorado. I thought this was the sunshine state."

Michael sat up straighter, his hands tightening on the wheel, his body tensing. The brakes weren't holding. Again he tapped, then pressed all the way to the floor. Nothing. The van was racing down the incline.

Fallon couldn't help noticing their excessive speed on wet pavement. "Michael, is something wrong? We're going so fast."

"The brakes aren't grabbing hold."

"What? How can that be?"

Up ahead in their lane, a camper was wheezing along on the sloping pavement. In the passing lane were several cars almost bumper-to-bumper, moving more slowly due to the rain. He had to do something before the gathering momentum would hurl them into another vehicle.

"Brace yourself, Fallon. I'm going to steer us off onto the shoulder."

"Oh, my God!"

Chapter 9

"Hey, buddy, you were damn lucky," Charley said as he stepped out from beneath the van suspended up on the hoist in his garage.

Leaning against the doorjamb of the mechanic's shop, Michael didn't feel all that lucky. True, they hadn't hit another person or car. No one had died and, except for his sprained ankle, no one had gotten hurt. But the skid off the highway onto the asphalt shoulder had sent the van banging against the concrete retaining wall several times before Michael was able to get the vehicle under control enough that it rolled to a stop.

"How so?" he asked.

Charley wiped his greasy hands on an equally dirty rag as he shook his head worriedly. "Someone out there doesn't like you, buddy. I thought you ought to know."

Seated in the lone chair along the wall, her trembling barely under control after their harrowing incident, Fallon heard the mechanic's words and walked over. "What do you mean?"

Charley adjusted his blue baseball cap more comfortably on his dark head. "Someone poked a hole in your brake line."

Michael straightened, then drew in a sharp breath as his ankle protested the weight shift. In getting out of the van that had ground to a halt at an angle, he'd stepped onto light gravel covering a pothole and sprained his ankle badly. That, it appeared, was the least of his problems. "Are you sure?"

"You bet I am." Charley ducked his head under the van and pointed upward. "See there? That's a hole made by something sharp and pointed, like an ice pick or a nail punch."

Michael stuck his head under and tried to see where the mechanic was pointing. It wasn't easy to see the line, much less the hole. "Maybe I drove over a rock with a sharp edge," he offered, unwilling to believe the other scenario.

"Not possible. That would have made a jagged tear." Charley's blackened finger pointed to the exact spot. "This here's a fairly small but deadly round hole, one made deliberately." He ducked back out and waited until the customer had straightened. "Someone knew what they was doing, too. They made it small so you'd be driving along for several miles with the brake fluid slowly leaking out. You wouldn't notice it for a while. Then, once the fluid was all gone, the brakes wouldn't hold. Bingo! Accident."

Michael saw that Fallon had turned nearly as white as her slacks. He slipped his arm around her waist before turning back to Charley. "I don't see how this could have happened. I keep the van in top condition. Just had it serviced last week. My regular mechanic didn't notice anything wrong."

Charley sent him an impatient look. "You're not hearing me, buddy. This had to have been punctured a couple of hours ago. Three or four, tops. Otherwise, all the fluid would have slowly dripped out and you would have noticed soon as you touched the brakes first time. When did you start out?"

"Less than an hour ago."

Charley nodded sagely. "You see? The heat of the engine warms the fluid and it flows faster. Where'd you have it parked? Had to be somewhere where just anyone could get to it real easy."

Fallon looked up at Michael. "You didn't pull into the drive last night because Jonathan's car was there. Did you garage the van after he left?" She remembered that her rental car was still taking up half of the garage space.

Michael shook his head. "The van sat out in front all night."

"So," Charley went on, "you want I should call the cops and report this?"

They were halfway between San Juan Capistrano and Lake Elsinore. What good would it do to involve local cops? What could they possibly do but fill out a report? "I don't think so. How long will it take you to fix it?"

Charley wrinkled up his forehead, calculating. "Depends on how fast I can get the parts. This ain't exactly a new-model van and we're not real close to a big city. I gotta call around."

"Would you, please? We'll wait over there until you can give us an estimate." Michael walked Fallon back to the chair, but she wouldn't sit down.

"Don't you think you should call Sam Damien, at least?" Her hand gripped his. "Michael, someone put us in jeopardy. They wanted to... to hurt us."

He pulled her close, wanting to deny the truth for her sake, but needing to face facts. "It does look like that." Through the open garage doors, he watched the rain splash onto the concrete apron and tried to think. Who would go to so much trouble to cause an accident? And why?

"I shudder to think what might have happened if you hadn't been able to get us stopped before that curve. We could have gone right over and—"

"Stop! It's not going to do any good to worry about what-ifs." The car phone hadn't been damaged and he'd been able to call Information to get a tow in to the nearest two-pump gas station that luckily had a mechanic on duty. "What did Charley say the name of this town is?"

Fallon stepped back from him, realizing her hands were shaking again. How had she gotten into this mess? Bad enough to put herself at risk, but in her zealous search for her sister, she'd somehow managed to endanger Michael's life.

She studied his face—his strong, handsome face—and noticed his worried frown. She would never forgive herself if something happened to Michael. "This is all my fault. It has to be connected with Laurie and that private investigator or T.J. or one of the others we've met since my arrival. Oh, God, I'm so sorry, Michael."

He turned to her and stroked her cheek. "We don't know that for sure. In any case, I'm the one who insisted on going along. Besides, I've made a few enemies in working with runaways. It could have been anyone."

Only he didn't believe it was. He remembered the Cadillac that had passed them in such a hell of a hurry when they'd first gotten on Interstate 5. He'd caught only a glimpse of the driver, a bearded man. Sherlock had told them that Raymond Hopkins, the private investigator, had a dark beard and had driven up in a big old Cadillac. And that same bearded man had asked Rollie what kind of vehicle Michael drove and where Michael's House was located.

Coincidence? Highly doubtful. Had Hopkins tailed them, playing tag with the van, believing himself to be anonymous, then waited for the crash from a safe distance? A chilling thought.

Yet if that was the case, why did this P.I. hired by Roy Gifford want to kill or frighten him, knowing full well he would be with Fallon most of the time? Surely her stepfather didn't want to harm Fallon. Or did he? Was it possible that they were getting too close to some real answers, answers that would somehow incriminate Roy in something shady? Like paying a chunk of money to his other stepdaughter to disappear without his wife's knowledge, then paying Hopkins to cause an accident and he would be rid of Fallon, too?

But why?

Surely peace of mind—if that was what he was after, since the two sisters seemed to rankle him—wasn't worth committing murder. Despite Fallon's protests, Michael still hadn't dismissed the idea that Roy might have molested Laurie. During her brief visit to Michael's House, the girl had had such a haunted look about her.

Perhaps Roy was worried that Fallon would locate Laurie who might break down and reveal his rotten side. He had a fairly important position with the IRS, according to Fallon, and such a revelation would cause him to lose his job, plus his retirement pension, and certainly his wife's devotion. The more Michael thought about it, the more he believed that his theory wasn't all that far-fetched. And he was beginning to think that Roy was a whole lot more dangerous than Fallon thought him to be.

"What are you thinking?" Fallon asked, wondering at his lengthy silence. "If you want to return to San Diego and drop the whole thing, I'll understand. You have your own obligations and I've dragged you away from them long enough. I'll just pick up my Mustang and go look for Niko on my own. I appreciate all you've done so far and—"

"What makes you think I'd let you go on alone, especially after this?" His voice was low, his eyes serious. "Do I strike you as the sort of man who doesn't finish what he starts, who walks out on someone he promises to help when the going gets a little tough? Is that what you think of me?"

"No, of course not. But you certainly didn't bargain for this—someone deliberately sabotaging your van."

"You're right. I didn't. And neither did you. But I think I'm far more prepared to handle someone who wants to play rough than you are." Michael frowned thoughtfully, wishing he knew for sure that his theory was right. He needed some answers. Stepping aside, intending to pace, he felt a sharp pain spiral up from his ankle. Damn inconvenient to have this sprain right now, he thought with annoyance.

"Maybe we should reconsider and call Sergeant Damien," Fallon suggested again, at a loss as to what avenue to try next.

"What good would that do, Fallon? All right, so this mechanic says someone deliberately put a hole in our brake line. What proof do we have that it wasn't done by some kid who's been turned out of Michael's House for not following the rules? Or someone who lives in the neighborhood and doesn't like a home for runaways nearby, so he thought he'd give me a scare, a warning? Sam's too busy to deal with what-ifs. When we can give him something concrete to work with, then we'll call."

Fallon brushed back her damp hair. "I suppose you're right." She saw him take a few tentative steps, favoring his right foot. "I hope you haven't broken any bones. Maybe we should get your ankle X-rayed."

Irritated by the suggestion as well as the plight of his van, Michael realized his tone was harsher than he'd intended. "No, it's fine. *I'm* fine." Squaring his shoulders against the pain, he limped over to where Charley was hanging up the phone. "What have you found out?"

"Maybe by tomorrow, the next day for sure," Charley answered. "Best I could do. You want I should go ahead?"

Michael scrubbed a hand over the face he hadn't taken the time to shave this morning. Two days, shot. He knew that Fallon wanted to check out Niko's and see if Laurie was there. He also knew he could call Donovan and have him bring up Fallon's car or he could rent one somewhere in this small lake town. Or a call to Jonathan would have someone there with any vehicle he wanted in under two hours.

But his ankle was hurting like hell, and despite his protests to Fallon, it was raining and he didn't feel like going on the chase today. Still, it was her sister in danger and so he had to offer her a choice.

"Okay, order the parts," he told Charley, since either way, he would have to have the van repaired. He hobbled back to Fallon and carefully outlined their options.

Her eyes studied his as he talked. Sometimes they spoke more loudly than his words. "We've waited this long, I don't think a short delay will matter that much." She truly didn't want to continue without him, not after what had just happened, and she could see he wasn't up to continuing today. While it was true that she felt a restless urgency to get going, her empathy for Michael in pain was greater. "Why don't we find a place to stay and wait for the van to be repaired?"

He was amazed at how well she'd read him without his having to actually ask. He called to Charley over his shoulder. "Do you know of a hotel or motel around here where we could wait for the van to be ready?" While not exactly in the middle of nowhere, they were on a side road off a two-lane highway. He hoped there was *something* not too far away.

Charley removed his cap and scratched his head thoughtfully. "There's a motel off the highway about five miles north, a Best Western, I think. Or you could try Perkins Bed and Breakfast up in the mountains, about ten miles inland. If you call them, Old Man Perkins will come get you. The place is family owned, kind of private. I hear tell the food's like down home."

Michael let out a tired sigh. "Sounds perfect."

Perkins B and B was up a winding road and almost hidden by thick foliage and dense trees. It was a two-story house with a vaulted-ceilinged attic room that had its own bath, which turned out to be vacant and their first choice. Stretching out on the large pine four-poster bed, Michael listened to the rain dancing on the slanted roof just overhead and sighed. Folded at the foot of the bed was a goosedown comforter for chilly nights, and a beehive fireplace occupied one corner for the really cold spells. Michael found himself wishing the rain would turn to snow and they would be marooned for a month, although he knew the thought was foolish.

He listened to Fallon turn off the shower and glanced down at his right ankle wearing an ice bag and propped up on two pillows. She'd insisted on taking care of him even before changing out of her damp clothes. He couldn't remember the last time someone had fussed over him—certainly, no one since he'd reached adulthood. When he'd moved in with Jonathan, the Redfield housekeeper had tried when Michael had gotten the occasional cold, but he'd discouraged her every attempt. Michael smiled, remembering that he'd thought himself too macho to accept help, coming off the streets as he had.

His mother had been the last one to tuck him in, to put a cold cloth on his head when he'd had one of his bad headaches, to bring him herbal tea when he'd had the flu in winter. The memory of her lovely face—her beautiful smile, her dark eyes—floated into his mind, and his own smile was tinged with sadness. Here he was, a grown man of thirty-two, a successful man by most standards, and yet he still missed his mother.

Freud would have a field day with that, Michael decided.

Probably his reluctance to accept female fussing had a lot to do with his difficulty in trusting. Trust was something he was very sparing with. Give it freely, Michael felt, and you were bound to get burned.

At first when he was on the street on his own, he'd trusted with the innocence of youth. But he'd learned quickly that people weren't always what they seemed. He'd been lied to, stolen from, beaten up. So, yes, he supposed he was jaded, but a man had to protect himself.

He'd worked hard to make himself into the sort of man *he* would respect and admire. Now, when he looked in the mirror, he saw the man he'd made himself from the raw material of an orphaned boy who'd run from the law, cheated and stolen to survive. But he *had* survived and become educated, responsible, sought after.

Yet occasionally, he still caught glimpses of the frightened teenager he'd been, hidden behind the confident facade the world viewed now. And he wondered who else saw what he did.

Most of all, he wondered what Fallon saw the many times he caught her studying him. He could tell that she was attracted; that she wanted him, as he wanted her. They'd proved that they were sexually well suited. But lately, in her eyes, he saw more. Too much more.

She was beginning to care in a way that hinted at thoughts of permanence, and he couldn't allow that. He didn't want to hurt her, but he had no intention of getting involved again with the end result being marriage.

There were people, Michael was convinced, who weren't intended to marry. He was one and probably Jonathan was, too. If Jonathan's wife had lived longer, probably their marriage would have foundered because of his devotion to his work. Michael was equally devoted to his. Men like that made lousy husbands. Fallon deserved better. He would study her carefully, watch for signs and, if it came to that, he would have to find a way to explain how he felt before it was too late.

But not today. Today and tonight and hopefully tomorrow, they could just lie back, listen to the rain and enjoy each other. He'd already called Opal and Donovan and, thankfully, things were under control back at the house. He hadn't taken time off to just do nothing since they'd moved into the new building five years ago. He shouldn't feel guilty over a couple of days.

He and Fallon hadn't been alone, really alone, in too long. He wanted to hold her, to feel her heart beating next to his, to make love to her until they were both too exhausted to move. He wanted to explore all the ways he knew to pleasure her. The shower had probably relaxed her, chasing away the anxiety of the near accident. She'd been stressed-out for too long, between dealing with her parents and handling the search for Laurie. She needed R and R as badly as he.

He wouldn't bring up anything too distracting or disturbing, Michael decided. The truth was, he didn't want her taking off without him, as she'd done the day he'd been at the hospital with Wendy. He didn't want her to get angry with him and leave, either. He wanted her in his life, but not necessarily as a wife. But would that be enough for a woman like Fallon?

He knew nothing of her past loves, and she surely must have had some. Deliberately, he hadn't told her about his and guessed that she'd intentionally kept her own secrets.

The thought of her with another man didn't sit well with him, and his reaction surprised him. He'd never been the jealous sort. But then, he'd never before wanted a woman as much as he wanted Fallon. He was painfully aware of the dichotomy of being unwilling to plan a serious future with her while being unable to stand the thought of her with someone else.

The bathroom door opened and Fallon stepped into the room in a cloud of steam, dressed in clean jeans and a cotton sweater. It was definitely cooler up here in the mountains. He watched her toss the clothes she'd been wearing earlier into her suitcase before coming over to check his ankle.

"How does it feel now?" Fallon asked.

"Better. Where'd you learn about treating sprains?"

"In college, actually." She sat down on the edge of the bed. "I dated a premed student. He taught me about the *R-I-C-E* method. Rest, ice, compression and elevation."

Michael found himself wondering what else the premed student had taught her, but decided not to ask. Never ask a question if you fear the answer, someone had once told him.

Fallon removed the ice bag from his ankle. "I think that's enough cold treatment. Mrs. Perkins gave me an elastic bandage to wrap it with." She went to the dresser and got the bandage, then went to work. "Let me know if this is too tight. I don't want to cut off your circulation."

Feet are very sensitive, Michael discovered as she wound the bandage over and around, her hands gentle. He wanted those hands on other parts of his body—up higher, with a bolder touch. And he wanted his hands on her, seeking, exploring, enjoying.

"I've been thinking," Fallon said. "I want to make a couple of calls. I've got Raymond Tompkins's card. I'm going to call his office and see if he's back in Colorado."

"What are you going to ask him? Something like, Mr. Tompkins, when you were in California, did you happen to poke a hole in the brake line of Michael Redfield's van?"

She sent him a withering look as she fastened the end of the bandage with a metal clip. "Hardly. I have lots of questions." Carefully, she placed his foot back onto the thick pillows.

Michael sighed. Perhaps he should just get this over with. "Why don't you get the number and let me try?" He reached for the phone on the bedside table and placed it on the bed.

Slightly annoyed, she went to get the card. "Do you think a man will get further than a woman? Is that it?"

"Not necessarily. I think I've had more experience questioning evasive people than you."

Reluctantly, she handed him Raymond's card. Using his phone credit card, he put through the call. A man answered on the third ring.

"Tompkins Agency." The voice sounded middle-aged, nasal, impatient.

"Is this Raymond Tompkins, the private investigator?" Michael asked.

"Yes. How can I help you?"

First things first. "Do you have a client by the name of Roy Gifford?"

"Never heard of him. Who are you?"

Michael introduced himself and explained that he operated a home for runaway teens in San Diego. "Have you been in California recently searching for a young girl by the name of Laurie McKenzie?"

"No." The man sounded irritated. "Who gave you my name?"

Wincing as he shifted his ankle, Michael sat up. This was one he hadn't considered. "A man has been passing out your cards around San Diego saying he was sent by Roy Gifford to find his runaway daughter. And you say you have no knowledge of either?"

"Right. My cards are easy enough to get, I suppose. I hand them out to clients and prospective clients." The man's curiosity overrode his reluctance. "What does this guy look like?"

"Tall, in his forties, with dark hair and a full beard. He favors Western clothes and drives a big, older Cadillac."

There was a pause, then finally Tompkins spoke. "I'm five foot seven with gray hair, weigh about 145 and I'm fifty-two. I drive a Toyota. I don't know who the man you describe is, but I'm not pleased to hear he's impersonating me. I've been a licensed private investigator in Colorado Springs at this location for over twenty years. I specialize in insurance fraud, not missing persons."

An idea struck Michael. "Do you ever do any work for the IRS?"

"I handled a couple of cases for them locally a while back. As I mentioned, suspected insurance fraud." His voice wasn't quite so unfriendly. "Sorry I can't help you more."

"Thanks for trying." Slowly, Michael hung up and filled Fallon in on the part of the conversation she hadn't heard.

Fallon was clearly puzzled. And getting angry. "Roy told me he'd hired Raymond Tompkins, a local investigator with a good reputation. He must have heard about him through his job. Yet Tompkins never heard of Roy."

"So, if Tompkins isn't his name, then who is our tall, bearded impersonator in the fancy Western duds driving a big, old Cadillac?"

"Good question. I think it's time I called my dear step-father again."

"I agree. But first, let's call the number on the back of that card, the motel where this bearded guy asked both Sherlock and Rollie to call if they saw Laurie."

Fallon turned over the card and read him the number.

It took less than five minutes to learn that an R. Tompkins had checked out of his room last night, paying his charges in cash. The description Michael requested revealed that the man who'd occupied Room 8 was tall, bearded and usually wore jeans and a bolo tie. He drove an older-model white Cadillac. Michael asked if they'd made note of the license number and the clerk read it off to him. California plates.

For the second time, Michael hung up the phone with a perplexed expression on his face as he relayed the gist of his conversation to Fallon.

"I can't imagine that there'd be two men named Raymond Tompkins involved here," Fallon said, thinking out loud. "That leaves us exactly where we were before—nowhere."

Michael was thoughtful. "If he checked out last night, he could have driven to the house, hung around and waited until Jonathan left and the lights were out before tampering with the van. If, in fact, it was him." He decided to tell her the rest, about seeing a fast-moving Cadillac pass them on Interstate 5 with a bearded man behind the wheel.

"Why didn't you tell me sooner?"

"What for? To worry you more? Besides, do you know how many Cadillacs travel along Interstate 5 daily? I didn't make the connection until a while ago. We still don't know whether or not it's a coincidence. I didn't check the license plate, but a lot of Californians have beards."

"I don't believe in coincidence."

That made two of them. "I'm going to check on this license-plate number," he said, phoning Information for the number. The call took ten minutes. He hung up with a frown. "The number's no longer in use. Tompkins gave the Motel 6 clerk a phony number."

"Why am I not surprised?" Fallon reached for the phone. "I'm calling Roy." She glanced at her watch and saw that it was one o'clock. Roy often ate lunch at home even on weekdays—another of his penny-pinching ways. Impatiently, she put through the call, and was disappointed when her mother answered the phone sounding oddly cheery. "Mom, it's Fallon."

"Oh, yes, Fallon. Did you locate Laurie?" The worried tone was back.

"Not yet. Is Roy there?"

"No, dear, he's not. He took Danny out to lunch." There was a definite upbeat sound in Jane Gifford's voice again. "He's home for a few days and, oh, Fallon, you ought to see him. He's *so* handsome in that uniform. They shaved off all his curly hair, but even that looks good on Danny. We've been having such a good time showing him off to all our neighbors. Danny's really disappointed that you can't be here."

"Yes, well, as you know, I'm here looking for Laurie, your daughter." That was mean and Fallon immediately felt ashamed. But damn it all, did they have to strut Danny around like some returning hero when Laurie could be in major trouble?

Jane sniffled. "I haven't forgotten, Fallon. You know how much I appreciate what you're doing for us. When we told Danny that Laurie still isn't back, he was stunned. Have you had any leads, any at all?"

"I'm working on a couple. Mom, I need to talk with Roy. When will he be back?"

"I'm not sure. He said something about taking Danny in to his office after lunch to meet some people. And then tonight, we're having a backyard barbecue with some of the neighbors coming over. I'm making the potato salad right now. I do wish you could be here."

"Yes, so do I." So she could take Roy aside and ask him what in hell was going on. "Maybe I'll try to catch Roy at his office later. Would you give me his number, please?"

Jane recited the number from memory, then paused. "Fallon, what do you want to talk with Roy about?"

"About the private investigator he hired."

"Oh. I believe Roy mentioned that he talked with Mr. Tompkins and told him to return home."

Fallon felt a wave of exasperation. She hadn't realized until this whole thing began how little Jane knew about all that Roy did. "Have you ever met this man, Mom?"

"Why, no. But Roy speaks very highly of him."

Which meant absolutely zero. "All right, Mom. When you see Roy, tell him I need to talk with him."

"Fallon?" Jane said, somewhat timidly. "Please be careful."

Suddenly alert, Fallon frowned. "Why would you say that?"

"Well, because I'm sure you're having to deal with all sorts of people while you're searching for Laurie. I mean, Roy says that people who run those houses for teenage runaways are just in it for the money, that they don't care a bit about the kids. He says that some of them are drug addicts and sex offenders and worse. I pray every night that Laurie isn't involved with those...those seedy individuals."

Fallon felt bone weary. It was becoming increasingly clear that her mother didn't live in the real world, but rather in one Roy had created for her, and that she was totally blinded by his influence. Fallon had been gone from home so long that she hadn't truly realized this. Jane Gifford had handed over more than her freedom to her second husband; she'd given him carte blanche on what to think and how to perceive the world. "I'll be careful. I'll call again when I know something more." After their goodbyes, Fallon hung up.

This time, it was her turn to tell Michael the other side of the phone conversation as she flopped onto the bed alongside him. "It's difficult for my mother to concentrate on anything else when the heir apparent is on the scene." She heard annoyance in her voice and irritation, but not jealousy and certainly not envy. Her mother's and Roy's devotion to Danny wasn't really Danny's fault. He couldn't help the way they fawned over him as if he were still a cute towhead toddling around flashing his dimpled smile. Still, Fallon couldn't help resenting Danny on Laurie's behalf.

What angered her was her mother allowing Danny's visit to overshadow her concern for Laurie. Dammit, Laurie was her own flesh and blood, out there somewhere, possibly in need, probably lonely and lost. And her mother was making potato salad and planning a barbecue for her husband's son.

Mindful of his wrapped ankle, Michael turned onto his side and reached to trail two fingers along the silkiness of Fallon's cheek. "You're upset, naturally. It's always been like that, hasn't it, Danny getting the lion's share of love and attention in that house?"

She brushed back her hair as she turned toward him. "Yes, but I hadn't realized things were quite so lopsided until this whole thing happened. I wonder if that's why Laurie left—because she knew she'd always be second best."

There was more, Michael was certain. But right now, his concern was Fallon. "Tell me what you want to do—continue looking for your sister as soon as the van's fixed or go to Colorado to confront your stepfather and maybe get some answers out of him. Either way, I'll go with you, if you want me along. But it's your call."

Tenderness welled up inside Fallon, almost overflowing with the tears she tried not to shed. Michael Redfield was a busy, committed man with many people counting on him, yet he'd delegated responsibility to others so he could help her. He'd spent nearly every waking hour since she'd arrived planning and organizing the search, using his experience and knowledge, questioning people, tracking down leads. And here he was with a van someone had probably tampered with and a painful ankle, all because of her.

But still, he told her it was her call and he would go along with whatever she chose to do.

She reached to bury her fingers in his thick blond hair. Fallon wasn't certain how it had happened, or even when, but she felt a rush of love for him. How clear it was, now that she'd thought it through.

Once before, she'd shared his bed, both of them filled with frantic passion. Now, she would share it with tenderness and a love she knew instinctively she couldn't confess. Michael loved many but had no room in his heart for one special love. He'd made his views on love and marriage quite clear when they'd discussed Tim's wedding plans. Michael wanted no commitments, believing he could be married only to his work. She couldn't change that, just as she couldn't change her feelings for him.

With that in mind, she let her touch turn into a caress. "You're so good to me. Why?"

He smiled and the dimples she loved shifted into deep grooves. "'Cause you have eyes greener than any emerald

I've ever seen and skin so soft I can't seem to stop touching it." His gaze roamed over her face as he shifted closer, slipping his hand down to cup her chin. "And your mouth. Lord, what a mouth. Wonderfully soft and feminine—yet, I know how wild those lips can get, how crazy they make me, how cleverly they arouse me."

Fallon closed her eyes briefly, feeling a pleasure she knew would end in heartbreak. Something was better than nothing, she reminded herself.

Michael touched his lips to hers, lightly, playfully. Then he placed a kiss, first to one corner of her mouth, then to the other. Her sigh drifted out between her parted lips, lazy yet tantalizing, her breath as sweet as any honey he'd tasted.

"Why Mr. Redfield, are you trying to seduce me?" she asked, her voice smoky with the beginnings of passion.

"Damn right, I am." His fingers caressed the satin of her throat, the back of her neck, then traced the contours of her ear before his lips followed the trail. He breathed into her ear and felt a shiver take her as her hands bunched in the cotton of his shirt. "How'm I doing?" he whispered.

"Mmm, but you don't have to work at seduction. Not with me, never with me." Her hands tightened, clutching his arms. "Make love with me, Michael. I need you today. Badly."

He could feel heat throbbing throughout his body. "No more than I need you." He shifted to kiss her again as he gathered her to him.

The night they'd spent making love, Fallon reflected, had been wildly exciting, both of them trembling with repressed passion from the days they'd spent wanting one another, until they'd all but torn their clothes off in their haste to be skin to skin. But things had shifted between them since then with all they'd been through together, changing their outlook, deepening their feelings.

His kiss was poignantly tender, sweetly gentle, deliciously stirring. Her heart overflowed with feeling as she returned his kiss, and she felt tears gather in her eyes. He seemed to sense the change and drew back to gaze at her, to study her. Afraid he might notice the love she felt almost brimming over, she dropped her eyes, slipped her arms around him and pressed her head to his chest.

Fragile. Michael was overwhelmed by how fragile she was, her body slender and delicate. But more important, he realized how fragile were her newly awakened feelings. Passion. It was only passion he'd seen in her eyes, he decided. *We have nowhere to go,* she'd told him once, and he'd agreed. No demands on one another, except here, together in bed. Losing control here was acceptable, even desirable. But not elsewhere.

Relieved that he'd seen what he wanted to see in her eyes, he began undressing her slowly, to draw out the pleasure. She lay back, oddly docile, uncharacteristically submissive, watching his every move. As more and more of her golden skin was revealed, he realized how perfect she was, how elegant her features were, how delicate her bones. His hands seemed rough and clumsy to him as he fumbled with the zipper of her jeans, the buttons on her sweater.

And when the last silky item was tossed aside, he narrowed his gaze, fascinated with the beauty he saw. "You're so lovely," he whispered. "So very lovely." His hands skimmed over the slope of her shoulders, along her graceful arms, then back up to trace around the ripe curves of her breasts. His breath almost backed up into his throat, as his hands trailed lower.

Fallon felt her skin quiver in anticipation, in need. No one had ever touched her like this—with such devotion, such tenderness. She felt drugged, achy. As his fingers danced along her legs, she felt as if he were committing each separate part of her to memory, such care did he take in touching her. Her arms felt heavy, her mind giddy with the wonder of his loving.

As his lips settled on the vulnerable column of her throat, she gasped at the pleasure. His hands were kneading her breasts and the drugging sensations went on and on. Stunned by her own desire, she whispered his name in a voice she didn't recognize.

But the balance wasn't right, Fallon thought as her hands tugged at his shirt, finally pulling it off over his head and

tossing it aside before wrestling with the snap at his waist.
"Too many clothes," she murmured.

As impatient as she, Michael yanked off the rest of his
clothes, an involuntary grunt escaping when pain shot
through his ankle at his hurried movements. But the ache
was nothing compared to the need that had his mouth returning to claim hers.

Amazed. He was totally amazed at what just kissing her
could do to him. Her hands merely rested on his shoulders, yet they felt like fingers of fire on his skin. Dazed with
longing, he rolled onto his back and took her with him.

Now she was free to love him more openly, and she did,
trailing her lips over his shoulder, up his throat, then down
again to bury them in his chest. She took tiny nipping bites
as she tasted and tested, then kissed away the small hurt
while her hands streaked over his ribs.

She took her mouth on a heated journey, covering every
inch of him, wanting him to feel all that he'd made her feel.
She heard the deep sounds of his pleasure and felt a thrill
she'd never known—the thrill of seducing the seducer. With
a low, throaty chuckle, she returned to kiss his waiting
mouth.

Michael heard the rain pounding on the roof and knew
he would never again lie under the eaves without remembering this moment and the woman who could make him
forget his own name. Her scent, fresh from her shower,
lightly floral and enormously captivating, wrapped around
him, drugging his senses. The taste of her mouth as she
deepened the kiss was richer than any wine he had drunk.
The feel of her sprawled on top of him was sending him
over the edge.

Too quickly.

He reversed their positions and put his hands to hers,
palms touching, stretching them up over her head. Her eyes
were deep green and dewy with need. He saw them turn
cloudy with a kind of dazed pleasure as he touched his chest
to hers, brushing against her pointed breasts with feathery
strokes. His thumbs at her wrists felt her pulse pound like
the thunder rumbling in the afternoon sky. He dipped his

head and kissed her eyes closed, wondering what it was about this woman that made him feel so different.

At his mercy. She was totally at his mercy, Fallon thought as she gave herself over completely to Michael's lovemaking. Willingly, happily, she relinquished control and let him lead. Never before had she trusted her vulnerability so completely. Never before a follower, she suddenly became one, for she sensed he knew things she had only imagined. Then, with lips and teeth and tongue, he slid down and showed her pleasure she had only dreamed of.

He was branding her, searing her with hot, moist, open-mouthed kisses that set her soul on fire. His fingertips whispered over breasts grown heavy and full from his touch. As he slid lower, she felt the scrape of his unshaven face brush against the delicate skin of her thighs. He bent to her as her hands thrust into his hair and her soft moan drifted to him.

Then she arched and cried out as the first fierce wave slammed into her. Relentlessly ignoring the sounds she made—whether plea or protest, he wasn't certain—he sent her up again, higher and higher still. He watched the sensations rip through her as she struggled to catch her breath. Pleased with himself, he traveled back up and captured her mouth.

Fallon felt buffeted, battered, defenseless. She felt boneless, weak, drained—yet she wanted him even more, wanted to be one with him. Her hands on his back felt the tension in him, the control he was hanging on to by a slim thread, the sensual heat that rose from him in waves. She knew he had to be ready to explode, but her heart was pounding so that she couldn't speak, not yet. So she used her hands to convey her meaning, to adjust their bodies, to finally guide him inside her.

Michael's muscles trembled with the intensity of his effort to go slowly, to stay in control, to give as good as he got. Her eyes were open and on his, urging him on, yet letting him chart the course. He moved within her and with her as if they'd been lovers for years instead of days. He

shifted her so he could go deeper, filling her with all he had
to give; deeper and faster and harder, as he watched her
eyes lose focus and drift closed.

When at last they flew over the edge, they flew together.

Chapter 10

The rain had stopped sometime while they'd slept—Fallon wasn't sure just when. Awakening still snuggled in Michael's arms after the loving, cozy under the feather comforter they'd pulled up against the chill, she felt warm, languid, pliant. She couldn't help imagining what it might be like to fall asleep like that, night after night. What would it be like to have all that charm and attention and passion focused on her regularly? Michael had been a tireless lover in bed despite his injured ankle. He was skilled, sensual, thrilling.

But he wasn't hers, Fallon realized, as she let her gaze linger on his face, aware again of the strength and determination visible there even in sleep. Perhaps he cared in his own way—about her safety, her feelings. But the feeling of rightness, of belonging that she knew within his arms spoke of emotions he might never verbalize, even if he felt them.

Was it experiences from his past or his commitment to his work that had formed his somewhat-skewed opinion of marriage? she wondered. She remembered overhearing Jonathan mention a woman named Paige Hanley, and Michael's heated reaction to the name. Was she someone who'd influenced his feelings about wedlock? When they'd discussed Tim's forthcoming marriage just before the van's brakes had given out, Michael's opinion of that institution seemed to hint at feelings of entrapment, financially and otherwise.

Who or what had made him think that way?

Slowly stretching so as not to disturb him, she wondered if she could get him to talk more on the subject. Not that she was ready to go shopping for bridal gowns, but she knew her feelings for Michael ran deeper than they had for any other man she'd known, including Jeff Raynor. Even the realization that what she felt for Michael was love as she'd never before known it, she was experienced enough to recognize that that sometimes wasn't enough to make a good marriage.

Had she ever been exposed to a really good marriage? When her father had been alive, there'd been moments. Jim McKenzie had been a loving man but an irresponsible one, whose concern for his family hadn't been enough to make him want to work long and hard to keep food on the table and a roof over their heads—one that didn't leak. Yet, although Fallon had been young, she'd witnessed an almost-tangible love between her parents.

Certainly the union of her mother and Roy wasn't based on love. She had a few friends who'd married since college—one already divorced, another on a rocky road and a third who never commented on either her spouse or her marriage. What, then, did she really know about matrimony? Precious little.

Too soon, Fallon decided, to be thinking of such things as "forever" and cottages by the sea and a ring on her finger. Instinctively, she felt that Michael might never be drawn to that sort of commitment, even as time progressed and they were together more. It was a foolish dream anyhow, she thought with a sigh. "Happily ever after" happened only in the occasional movie or book.

Again, she shifted, turning so she was inches from his sleeping face. *You'll get no traps set by me, Michael,* she silently promised. *There are no strings attached to my feel-*

ings because I won't even allow myself to verbalize them.
She touched his unshaven cheek, pleased at the very male
feel of him. *But oh, let me feel them, please.*

He'd sensed for some minutes that she was awake, and
wondered what she was thinking. That she would like to be
out looking for Niko instead of stuck here with him, probably. That she'd made love with him willingly, but now it
was time to get moving. Michael knew he'd given her
pleasure and, for that short period of time, had had her full
and undivided attention. But he detected a restlessness in
her now, an impatience to leave his bed that disappointed
him even as he puzzled over why he should feel that way.

He'd never been one to invite a woman to stay hours afterward with him, or overnight, even. Two mutually con-
senting adults who gave and received pleasure, then moved
on—that was his preference. Why, then, was it that, even
in the drowsy vulnerability of sleep, he'd found himself
reaching out for her, wanting to keep her close, wanting her
to stay?

Puzzled at his own reactions, Michael opened his eyes
and stared into her serious green gaze. He cleared his
throat, unable to read her expression. "What are you
thinking?" he asked, almost afraid of the answer.

"I'm thinking about you. Only you." Her voice sounded
husky and foggy from sleep.

That surprised him—that she'd been lying there thinking only of him. He was unprepared as to how to respond.
Feeling too warm, he turned back the heavy comforter and
his eyes automatically slid to her breasts, rosy from his
scratchy beard. He touched a finger to one. "I marked
you."

Instantly, Fallon felt heat form just beneath her skin
from his touch. Yes, he had marked her, but not in the way
he meant. She noticed a tiny love bite on his neck and raised
a hand to trace it. "And I marked you, as well."

"Mmm, that hasn't happened to me since high school."
She drew the sheet around her, not nearly as comfortable lying beside him unclothed, now that he was awake.

He'd given her an opening and she snatched it. "What were you like in high school?"

"You mean aside from being a lousy student who kept skipping classes?" Michael stretched out on his back, raising one arm and placing his open hand beneath his head. "I was a late bloomer, if you're talking about boy-girl stuff. I was so busy being angry at authority and the world in general that I hardly noticed girls until I got to California."

"And then what happened?" Fallon prompted.

He shrugged. "I noticed a couple, I guess." He turned his head toward her. "You know, your average hormones-raging teenager. Very typical, I'd say."

He was being open and talkative, so she decided to go for it. "Have you ever been in love?"

Michael's expression tightened. "Yeah, once. Love's a near-fatal disease. I succumbed but survived, and learned a valuable lesson. It's not for me."

She'd guessed as much, yet was surprised at how the answer she'd been expecting disturbed her. "Who was she?"

Michael forced himself to step back from the remembered anger and turned to her, his smile once more in place. "No one important." He skimmed his hand along her bare shoulder. "So what do you want to do next, go find something to eat or indulge in a more interesting activity?" He bent to place a kiss on the same shoulder.

She'd come too far to turn back. "Michael, will you tell me about her?"

His frown came swiftly as he lifted his head. "Why? Why do you want to know? You haven't told me anything about the past men in your life."

That was fair enough. "All right, then, I will, but there haven't been many and they weren't particularly exciting. What do you want to know?"

Actually, she'd opened up a subject he'd been wondering about for some time. "Have *you* ever been in love? And who was he and why didn't it work out?"

Fallon drew in a thoughtful breath. It wasn't that her close call was any great secret, but she still couldn't speak of that time without rancor. "I fell in love once, too, and it left me a bit battle scarred. I met Jeff Raynor at a party a nurse friend of mine gave. He's a doctor, an internist, and he was a partner in a very busy practice. I was fresh out of college, starting my first real job, and very impressionable."

Nine years older than she, Jeff had been so handsome, so charming, Fallon remembered. And he'd romanced her feverishly for several months. As inexperienced as she'd been, having dated mostly college boys up to that time, she'd been flattered and overwhelmed.

"He had a lot of charisma and I fell for him like a ton of bricks. After six months of dating exclusively, he asked me to marry him and I said yes. Apparently, just like a cliché, I was so nuts about him that I hadn't allowed myself to see his faults, to admit he even had any. Or maybe I just overlooked them all. I don't know."

"We have a tendency to do that when we're young and think we're in love," Michael commented, realizing he sounded as cynical as he felt.

"It wasn't until we started planning our wedding that I began to notice things. Like we always went to the restaurants and plays that Jeff chose. We spent time with *his* friends, never with mine. But when I mentioned how I felt, Jeff told me that naturally, being older, he was more experienced, knew the best places to go, the right people to know. Like a dope, I accepted his explanation. Then one day, he asked me to take a ride with him. He drove me to this house he'd picked out and bought without so much as consulting me, a house he informed me we'd move into after the wedding. As I stood there in absolute shock, he stunned me further, saying that he'd decided it was time I quit my 'little job' and prepared myself to be the wife of a successful doctor."

Michael recalled how she'd accused him of trying to control everything, to make her decisions for her. Now, he could see where she was coming from. "I can just imagine how you felt about that."

"I was furious. The house was beautiful, but that wasn't the point. And to have the job I'd worked so hard to get dismissed as some little hobby was the topper. In a very dramatic gesture, I threw his ring at him and broke the engagement." She sighed, shaking her head. "But I hadn't learned my lesson yet. Jeff kept coming around, begging me to reconsider, swearing he'd changed. He put the house he'd chosen on the market and said we'd pick one out together. He only wanted my happiness, he said repeatedly. Like a fool, I believed him."

"I'm not surprised. Remember, I told you that love makes you do stupid things?"

Fallon looked into his eyes. "Not always, Michael. Love with the right person can be wonderful. It's not a trap with the right person."

"I've yet to see an example of that in living color," he said skeptically. "Go on with your story."

"I took back his ring and we went on with our planning, doing it all together, or so I thought. Then one day, my manager called me in and asked why I wanted to leave my job just when I was doing so well. Again, I was stunned. He told me that Jeff had stopped in and told him that I'd only taken the job to fill in my time before marrying and that I planned on quitting so I could run his house and have his children."

"He's not a man to give up easily, is he?"

"Not at all. That evening, I was waiting for him to pick me up and he came rushing in all excited and handed me the tickets he'd just picked up, tickets to Hawaii where we were going to honeymoon. We'd never once discussed Hawaii, but he'd run across a friend who'd highly recommended the honeymoon package so, without a single thought of checking with me first, he arranged the whole trip. Between that and his chat with my manager, I really blew."

"You tossed him out on his ear?"

"More or less. I'd lived with a dominating stepfather for eight years. The last thing I wanted was a control freak for a husband." She rose on one elbow, needing to make him see. "It's an insult, I feel, for one adult to take over the relationship and make decisions that will affect both of you. Jeff and Roy feel they know what's best for everyone and so they need to call the shots.'' She let out a huff of air. ''Very infuriating.''

He could see that she had plenty of residual anger. Still, he wanted to ask. ''Do you think I'm a control freak?''

She took her time answering. ''I did, at first. I think some of that comes from the fact that you work with kids who need an adult to make some decisions for them, and you got into the habit. I've seen you with other adults, though, and I've changed my mind.'' She couldn't help a smile. ''But you bear watching in this department.''

''Thanks a lot.'' But he was smiling, too. ''It's a tendency I have, I must admit. But nowhere to the extent that your friend, Jeff, had. So, was he the only one you've cared about?''

Fallon nodded. ''Yes, and that was four years ago. Jeff's now married to a little mousy woman who, I hear from friends, lets him choose her clothes, plan their menus, everything. I couldn't live like that.'' She wiggled into a more comfortable position. ''All right, your turn.''

Again, the shadows returned to his face. ''My experience is a lot grittier. You, at least, woke up before real harm was done.''

That didn't sound good. Fallon waited, allowing him to collect his thoughts.

''You probably don't really want to hear this. There's been a lot of water under the dam since all that happened.''

''Yes, I do want to hear,'' she said quietly.

He hadn't really thought she would say no. Maybe he didn't want her to. Maybe it was the best way to explain himself to Fallon. ''Because of the years I'd spent on the streets, it took me a while to catch up on my education. I was twenty when I entered college, although I finished in three years. Despite all the places I'd been, I'd never met a woman who truly interested me. Not until Paige Hanley.''

At last, she would learn about this mysterious woman, Fallon thought, trying not to reveal her keen interest.

His eyes were gazing out the window at the setting sun, but what he saw was something entirely different. "She was beautiful, tall and willowy, with this great auburn hair."

Fallon's eyes grew wide, recalling that Jonathan had mentioned Paige's resemblance to her. Was that why Michael found her attractive, because she looked like his first love?

"Well, what can I say? I was young and ripe to be overwhelmed, I guess. I couldn't believe she cared as much as she said she did." He gave a bitter laugh as he raised his knees, tenting the sheet. "I should have followed my instincts. When it's too good to be true, it usually isn't."

"You're probably right."

"Anyway, for the first time, I asked Jonathan for something more than he'd offered. He'd paid for the dorm and I all but begged him for my own apartment. He hesitated, and lectured me, even though it all went over my head, but finally gave in. The ink wasn't dry on the lease before I'd moved Paige in with me.

"You can probably guess the rest. Two months later, she told me she was pregnant. She played it cool and waited until I insisted we get married." He met her intense gaze. "You know how I grew up, losing my father when I was fourteen, having to live hand-to-mouth for years. I wasn't about to allow a child of mine to go through that. I went to Jonathan and promised him I'd pay back every dime if he'd help me. To his credit, he didn't lecture me again, just made the arrangements."

"So you married her?"

"Yes." Michael fell into momentary melancholia, remembering all the feelings he usually kept buried. "Jonathan gave us a nice wedding—not nearly as large as Paige and her mother wanted, but plenty big enough for me. I hardly remember any of it. I knew I didn't love Paige. Hell, I don't think I loved anyone. I was grateful to Jonathan and good friends with Paul, but love? I'd left any feelings of love behind in Michigan along with my childhood, when my family was taken from me years ago."

As she had once before when he'd talked of his youth, Fallon felt a deep sadness for the boy he'd been, but decided to let him continue at his own pace.

"Jonathan continued with the checks, supporting us both in a larger apartment. I stayed in school, but Paige quit, saying she had morning sickness. But it didn't keep her from shopping almost daily with her mother, using my charge cards. Then one day, I came home and found her in bed all rolled up in a ball. She'd lost the baby, she told me."

"Oh, no." The child had been the only reason he'd married her. "How did you react?"

"Not good, I'm afraid. She stayed in bed crying and I tried to comfort her, but my heart wasn't in it. First chance, I went to Jonathan again, hat in hand, and asked if perhaps I should think about a divorce. He told me to wait awhile, that moving too fast would devastate the girl when she'd just had a terrible shock. Reluctantly, I agreed."

Michael found himself smiling finally. "I have to hand it to Jonathan. He's a fox. He'd used his connections and had Paige checked out, discovering that she'd never been pregnant at all. Actually, I'd been suspicious because I *always* use protection, but I figured no method is foolproof."

"You didn't ask to see the doctor's report?"

"No. But we found out that she lied anyhow, using her knowledge of my background to get me to marry her, that I wouldn't walk away from my own child, hoping to get her hands on Jonathan's money eventually. Apparently she figured that Jonathan and I were tied together financially, that I was his adopted son because of the name, which isn't so."

"So what did you do?"

"Got a quiet, uncontested divorce. I had no assets in my name, so she wound up with nothing. I wound up feeling betrayed." Michael shook his head. "And that was my first and last experience with Cupid's arrow."

Sitting back against the pillows, Fallon studied his face and saw the resentment he still carried. "That was a terrible thing that happened. But surely you know that few women would go to such extremes."

He raised a questioning eyebrow. "And surely you know that all men aren't controlling."

Fallon found a smile. "Touché. I guess we've both been burned once."

"I, for one, don't intend to repeat that mistake." Michael shifted, moving closer to her. "When two people enjoy being together, in bed and out, what more is there? Getting legally entangled with marriage documents and such is unnecessary. Unless you want a houseful of kids, which I certainly do not. I've got all the kids I can handle at the house."

Another brick wall. He kept tossing them up. She drew in a shaky breath. So she'd just have to keep tearing them down, Fallon decided. It was a dirty job, but someone had to do it.

Turning toward him, she let her hands roam over his broad chest, the muscles of his back and shoulders. As always, his strength drew her and his devotion to his kids, the responsibilities he took on on behalf of others, the integrity of the man he'd become. All of that made up what Michael Redfield was, and those qualities aroused her as much as his body, his wonderful mouth, his deep, deep dimples, his clever hands.

Unable to hold off any longer, she pressed her lips to his.

Michael laid her back on the soft bed, leaning over and giving himself up to the kiss, gently but thoroughly. No woman had ever aroused tenderness in him the way Fallon did. She'd been hurt, as he also had been—betrayed and deceived. Yet here she was, up at bat again, risking herself, as he was.

Only this time, neither would get hurt. Michael promised himself that, as he wound his arms around her and took her deeper.

Niko Eustasius was a second-generation Greek with black hair and dark eyes, almost Hollywood handsome. He held court in a red fake leather booth at the back of his restaurant, sipping ouzo and watching the customers come and go. Facing the lake, the place was popular with locals and tourists alike. The food had to be good, Fallon thought as she inhaled the spicy scented air, since a lunchtime crowd filled the place to nearly overflowing.

The sun had been shining brightly when the mechanic had finally called and said the van was fixed. Fallon sensed a reluctance in Michael to end their nearly idyllic stay at Perkins B and B in the mountains, a reluctance that she shared. They'd spent two days and nights in the cozy attic room, leaving only to get something to eat in the comfortable dining room downstairs.

They'd shared with one another more than their bodies, talking almost nonstop about their less-than-wonderful childhoods, their memories of their parents and siblings, the hodgepodge past that had formed them into the adults they were today. Fallon felt as if she knew Michael better than when they'd left San Diego, and yet the moment they'd gotten into the van, he was once more the dedicated, somewhat-distant guardian of runaways, bent on the search.

That was what she'd wanted, of course, Fallon reminded herself; a knowledgeable man experienced in dealing with street kids, who would help her. But somewhere along the way, she'd begun to view him in another way, too—as the tender lover she'd been subconsciously seeking all her adult life. Even as she now watched him study Niko from across the room, she wondered if Michael ever let anyone get really close to him.

Michael thanked the bartender for pointing out Niko and, with his hand at Fallon's back, walked over to the owner's booth, still favoring his wrapped ankle. "Niko?" he asked, as the man's almost-black eyes assessed them both.

"Yeah, that's me. Do I know you?"

"Not yet." Michael held out his hand in a friendly gesture. He needed this guy's cooperation, so it would be wise to win him over. "Michael Redfield, and this is Fallon

McKenzie. We just want to ask you a couple of questions. Do you mind if we sit down?"

The dark eyes narrowed. "Are you cops? I thought I knew all the local cops around here."

Michael shook his head. "We're not with the police."

Niko waved a manicured hand and invited them to join him.

"So, what do you want to know?"

Fallon slid into the booth ahead of Michael and reached into her shoulder bag for the picture. "Have you seen this girl?"

Niko studied the photo, his face expressionless, then looked up at Fallon. "Why are you looking for her?"

"She's my sister."

"Yeah, so?"

His challenging tone took Fallon aback, but she persisted. "Laurie's only sixteen and she's run away from her home and family in Colorado. We love her. We want her back."

Niko threw back the last of his ouzo and signaled the waiter before speaking. "Look, lady, I was a runaway, living on the streets for years. My old man tried finding me, even offered a reward to get me back so he could beat the hell out of me some more. I'd have broken the kneecaps of anyone I met who would have turned me in." He slid the picture back across the Formica tabletop. "I don't rat on my friends."

"Then she is a friend of yours?" Michael interjected.

Niko took the fresh glass from the waiter and didn't invite them to join him in a refreshment. "I didn't say that."

Michael braced his arms on the table and leaned forward. "Look, Rollie at the Rodeo Bar in San Diego sent us to you. He said you were good people, that you help runaways. So do I. I run Michael's House not far from the Rodeo. You can check me out, if you like."

Squinting, Niko studied the blond man, considering. "Yeah, I heard about you. The kids say you're okay."

"Glad to hear it. We have reason to believe that Laurie's in trouble. She left under suspicious circumstances.

Fallon's honestly trying to help her. We just want to talk with her. If she doesn't want to go back, I won't force her. You have my word."

Taking his time, Niko took a long sip of the clear liquid, sliding his eyes from one to the other thoughtfully. "She's a good kid, but she trusted the wrong person."

Fallon felt her heart lurch into her throat. He knew Laurie, maybe knew where she was this very minute.

"What wrong person?" Michael wanted to know.

"A young punk goes by the name of T.J. He's owed me money for some time. He borrows from everyone. The kid's bad news."

Sensing Fallon's tension, Michael gripped her hand beneath the table. "Have you seen either of them lately?"

Niko nodded. "Like I said, T.J. owed me and he knew better than to welsh. He showed up here coupla nights ago and paid up." Niko angled his chin toward the picture still on the table. "She was with him."

Fallon closed her eyes briefly, grateful that they were on the right track.

Michael had more questions. "Who did you mean when you said she trusted the wrong man? T.J.?"

Niko ran a hand wearing a large pinkie ring along the smooth line of his glossy hair. "She's small-town, easily snowed. T.J. took her for every dime she had, and she had plenty."

Fallon felt a rush of anger rising. "You mean he stole money from her?"

The Greek shook his head. "That's not how the punk works. He finds a young girl, pretty, new to the scene. He moves in on her, convinces her she can't survive without him. Makes up stories about his rotten childhood to get her sympathy. Now she trusts him. If she's got money, he persuades her to give it to him. If she doesn't, he sets her up, if you know what I mean."

Fear clutching at her heart, Fallon looked straight at Niko. "No, what do you mean?"

Niko's eyes shifted from Fallon to Michael and back again, clearly uncomfortable. "He acts as her pimp, what else?"

"Oh, God," Fallon murmured.

Michael pressed her hand. He'd told her from the beginning that she was going to learn things she didn't want to know, yet he couldn't help but feel for her. He went after Niko for the rest. "You said that Laurie had money, plenty of it. How do you know?"

"I know because we sat in this very booth and she peeled five C-notes from a wad of money and gave them to me—the money T.J. owed."

Fallon brushed back her hair with a shaky hand. "I can't believe she let that . . . that vermin convince her to pay his debts. Why did she trust him?"

Niko shrugged. "Because she wanted to believe. T.J.'s a creep, but he bats a thousand with the girls."

Fallon turned to Michael, her eyes distressed. "That must have been the envelope of money that Rollie saw Tompkins give Laurie at the Rodeo."

Michael nodded. "Where'd they go after he paid you off?" he asked Niko.

"They took a room in my motel, Neptune's Nest, around the other side of the lake. Next day, she came to me here, told me T.J.'d stolen her money while she was sleeping and left her high and dry."

"Oh, no," Fallon groaned, then gave in to her fury. "I'd like to get a hold of that kid."

"Get in line," Niko said. "He's not real popular with me, either. I hate it when someone fleeces the kids. I warned your sister that day she was here shelling out money for T.J. You think she listened to me? Hell, no."

"You said she came back to see you after T.J. left," Michael went on. "What did she want?"

"A job."

"Did you give her one?"

"Sure." Niko's eyes scanned the room before he jerked his head in the direction of the side section. "She's over there, waiting tables."

Fallon gasped out loud, unable to believe her ears. Half rising, she craned her neck around Michael, searching the restaurant. In moments, she spotted a young slender girl with a chestnut ponytail wearing a white blouse and black skirt like the other waitresses. Then she turned and Fallon took in the pale face, the dark eyes, the defeated look. "It's Laurie."

"She didn't even have enough to buy her uniform," Niko added. "I popped for it and gave her an advance so she could pay her rent. She said she's tired of living on the streets."

"Please, let me out," Fallon said to Michael, hemmed in as she was by him on one side and Niko on the other.

Niko reached out and touched her arm. "Remember what I said, you're not to force her to go with you. I'll be watching."

She didn't know whether to be annoyed with him or grateful that he was looking after her sister, in a manner of speaking. "I'll remember," Fallon told him as Michael got to his feet.

Michael gave her a quick hug. "I'll wait here."

Laurie was standing by the food counter, placing an order by clipping the slip to the turnstile used by the short-order cooks. Slowly, Fallon walked over, her pulse pounding. She stopped a foot from her sister and waited.

Wearily, Laurie rubbed along the back of her neck, then turned to check out her station for new arrivals. What she saw in front of her stopped her in her tracks. "Oh, my God," she whispered.

"Laurie," Fallon said softly, her eyes filling.

Struggling to hold back tears, Laurie blinked, then looked behind Fallon. "Is anyone with you? Did…did Roy send you?"

"No one from home except me. I came because I've been worried sick about you. Are…are you all right?"

Laurie's young face crumpled. "No," she sobbed, then flung herself into Fallon's arms.

* * *

On the bench seat of the van, behind Michael who was driving, Fallon sat with an exhausted Laurie's head in her lap, her fingers brushing back her sister's oddly dull hair. "Try to get some sleep, honey. When we get to Michael's House, you can take a long shower, wash your hair and stretch out in a comfortable bed."

"I don't think I can sleep, even though I'm really tired," Laurie said, her young face wrinkled in concern. "Maybe I shouldn't have come with you." She choked back a sob that kept wanting to escape. "I just don't know what to do."

"You said you didn't want to stay at Niko's waiting tables," Fallon reminded her. They'd managed to convince the obsessively watchful Greek that Laurie was leaving of her own accord—but just barely. Niko had hugged her and told her to come back anytime if she felt the need, and he would have a job for her. He'd then shot a look at Fallon as if in warning. Exerting great control, she'd managed not to tell the overly protective man that he wasn't Laurie's father and that he'd only met her days ago, so he could hardly be expected to know what was best for her.

"I know." Laurie let out a ragged sigh. "It's really hard work, being a waitress."

"Don't I know," Fallon agreed. "I waited tables for two years when I was in college. I didn't want to be beholden to Roy for my expenses."

Hearing her stepfather's name, Laurie stiffened. "You're sure Roy didn't send you?"

Fallon frowned down into her questioning face. "Why would you think I'd lie to you? I never have before."

"I know. I've gotten paranoid, I guess. The way I've been living lately, well, it makes you distrust everyone."

Fallon debated about discussing the punk Laurie had been hanging out with for weeks, then decided she might as well get it over with. "This T.J., I understand he stole some money from you."

"Who told you that?" Her tone was defensive.

"Niko. Is it the truth?"

Laurie studied the chipped nails of one hand. "I was stupid to trust him. Like I said, it's hard to know who you can believe."

"Where'd you get so much money, Laurie?"

She gazed out the window. "I closed out my bank account back home."

"Yes, I checked with them. A hundred and sixteen dollars. But you gave T.J. five hundred to pay off his debt to Niko, and you had money left over." She was putting Laurie on the spot deliberately. Fallon felt she'd turned her life upside down for her sister. Laurie owed her a few answers.

Laurie sat up, distancing herself from Fallon. "I worked a couple of jobs here and there." Her eyes swung to her sister, suddenly filled with accusation. "Is this why you hunted me down, to interrogate me?"

Fallon's guilt surfaced as she tried to understand. "Of course not. But you can't imagine how worried we've been. Mom has been crying nonstop since you left." Which wasn't exactly the truth, but despite her pleasure over her stepson's visit, Fallon knew that their mother was still concerned about Laurie. "I'm just trying to figure out how you managed to live all this time, how you supported yourself."

Laurie crossed her arms over her chest in a protective gesture. "Well, I wasn't turning tricks, if that's what you wanted to know."

Chagrined, Fallon placed her hand on her sister's rigid arm. "Oh, Laurie, I never thought that." But she had feared that her sister might have been forced to do things she ordinarily wouldn't, just to survive. However, they were getting nowhere, so she decided to back off, for now. There would be plenty of time to talk later.

Laurie stared ahead, her defiant gaze settling on Michael, who hadn't said a word since they'd left L.A. "Are you involved with him?" she asked Fallon.

Back at Niko's, she'd introduced Michael to Laurie, even though she knew they'd already met, explaining his presence, but perhaps Laurie had been too upset emotionally for the information to register. "Michael runs a house for runaways in San Diego and—"

"I *know* that." Exasperation tinged her sister's voice. "A girl I knew back home gave me the number of his place. I even spent a night there a while back with someone I met when I first got to San Diego."

"Yes. Emma. Michael told me. I found a piece of paper with his phone number on it in your room. That's how I traced you." Michael had warned her that her sister would change after living on the streets, and he'd been right. Gone was the shy, sweet girl, replaced by a testy young woman with a definitely belligerent attitude.

Laurie was silent for a couple of minutes, then turned to her sister, keeping her voice low. "You didn't answer my question. Are you involved with him?"

Tamping down her temper, Fallon met Laurie's gaze, unwilling to discuss her feelings for Michael with her rebellious sister. "Laurie, I came to California with only one thought in mind—to find you. That's the reason for my being here, and nothing else."

Laurie seemed to deflate a bit. "How is Mom?"

"Like I said, worried, weepy, frightened for you."

Laurie swung back, once more challenging. "And what about Roy? What does he think about all this?"

Fallon decided to take the line of least resistance. "Well, he hired a detective to locate you, so he must be concerned." Which, again, wasn't the whole story. Fallon waited for Laurie's reaction.

"What detective?"

"Didn't you meet with a tall bearded man named Raymond Tompkins in the Rodeo Bar a few nights ago?"

"Was he a detective?"

"That's what he said he was."

"You talked with him?"

"No. Rollie, the Rodeo bartender, told us that he saw Tompkins give you an envelope of money. What was that all about?" Again she waited, this time for an explanation.

"Damn, is there anyone else you've set to spying on me? I can't believe this. Did you pay Rollie and Niko and whoever else for information on me?" Angrily, Laurie curled up in the corner of the bench seat, as far away from her sister as possible.

Apparently Laurie had learned to be maddeningly evasive since leaving home, Fallon realized. She hadn't explained the money, the so-called detective or her relationship with T.J. except in the broadest terms. And she exploded into anger whenever Fallon got too close with a question she didn't want to answer. "I didn't pay anyone for information on you. Michael has connections and we talked to a few people, finally tracing you to Niko's. Are you angry that I found you?"

"No, but I'm not happy with the way you went about it."

This teeter-totter of emotions was enough to test the patience of a saint, Fallon thought. "Laurie, I want to ask you something."

"Isn't that what you've *been* doing? What's one more?"

She's been through a lot, Fallon reminded herself. There had to be a reason for all this and if she learned what it was, maybe she would understand her sister better. "Why did you leave home?"

Laurie pulled her legs up onto the seat and leaned her head onto her bent knees. "I don't want to talk about this anymore right now. I'm too tired." With that, she closed her eyes.

Feeling her frustration increase, Fallon moved up to take the passenger seat opposite Michael. Turning to face him, she mouthed a brief message to him: I give up.

Without saying a word, Michael reached over and took her hand, letting his touch silently convey his understanding.

Fallon tapped lightly on the bedroom door, then opened it without waiting for the invitation she wasn't sure would be forthcoming. Laurie had slept the rest of the way back to Michael's House, eaten a sandwich that Sukey had made especially for her, then taken a long shower. Now, lying between clean white sheets, she looked more like fourteen than sixteen, more like the sister Fallon remembered.

She stepped to the bed and sat down on the edge, noting the shadows of fatigue beneath Laurie's big eyes—eyes that measured her in a way they never had before. "How are you feeling?" Fallon began.

"Tired, but better." Laurie watched her fingers trace the hem of the sheet as she searched for the right thing to say. "I'm sorry if I said some things that hurt you. I never meant to. You've always been good to me, Fallon."

"That's probably because I love you. I always have."

Tears sprang to Laurie's eyes and she found herself blinking. "I love you, too."

Fallon took her hand, then noticed that something was missing. "Your opal ring. Did you lose it?" Michael had mentioned that she'd been wearing it the first night she'd shown up on his doorstep.

Laurie's cheeks turned pink with embarrassment. "I gave it to T.J. to hock. He said he'd pay me back, but..." Twin tears trailed down her cheeks. "I'm not a very good judge of people, I guess. I've trusted the wrong ones and been mean to you when you were the one person I could always count on being in my corner."

Fallon felt her heart twist for the confused and frightened girl. "I try to be, Laurie. I've been thinking that we disappointed you, all of us, and that's why you left. Roy's so damned strict and Mom doesn't ever stand up to him. And then I didn't let you come visit when you wanted to, and—"

"No." Laurie laced her fingers with her sister's. "It wasn't you, never you. It was... just things. Things piled up and I didn't want to stay there anymore."

"Are you saying you don't want to go back to live with Roy and Mom?"

Sniffling, Laurie nodded. "Please, don't make me do that."

"I won't. How about coming to live with me?" Lord, could she do this? Could she handle a sixteen-year-old who'd already run away once? Yes, Fallon thought, she would manage somehow. She loved Laurie, and love could see them through her sister's growing pains.

"Do you mean it?" Laurie asked hesitantly. "You want me?"

Deeply moved, Fallon leaned down to hug her sister tightly. "Of course I want you."

After a few moments, Laurie eased back, frowning again. "What will Mom say?"

"You let me handle Mom." Jane Gifford wouldn't be happy about the situation, would take on the blame herself when in fact Fallon was certain that Laurie was running from Roy's obsessive ways. But their mother would get used to the idea in time. At least, she would know her younger daughter was safe.

Fallon reached to open the drawer of the nightstand and removed the twirling ballerina that Laurie had left on her first visit to Michael's House. "I thought you might want this back."

Laurie gazed at the delicate figurine inside the dome with sad affection, but shook her head. "I left it on purpose. I think I need to grow up, to leave childish things behind me."

"Okay, if you're sure." Fallon replaced the ballerina, wondering at this new sign of maturity. Leaving behind something their father had given her seemed so drastic, as if Laurie wanted to sever all ties to her past.

She studied her sister thoughtfully. "Maybe we should take you to a doctor tomorrow before we fly back. A checkup wouldn't hurt, considering the way you've been living these past weeks."

A trace of Laurie's defiance returned. "Is that a subtle way of asking if I might be pregnant or have some sort of disease?"

It honestly hadn't been, but maybe she had a valid point. "Is that a possibility?"

"I made sure T.J. used protection." She saw the shocked look Fallon tried to keep from showing. "Surprised that your little sister's not as pure as the driven snow? Don't be.

It's not as if I left home a virgin." The bitterness came through, despite Laurie's efforts to keep her voice neutral.

Oh, God. Fallon's worst fear, the thing that Michael had insisted might be so, had finally surfaced. She had to ask. "Laurie, did Roy molest you? Because if he did—"

"Him?" She gave a short, humorless laugh. "I wouldn't let that man touch me for a million dollars in pure gold."

Relief flooded Fallon. She must have had sex with someone else. Some high-school boy, probably. While Fallon wasn't thrilled that her sister was sexually active at sixteen, that was far easier to handle than a stepfather who would take advantage. She wouldn't question her further on this right now, believing that Laurie was entitled to some privacy. "I didn't think so."

"I guess you're disappointed in me, right?"

"I think sixteen's a little young for sex, but . . ."

"You know what? So do I. But what's done is done."

Cynical at sixteen. What a shame. "Listen, Laurie, we'll get past this, all of this. I'll take you to Denver and fix up the spare room for you. There's a high school not terribly far from my place. You're bright, you'll adjust, make new friends." When Laurie said nothing, Fallon stood, realizing that her sister needed sleep more than another lecture. "We'll do things together. Maybe Mom will drive up and visit us. Without Roy."

Laurie's smile was sleepy. "I'd like that."

"And we can drive to the academy and see Danny. He's home visiting, right now. Mom said he asked about you and wished you were there."

Laurie didn't comment, just closed her eyes.

Fallon decided that her sister had lost the battle to stay awake. The poor kid was beat. Quietly, she left the room, closing the door behind her.

It would work out, she told herself. She hadn't planned on taking in a sixteen-year-old but, as Michael had once said, you had to play the hand life dealt you.

Feeling better than she had in weeks, Fallon went downstairs to look for Michael.

*   *   *

In the morning, Laurie's bed was empty and her piti-
fully few belongings were gone.

*If someone had told me when we set out to search for
Sloan's son that I might find joy in the rugged mountains
of Mexico, I would have laughed. But I have.*

*A miracle has happened. I've fallen in love with Sloan,
and he with me. This beautiful person is like a gift I never
dared hope for, much less realize. He is kindness personi-
fied—a big, rugged man with a tender heart. His love for
his child, his willingness to put his life on hold, to do anything it takes to find his boy, only makes me love him more.*

*I was only sixteen when Lance and I married. Michael
was born six months later. Although we were in love and we
were a happy little family, the endless hard work of running a farm and raising a baby when we were scarcely more
than children ourselves left little time for the two of us.
Then Lance's mother died and his father changed, griev-
ing so much that within a year, he, too, was gone. The two
of us never had time to talk, to be foolishly romantic, to
have fun together. We were always working, always tired.*

*I loved Lance, but we never were able to share the deep
friendship I now know with Sloan. For weeks, we've been
together, alone, just the two of us for the most part, except for the occasional stranger we meet along the way. His
illness drew us closer and the obstacles we've had to over-
come on our journey have forged a bond that's very strong.
I don't think there's a subject we haven't talked over, a
thought we haven't shared.*

*For me, loving Sloan has been like an awakening. I can
scarcely believe how sensual and uninhibited he makes me
feel—at my age. I know he's also the reason my energy level
is so high. I want desperately to find Christopher, to find
him well taken care of and to be able to disentangle him
from his heartless mother.*

*Right now, the future is uncertain for both Sloan and me.
It would be foolish to make plans when a large part of our-*

selves—our children—isn't with us yet. But one day, when all these terrible days and nights are but distant memories, I pray that there'll be a future for us, together with all four children.

Chapter 11

Fallon sat slumped in a chair across the desk from Michael. Her hands were curled around a mug of hot coffee and yet they still felt cold and clammy. "Why? I just want to know why. Dammit, I thought we'd squared things last night. She hugged me with tears in her eyes, told me she loved me, told me she wanted to move to Denver and live with me. Then, bingo! She runs again." A shiver raced along Fallon's spine and she took a sip of coffee, wishing she could warm up.

Leaning back in his chair, Michael wondered what to say. It wasn't quite as if he could have predicted that Laurie would bolt. Yet it didn't surprise him. She had before. And he'd experienced the same thing with other runaways. After living on the streets for a while, some kids simply didn't want to stay in one place.

He'd overheard much of their conversation directly behind him in the van as he'd driven back yesterday, and had decided that Laurie was far from over whatever it was that had made her leave in the first place. She displayed anger, confusion, frustration. She vacillated between accusations and apologies, between exasperation and excitability.

In other words, she'd behaved very much like a typical teenage girl whose back was to the wall.

"I thought she sounded kind of defensive when I heard you two talking on the drive," he said, uncertain just what to say to Fallon, who was obviously blaming herself. "It could be that it wasn't anything you said or did, and merely that she has this need to run away—from questions, from authority, from anyone who dares to judge or criticize her."

"You think I was critical and judgmental?" Fallon didn't sound defensive, but rather as if she really wanted to know.

"I didn't say that." Straightening, he tossed down the pen he'd been toying with. "I'm pretty much in the dark on this, same as you, Fallon."

"But you must have some ideas. You've dealt with runaways for years."

He wished he could give her the answer she wanted, the right answer. The most he could do was try. "All right, let's try to analyze this. Tell me what you talked about last night in her room, everything that was said."

So she did, replaying the scene for Michael. But when she'd finished, she still had no clue. "Niko told us that Laurie had come to him looking for a job after T.J. stole her money because she was tired of living on the street. Yet I offer her a home, love and all that goes with it, and she runs." Unable to sit still another minute, Fallon rose, pacing to the window. "I can't remember my teen years being this difficult."

Michael was thinking over all he'd heard. "Did she seem at all enthusiastic when you mentioned that your mother could drive up without Roy and that you'd visit Danny at the academy?"

"No. She just closed her eyes, as if she was very tired and didn't want to talk anymore. I don't think she even heard me leave the room."

"And you didn't look shocked or get on her case when she told you she was no longer a virgin?"

"I certainly *was* shocked, though I don't think she could tell." She turned from the window. "Wouldn't you be if your sixteen-year-old sister who'd hardly dated, to the best of your knowledge, told you that?''

Michael wished he had a sister of any age. He would deal with the problems as they came up. But that wasn't what Fallon wanted to hear. ''So T.J. wasn't the first?''

''Apparently not.''

''And you believed her when she said that Roy hadn't touched her?''

''Absolutely. She was revolted at the very idea.''

Had that been a smokescreen? Michael wondered. Runaways often became very good liars in no time, as he himself had. And they denied their fears, even to themselves.

He reached for her hand, sat down in his desk chair and drew her onto his lap. ''Laurie's disturbed about something, I'm convinced of that. We just haven't figured out what it is, the same as with Daryl.''

Fallon had been so absorbed in her own problems, she'd forgotten that she'd found Michael having a long talk with Daryl last night when she'd gone looking for him. The boy hadn't looked good, so she'd left his office quickly. ''How did that go?''

Wearily, Michael shrugged. ''Like you, I wish I could get through to that kid. He got into a brawl at school with this older boy who stole the few bucks he had on him. Daryl didn't defend himself, just let the kid use him as a punching bag.''

''When I stuck my head in here last night, I noticed that his face was bruised and puffy. Why wouldn't he at least *try* to fight back?''

''Because he's certain he can't win. He's told me that his father used to slap him and his little brother around from the time they were toddlers. The brother is deaf in one ear from one of the blows. When you're small and defenseless, after so much pummeling, especially dished out by the very people who are supposed to love and protect you, you give up. The fight drains out of you. You take your lumps and try to remain inconspicuous in everything so nothing you do sets them off.''

Fallon had trouble believing that this sort of thing went on even today, although she knew it did. "This bully that picked on Daryl at school, could you find him and get something done about such an unprovoked attack?"

"I could, but Daryl doesn't want me to. The bully has friends and he's afraid they'd go after him in retaliation. The poor kid lives in constant fear, and I can't seem to ease his mind. I offered to see about getting him transferred to another school or to look into a foster home in a better neighborhood with a family I personally check out. But he just sat there staring at me with those world-weary eyes."

"Damn, it's so unfair."

"Yeah, it is. Which brings us back to Laurie. She's afraid of something, Fallon. Just like Daryl. And, because she's young and doesn't know what else to do, she runs. She doesn't feel safe."

"But I offered her safety. No one would hurt her if she was with me. I wouldn't let them."

Michael let out a sigh. "No one can protect another person a hundred percent of the time. I've offered relative safety to Daryl. He wants to believe and even buys into it for a while, until the next bully comes along. Then he's afraid again, reliving the nightmares again."

"But what on God's green earth is Laurie afraid of?"

"That's the big question. Yet sometimes, like with Daryl, even if you know, you can't make the fear go away. I'm arranging today to get counseling for him—someone more trained than I, someone not as close to the situation as I." He shrugged, feeling uncharacteristically downhearted. "Maybe it'll work, maybe not. I've got to try. Laurie might open up to a counselor."

"If she'd come back, I'd certainly be willing to try that." Fallon shook her head. "To think that when I first came here, I thought all I'd have to do is walk up to her, tell her I love her, that everything will be fine, and she'd happily climb on a plane and return with me. How naive can you get?"

Michael knew that I-told-you-so's weren't necessary. Fallon had learned a lot and changed even more. "Don't blame yourself. There's no right or wrong way, here. We try this or that, and if it fails, we try something else. People problems can't be solved like crossword puzzles." He had to ask, and was annoyed with himself that he dreaded to hear her answer. "What do you plan to do now?"

"I've got to call Craig Miller, my store manager. I thought I'd be flying back today with Laurie in tow, getting her settled and going back to work. Craig is relatively new and not nearly as human as our old manager was. He goes by the book and is always politically correct, but not very understanding of the people under him."

Michael felt a weight slip from his chest. She wasn't leaving, at least not now. He would deal with later later. "Then, you're planning on staying awhile yet?"

"I have to find her, Michael. I was so close, so very close. I have to give it one more shot. If this time, Laurie tells me she doesn't want to return, not to Mom's or to my place, I'll have to accept it. But I have to hear it from her." She slipped her arm around his shoulders and met his eyes. "That is, if you don't mind my staying on. I could rent a room somewhere and—"

"Mind? I *want* you to stay."

"Good, because I'm going to need your help again."

"I need yours, too. I think it's time we looked into this bearded guy who's masquerading as a P.I., the man who just might have poked a hole in the van's brake line."

The project seemed insurmountable to Fallon. "How on earth will we find him?"

"I've got a few ideas. A friend of mine's a police artist. I've done him some favors. I'm going to ask him to meet with Rollie and Sherlock, to take down the man's description and make a sketch. Then I'll take it to Sam and get copies distributed."

"I thought Sam was in the Juvenile Division?"

"He is, but he'll direct my request to the right people."

"You think our impersonator's a local man?"

"Could be. There certainly aren't two Raymond Tompkinses in Colorado Springs. How do you feel about trying

Roy again? Maybe if you confront him, we can learn something.''

"Right after I call Craig.'' Two phone calls she didn't want to make. The day was shaping up beautifully. For a brief moment, she shifted closer to Michael, absorbing his strength.

He buried his face between her breasts, inhaling the wonderful womanly scent of her. He knew how awful she felt, which was only one reason why he'd promised to help her. Yet he was reminded that once she found Laurie again, Fallon would have no more reason to stay.

And he found himself hating the idea.

Fallon kissed him lightly, then got off his lap.

Michael stood. "I'm going to meet with Opal and Sukey and see if there's anything I'm needed for while you make your calls. Come find me when you're finished, okay?''

"I will.'' Fallon slipped onto his desk chair with a heavy sigh. Nervously, she picked up the phone.

There were always details waiting for Michael's approval, especially when he'd been away awhile. He signed some checks, talked with Paul from the kitchen phone about medication for one of the kids, approved a food order for Sukey and checked over Opal's paperwork. Then he called Sergeant Damien and updated him, mentioning the bearded man he suspected of tampering with his car. Sam had been interested, as Michael had hoped, and took down a detailed description, then told him to get the artist's sketches over to him as soon as possible. He promised to put a good man on the case.

Nearly an hour had passed before he realized that Fallon hadn't emerged from his office. He went looking.

She was sitting in his desk chair, her back to the doorway, staring out the window, utterly motionless. He stepped closer. "Fallon?''

Slowly, she swung around and looked up at him. "He fired me,'' she said in a low, defeated voice.

He stepped around and leaned a hip against the edge of the desk. "Who, your manager? He fired you? On what grounds?"

She waved an impatient hand. "He rattled off a whole string of them, but the gist of it is that, and I quote him verbatim, 'You can't run a tight ship when your top people take off in an irresponsible fashion every time they get a notion.' End of quote."

"Can you go over his head and challenge his decision?"

"I suppose." She shoved both hands through her hair, leaning back. "But I'm not going to. I don't want to work for a man like him and even if I did, can you imagine what it would be like after I'd gone over his head? I've got a degree and four years' experience. I can find another job. But I have to admit, I feel as if someone just yanked the rug out from under me."

"Someone did, and unfairly at that. He could have offered you a leave of absence without pay—something."

"Could have, should have, but he didn't." Fallon shook her head as if to dismiss the whole incident from her mind. "It's probably for the best. I can concentrate fully on finding Laurie without worrying about Craig and his pettiness."

He wasn't sure if he should ask, but he had a practical nature. "How are you set for money?"

"I'm okay for a while. My rent's paid up and I've got enough savings to get me by until I find another job." Provided the search didn't take too long. "I've made some good contacts at a couple of other stores. I'm not worried about getting another job when I'm finished here." And even if she were concerned, she wouldn't want Michael to know.

She checked her watch. "I called Roy at work and they said he'd be back from lunch in forty minutes. I'm going to give it another try. I didn't want to leave my name in case the creep's trying to avoid my calls."

Michael moved to the chair across from his desk. "You don't mind if I listen?"

"Of course not." She dialed quickly and was put through almost immediately this time. Her stepfather's voice, as always, was controlled, authoritative. "Hello, Roy. It's Fallon."

"Fallon, where are you? Why aren't you back home? Your mother told me you called when Danny was home for a visit. I can't believe you're still off on this wild-goose chase."

How did he know she wasn't calling from her home in Denver?

And why hadn't he asked if she'd located Laurie? Maybe it was time to shock dear old dad. "I found Laurie," she said, dropping the bombshell.

Roy was slow to respond. "You did? What reason did she give for leaving?"

Not how was she, but what was her reason for running away. Interesting. "We can talk about that later. Something's very fishy here. Laurie stayed with me only a short time, then walked away again. I found her to be confused and troubled. I got the impression that something happened at home before she left. She absolutely refused to go back to your house. Any guesses?"

His reply was uncharacteristically hesitant. "Did she *say* something had happened?"

Answer a question with a question—an old ploy to put the onus on the other person. Two could play this game. She simply wouldn't answer his question at all. "Roy, why did you lie to me? I talked with the private investigator named Raymond Tompkins in Colorado Springs whose card I have. He never heard of you or Laurie. What's going on?"

Roy cleared his throat noisily. "I don't know what you're talking about. I heard about Tompkins through someone at work here and hired him to ease your mother's mind, as I told you the last time we talked. How dare you accuse me of lying? If anyone is, it must be Tompkins."

Highly doubtful, Laurie thought. What motive would Tompkins have? And he'd sounded genuinely surprised by her call. "Fine. When I return, you and I together with

Mom will have to pay Mr. Tompkins a visit at his office so we can get to the bottom of this."

"Listen, young lady, I don't like your tone." His tone was sharp and growing more annoyed by the minute. "It's time you stopped worrying about your thoughtless sister, stopped playing detective and got your fanny back to Denver before you lose your job. Or are you suddenly as irresponsible as she?" Roy made a disgusted sound. "I should have known you'd both turn out this way, considering what your father was like."

Fallon sat up so swiftly, her chair all but tipped over. "You leave my father out of this. Something's going on, Roy, and I'm not going to quit looking until I find out what it is. There's a man here who's assumed Tompkins's identity. He's tall with a dark beard and drives an older Cadillac. He's been seen with Laurie, giving her an envelope of money. A great deal of money. What do you know about this person?"

Roy's voice was brusque. "Did Laurie tell you about him?"

"Stop answering my questions with questions. You're not going to shake me off this trail by being evasive, Roy."

"Don't you threaten me, young lady." Roy was indignant. "I know nothing about anyone of that description. Obviously, Laurie ran away from you, too. Because she's reckless and undependable. Your mother and I have had it with coddling her, spending money on her. I'm through, finished. Don't call me about this again." The receiver slammed down.

"Damn him!" Fallon hung up, wishing Roy was in the room so she could tell him exactly what she thought of his attempt at righteous indignation. "Him, of all people, badmouthing my father. At least my father had integrity."

Michael went to her, tugged her to her feet and took her into his arms for a comforting hug. Then he listened while Fallon repeated Roy's lies. "If he's lying," he told her, "and it looks like he is, we'll trip him up, Fallon. I heard you tell him that you're not going to quit until you get to the bottom of this. I want you to know that I'm with you, all the way.''

Fallon looked into his sky blue eyes and felt a spreading warmth that drained away her anger. She wanted so badly to tell him how much she loved him—for supporting her in this, for all that he did for the kids who wandered through his life, for the man he was. But she held back the words and instead stepped closer into his arms.

For some time now, she'd avoided men who liked to take charge. But now, today, she was truly grateful for Michael's comforting presence. She felt tired and defeated, ready to let him take over. Just once, just this one time. "Thank you," she whispered. "I really needed to hear that right now."

He kissed her, feeling that quick flash of excitement that came every time his lips met hers. She opened to him, needy and willing, despite her worries.

He ended the kiss and noticed the fatigue in her face. "I'll bet you didn't sleep well last night, thinking about taking Laurie back to Denver. Why don't you go upstairs and rest while I track down a couple of leads on our bearded P.I.?"

Fallon shook her head. "I couldn't sleep. I need to go with you. This is *my* problem. Besides, two sets of eyes and ears are better than one."

He took her hand. "All right, let's go."

It turned out to be a very long day. Michael located his friend, Will Martin, but the artist wasn't available till two. They grabbed a quick lunch, then picked up Will before heading for Balboa Park. Fortunately, Sherlock wasn't difficult to find and, for another folded bill that disappeared like lightning into the pocket of his shabby jeans, he described the man who'd called himself Tompkins thoroughly enough that Will made several sketches. Michael didn't mind paying, for he felt they were on the right track.

From there, they went to the Rodeo Bar and got lucky again. Rollie had come in early to catch up on his beverage orders. He gave Will a description that matched Sherlock's to a T. Studying the sketches the artist had made in the park, Rollie nodded emphatically.

"Yeah, that's him. That sure is him, right down to the bolo tie."

Michael dropped Will at his place and they just made it to a print shop before closing. They had fifty copies of each of five sketches made, posted some in several neighborhoods as dusk approached, then dropped the rest off at the police station in an envelope marked to Sam Damien's attention.

Evening shadows were falling as they climbed back into the van. Michael noticed Fallon yawning behind her hand as he buckled himself in. "I think we're going to call it a night. What do you say?"

She wanted to keep going, to search each and every street, restaurant, park and bar, to look for Laurie so she could get the truth out of her this time. Fallon knew she wouldn't rest until she heard an explanation from Laurie's own lips. If something had happened at home—and she was beginning to believe it had—she was going to learn what it was. And she wanted to find the man who'd tried to harm Michael and her by sabotaging his van.

But not tonight, she realized. Before tackling anything more, she needed to rest, to regroup. They both did.

"I say you're absolutely right."

She'd given in without a hassle, which told him just how low her energy level and spirits were. He would try to raise them. As they drove toward his beach house, he picked up the car phone to let Eldora know they were on their way, hungry and tired, and then checked in with Opal to let her know where he would be.

Fallon laid her head back on the rim of the hot tub in Michael's backyard, stretched her legs out and slowly drew in a steamy breath. Overhead, stars filled a peaceful night sky and a restless breeze stirred the palm trees that formed a natural fence around both sides of the sloping lawn. King marched along the perimeter, sniffing occasionally at small creatures in the grass, guarding his territory.

Inch by inch, she relaxed, letting the tension flow from her, letting the burbling water steal away her fatigue. When they'd arrived, Eldora had had steaks sizzling on the grill, a Caesar salad tossed, crusty bread heating and a tart wine chilling. The woman was a wonder.

"I don't pay attention to the white-wine-with-fish and red-with-meat rule," Michael had said as he'd uncorked and poured. "I drink the wine that appeals to me at the moment."

Hadn't she known he would be unconventional, even in that? She'd eaten more than she had in a single sitting since that huge hamburger a couple of weeks back, then he'd suggested a dip in the hot tub to get out the kinks. Like two delinquent teenagers, they'd waited until Eldora had gone to her room on the far side of the house, then stripped and lowered themselves into the steaming water. Heavenly!

Fallon wiggled her one outstretched foot and felt Michael take it in hand, massaging with his strong, lean fingers. She smiled, feline-like, at the delicious sensation of a foot rub. Michael had lighted several chunky candles and their soft glow delicately danced and swayed in a soft breeze, the vanilla scent teasing her nostrils. From inside the house through the screened patio door, low, throbbing music drifted out from the stereo. A hazy half-moon played hide-and-seek with a few wispy clouds out over the restless waves that rolled tirelessly onto the sandy shore. On the cool deck alongside the hot tub sat two chilled glasses of wine. She couldn't think of another place on the planet that she would rather be.

She let her lazy gaze slide over him, his damp hair gleaming in the candlelight, his eyes more gray than blue, looking mysterious and seductive. Droplets of water gathered on his sleek chest and dripped from the curly hair nestled there. Then he shifted closer and she could feel his arousal against her wet skin, hear the sharp breath he drew in at the contact.

"I wanted to be alone with you tonight, just the two of us." He slipped a golden poppy he'd plucked from the flower bed earlier into her hair. "I hope you want that, too."

"Mmm, I do."

He scooped water into his palm and dribbled it down between her breasts, watching with a fascination he thought would never end. "We've been on the move, with people, for days now. I felt we needed some alone time."

Fallon sighed contentedly. "I couldn't agree more." And she wondered how she would come to this point so swiftly, she who'd never been impulsive or capricious or even very romantic.

"I have a confession to make," Michael whispered, one long finger drawing lazy circles around her breasts.

"What would that be?" she asked, too relaxed to really care.

"The first time I saw you, wearing that uptight little silk blouse, high-necked and long-sleeved, I wanted to rip it off you, to touch your skin, to touch you."

Fallon lifted her head, smiling. "Oh, my. That first time, in the backyard when I nearly fainted? Why, Mr. Redfield, aren't you the Big Bad Wolf thinking of taking advantage of a woman in distress?" She felt his smile against her throat as his lips pressed a soft kiss just beneath her ear. "Do you want to know what *I* was thinking at that moment?"

Michael raised his head. "I'd give up Saturday cartoons to know what you were thinking."

She chuckled low in her throat. "That you were too handsome and too damn sexy to be running a house for runaways. That half the teenage girls you meet must have tremendous crushes on you."

He gave a quick shake of his head. "Not so. I've not had one regard me that way. To them, I'm a helping hand, an authority figure, a big brother, maybe. Most of these kids are too troubled and mixed-up to think about schoolgirl crushes." He shifted her on the spa's seat, taking her onto his lap. "Besides, I'm much more interested in *big* girls."

"Who're you calling 'big,' bud?" But she let him adjust her in the buoyant water so she was straddling him, close but not too close, teasing both of them.

"Not you." His hands skimmed along her rib cage. "You're slender, soft, beautiful." He dipped his head to kiss her shoulder.

The moon slipped behind a cloud and they were left in shadow, the candlelight flickering across skin that was sleek and wet. The music thrummed, swelling with passion, the fragrance of oleander from the bushes nearby enveloping them.

Playfully yet seductively, Fallon let her hands wander over him, then move down to close around him. "And you're beautiful, strong, solid." She heard his husky laugh, then gasped as he again shifted her and slipped inside. She wrapped her arms around his neck and pressed her full breasts to his chest. His mouth was at her ear, filling it with his warm breath as he filled her with his heat.

Michael murmured things to her—hot, passionate promises of the pleasure they would find together—and she whispered back in soft, sensual responses, the meaning-less-yet-meaningful words that lovers share when they're as close as two people can get. He thrust gently upward, aided by the churning water, and felt her tighten around him. He was patient, not greedy, for they had the whole night to love and be loved.

The word echoed through his thoughts, reminding him that he'd deleted it from his vocabulary, recalling what a velvet trap love could be. He turned from the wayward wandering of those thoughts and instead, concentrated on feelings—the feelings that Fallon brought to him.

Passion and fulfillment, gentleness and desperation, awakening needs and trembling wants. She made him feel so much, want more than he should, reach for a happiness he wasn't certain existed. The weary warrior in him wanted to pull back, to retrench, to withdraw himself from a battle he was sure to lose. But the man in him, the lover inside that man, wanted only the tenderness she and she alone had shown him, the fantasy of a future with her always at his side, the happiness of a shared life.

He heard a low sound drift from deep in her throat and could hold back no longer. Taking her mouth first, he then took her—wildly, like a randy teenage boy who could never get enough.

Together, they drove each other on, moving toward the madness that would burn them like the smoldering flames. When at last release came, they shuddered, sighed and then kissed with generous affection.

Michael hit the button on the spa and adjusted the motor's speed. Bathed only in moonlight and gently rippling water, they stayed wrapped in each other's arms while the candles guttered out in a breeze that soon became a gusty night wind and finally sent them scurrying for big, fluffy towels to wrap around themselves.

Hand in hand, they crept like naughty children, quietly so as not to awaken Eldora, up to Michael's bedroom where they discarded the towels and snuggled under the covers. There they found that powerful waves as mighty as the sea now pounding against the shore engulfed them again. Insatiable, ravenous, greedy, they kissed and devoured, plunged and plundered, both swept up in a sensual battle that had no winner and no loser.

Afterward, exhausted but smiling, they cuddled together and dozed.

Until the bedside phone rang, disturbing Michael in the midst of a marvelous dream. Grumpily he answered, noticing that the digital clock showed that it was almost eleven.

"Michael—" Opal's serious voice came on "—I hate to disturb you, but I thought you'd want to know about this."

Immediately alert, he sat up. "What is it, Opal?"

"Wendy wasn't feeling well, so I was up with her. When I walked her back to her room, I noticed that Daryl's door was ajar. I went inside and saw that he was missing, his bed neatly made and his few belongings gone, except for his new white running shoes. They were sitting on the floor next to the bed. Michael, I'm afraid for him. You know he'd never have left those shoes behind, unless..." Opal sounded very worried. "Well, I don't even want to hazard a guess."

"Thanks for letting me know. I'm on my way." Michael hung up and tossed back the covers before glancing over his shoulder.

Fallon lay with her hair tousled on the pillow, her eyes sleepy and satisfied, blinking to bring herself fully awake. "What's wrong?" she asked, her voice thick.

Concerned though he was, he leaned down and kissed her, wishing he didn't have to leave her. Quickly, he told her about his conversation with Opal. "You stay here and rest. I'll be back as soon as I find Daryl." He rose and went to the closet.

Fallon, too, got up. "I'm going with you."

Michael reached for his jeans. "You don't have to. I—"

"Yes, I do," she said, gathering up her clothes. "What is your problem is *my* problem."

When had that happened? Michael asked himself.

"Is this usual for you, to go out looking for every kid who leaves unexpectedly?" Fallon asked as they pulled away from Michael's House after talking with Opal. "You did tell me once that no one stays if they don't want to."

"Daryl's different," Michael answered, heading for Balboa Park, which he figured was the best place to start looking. "I've known him awhile and I talked with him just yesterday about his problems. I thought we'd worked out a plan and, although he hadn't seemed real excited about any of my suggestions, he'd indicated that he'd go along with them."

"Sort of like me with Laurie," she reminded him. "These runaways can really get skittish." She glanced at his profile, saw the tension. "Do you have any idea why Daryl might have felt the need to leave again?"

"I wish I did. That's another thing—these kids get so used to hiding their feelings and thoughts that you can't even read their expressions." He turned onto Sixth Avenue, heading north.

Fallon agreed, remembering how she'd tried to figure out what Laurie had been thinking when they'd talked that brief time. Her expression had been guarded at best; not unfriendly, but not trusting, either. Almost as if she no longer trusted any adult. "I suppose, after years of mistreatment by adults, Daryl's unwilling to trust any grownup who tells him everything's going to be all right. He simply doesn't believe anymore."

"Yeah, I'm afraid you're right. And once you stop believing, once you lose hope for the future, what is there?" A muscle in Michael's jaw tightened. "I just hope he doesn't do anything crazy."

Fallon frowned. "Like what?"

He didn't want to put a voice to his fears. "The thing that worries me most is that he left those shoes behind. He really loved those shoes. I don't think he even has another pair." The nights were getting cooler. He remembered that the frail young boy had gotten sick once before, living on the street. If only they could find him before that happened again. If only he could convince Daryl that he did have a future.

If only, Michael thought. Two of the saddest words ever.

He pulled the van to a stop alongside the wooded area where most of the kids gathered at night, near the picnic table that Sherlock had designated as his own. As they stepped out, Michael saw that the heavy-set man wasn't around.

"Why don't we separate?" Fallon suggested. "I'll go one way and you can take that other path."

"No, it's nearly midnight. I don't want you walking alone in this park at night." He took her hand. "Just keep your eyes peeled. If he's here, one of us should spot him. He's smaller than most boys his age."

They walked all the way up to Laurel, then turned and swung back, strolling through the grass, ending up near the Organ Pavilion. It was there that Michael spotted Sherlock and waved him over.

"What's up, man?" Sherlock asked, nodding to both of them. "You're out kinda late."

Michael got right to it. "One of our kids left and we need to find him. His name's Daryl and he's pretty troubled." He gave Sherlock a description. "Seen him around tonight?"

Without thinking it over, Sherlock shook his head. "Nobody like that's been around here. But I heard down the grapevine that that other guy you're looking for is a local."

Fallon came alert. "You mean the bearded man that we had sketched?"

"Yeah, him. I hear tell his name's Wesley Greiner. Used to be a P.I., but he lost his license coupla years back. Some trouble with cops over ethical behavior, or so I heard."

Michael tried not to show too much interest. He had to deal with Sherlock occasionally, but he didn't trust him a hundred percent. "So, who told you about him?"

Sherlock shrugged one shoulder in the direction of the street. "A guy I know, name of Curtis. He's lived on the streets longer than me. He saw the poster you taped on that pole over there."

"Did Curtis tell you where this Wesley Greiner lives or where I could find him?"

"He's not exactly in the phone book, you know." Sherlock gave him a sly smile. "Curtis asked me if there was a reward coming."

He should have guessed. "Tell him if he can pinpoint the guy and when I go there, it's really him, I'll pay both of you."

Satisfied, Sherlock nodded. "I'll tell him. Meanwhile, I'll pass the word about Daryl. For him, it won't cost you. I know you mean to help the kid."

"Thanks, Sherlock." Michael tugged Fallon's hand away before she could say anything. He'd felt the tension from her while they'd been talking. They were almost to the van when he finally asked, "Something wrong?"

"That man bothers me. I can't help it. What a way to live."

Michael slid open the van door. "It's *his* life, Fallon. He probably wouldn't want to sell women's clothes like you do. Choices. Right or wrong, we get to make our own."

She wasn't exactly selling women's clothes these days, either, Fallon thought. She'd been gone less than two weeks and already it felt like two years—in one way. As Michael started the engine, she looked over at him. In another way, it seemed like only yesterday that she'd come here and unwittingly fallen in love.

"Where now?" she asked him.

"I'm going to drive around places I've seen Daryl in the past. I don't know what else to do."

Fallon buckled herself in and settled down for a long night.

They were climbing back into the van at about one in the morning, after walking the area around Daryl's school, when the van phone rang. Michael picked it up. "Yeah, Opal, what've you got?" He listened for several moments. "He didn't say anything else? Okay, thanks. I'll call him."

He glanced at Fallon. "Opal says that Sam called me, wants me to meet him at the station. I hope that means they've picked Daryl up again." His mouth a thin line, he shifted into gear. He had a bad feeling about this one.

Sergeant Damien looked tired as he glanced up from his desk when Michael and Fallon walked into his office. Wearily, he removed his glasses and ran a hand over his eyes as with the other, he motioned them to sit.

"It's bad news, isn't it?" Michael asked, unable to rid himself of the sense of foreboding.

"'Bout as bad as it gets, Michael," Sam said, unable to muster the energy to be gentle. He'd been home and in bed only two hours when the call had come. He'd been a cop working with kids too long, had seen too much. Some days, he was sure it was a hell of a way to make a living. This was one of those days. "Daryl stepped in front of a truck rolling down Harbor Drive. Probably died instantly."

"Oh, no," Fallon said softly, and reached for Michael's hand. It was cold, clammy.

Sam went on. "I got the driver downstairs, but we're going to let him go. There were two eyewitnesses who were strolling back to the Marriott. They said the kid was standing shoeless on the curb, looking like he was planning to cross the street. They watched him because he looked so young to be out alone so late. Next thing they know, Daryl calmly stepped in front of the barreling truck."

Wordlessly, Michael closed his eyes on the mental picture. He was vaguely aware of Fallon squeezing his hand. He drew in a deep breath, then opened his eyes. "I'll...I'll see to the funeral."

"You don't have to. I..."

"I *want* to." Michael stood. "Thanks for letting me know."

Sam put his glasses back on and studied the man he'd known for fifteen years, from boyhood to the present, and he ached for him. "Michael, it wasn't your fault."

Dazed, Michael nodded. "I'll be in touch." He walked down the hall with Fallon, letting her lead him back to the van, his eyes picturing a young boy's smashed body under an eighteen-wheeler. What had been going through that poor despairing child's mind when he'd stepped off that curb?

"I'll drive," Fallon said at the van, holding her hand out for the keys. She'd thought he would fight her, but Michael handed the keys over and slid into the passenger seat. She got behind the wheel, wondering what to say, how to comfort him. When she'd been exhausted and feeling bruised, he'd taken her to his beach house, held her and healed her. She would do no less. She put the key in the ignition.

Michael lay in his bed staring up at the ceiling, his face filled with pain. Next to him, Fallon lay on her side and twined her fingers with his, simply letting him know she was there, willing to talk if that was what he wanted, able to be quiet if that was what he needed. She struggled with her own demons, picturing her sister facing such despair, unable to find a way out so she would just give up. She chased the image away and concentrated on Michael.

"Once, about five years ago," Michael began in a low, soft voice, "we lost another one of our kids in much the same hopeless way. Her name was Rebecca and she'd run away from home because she was pregnant and afraid to tell her parents. I talked with her, Paul tried to help her, we all did. But there was no getting through to her. Finally, she found someone who did a shady abortion and she bled to death." He turned to Fallon, gripping her fingers. "I had some bad times on the street, but not like these kids do today. I never once thought of killing myself, only of surviving. Where'd I go wrong with Daryl?"

"You didn't. You tried, but he was beyond help, probably by the time you met him. You're not the problem, Michael, and you're not the solution. Aren't you the one who told me that when I first arrived?"

He let out a ragged sigh. "I guess so."

"You deal daily with troubled kids, most of whom have pretty awful lives. You have to know there will be some losses. You can't save them all, but think of the ones you do save. Think of Wendy who's recovered from losing her baby and back in school now, and Roxie who loves living at Michael's House, and all the others. They know you care about them and it makes a big difference in their lives."

"Yeah, I care. That's the problem. If you let yourself care too deeply, you can't help people. You need to be like cops and doctors, to stay emotionally uninvolved. Then, maybe you don't hurt so much when something like this happens."

She touched his face and made him look at her. "You don't think losing a patient hurts a doctor deep inside? And did you see Sam's face tonight? How many kids like Daryl has he seen and then had to call someone to come pick up the broken pieces?"

Michael narrowed his eyes. "That's exactly my point. *If* you don't let yourself care, then you won't get hurt."

"No, you'll just be a robot, an unfeeling machine, an automaton. Is that what you want to be?"

His eyes were anguished. "Love's too damn difficult, Fallon. It makes life too hard."

She gave him a gentle smile. "You're wrong. Love's the only reason for living."

He wrinkled his forehead, realizing he had a pounding headache. "I don't want to think about this anymore tonight."

"Then don't." She eased his head over until his cheek rested on her breast, her hand gently massaging his temples, soothing away the headache she could see in his eyes. "Just close your eyes and rest."

He felt himself drifting, needing to escape. "I don't need love, Fallon. I really don't. I do just fine without it."

She rested her cheek on his soft hair. "Sure, you do." In all her short life, she'd never known anyone who needed love more.

Chapter 12

The man known as Curtis was small, wily and smarmy, with little fox eyes, Fallon thought. She hung back as Sherlock introduced them. Michael stood at least a head and a half taller than this creep who supposedly had information on the bearded man passing himself off as Raymond Tompkins.

"I recognized his picture," Curtis mumbled, wiping his nose on a dingy sleeve. "The poster says he drives an old-model white Caddy and likes to dress up like a dude. That's Wesley Greiner. I'd bet on it."

"Where can I find him?" Michael asked.

Curtis closed one eye and looked up. "How much you willing to pay?"

Sherlock stepped in. "I told you Michael will pay when he checks the guy out."

The beady eyes swung to the chubby man. "Who says I can trust him to come through?"

"*I* do," Sherlock said quietly.

Curtis thought that over and apparently decided he would have to live with it. "Wesley lives on Alabama off El Cajon Boulevard. There's an adult bookstore on the corner. His is the last house at the end of the block. You can't miss it. It's painted blue."

"You know him?" Michael questioned.

"Sort of." Curtis shuffled scuffed shoes in the dry grass. "He used to do P.I. work for this company I worked for, only the cops pulled his license. He takes odd jobs now. I stay away from him, mostly. He's a grifter."

"Okay," Michael said. "I'll check him out and be in touch." He nodded his thanks to Sherlock, then walked with Fallon back to the van.

"What's a grifter?" Fallon asked when they got under way.

"A con man. Pretty funny, isn't it? One con man saying he avoids the other one."

It was three days after they'd learned of Daryl's death and a day after the boy's forlornly sad funeral attended by only a handful of people from Michael's House. Fallon had been spending her days looking for Laurie in every conceivable place, surmising that she had to be waitressing somewhere, as she had been in L.A.; and her nights with Michael, keeping him from slipping into despair, from blaming himself for Daryl's apparent suicide.

Maybe finding the man who'd sabotaged his van would lift his spirits. "What are you going to do when you find this Wesley Greiner?" she asked him.

"Make him talk." Michael's mouth was a thin line.

"Shouldn't we involve the law? Sam's been pretty helpful." She didn't like the dangerous look on Michael's face.

"Eventually. I'm going to drop you back at the house and..."

"Oh, no, you're not. This is *my* battle, remember? This man came after you because of me. I'm going along." She saw his jaw clench and went on. "That is *not* negotiable, Michael."

"You could get hurt."

"So could you. Everyone has said this guy is big. You're in good shape, but I don't imagine you've got a black belt in karate or something similar. And I don't suppose you have a gun in the van, do you?"

He sent her a frown. "With kids in here all the time? Hardly."

"Okay, then, I'll walk with you, standing back a ways, holding your cellular phone. If he makes a wrong move, I'll dial 9-1-1 so fast his head will spin." To show him she meant business, she picked up the phone and placed it in her lap.

He tried to keep his lips from twitching. There was nothing humorous about their mission, but being backed up by a woman who probably weighed a hundred ten, armed with only a phone, struck him as slightly ludicrous. But he didn't want to insult her so he nodded solemnly and concentrated on his driving.

He hadn't been in El Cajon just east of San Diego proper in some time. The streets off the boulevard were named alphabetically after states and others were numbered. The area, sprinkled with cheap hotels and seedy bars, had definitely seen better days. Even so, he had little trouble finding Alabama Street and following it to the end.

"Well, it certainly is a blue house," Fallon commented as they rolled to a stop two doors from the cinder-block bungalow painted blue that stood out like a sore thumb, even in this nonconforming neighborhood.

In the driveway was parked an old white Cadillac, its hood propped up. A man in stained overalls was leaning in, tinkering with something. At the sound of their car stopping, he straightened and looked over. He was tall with a full beard, his hair thinning.

"That's our man," Fallon whispered.

Michael kept his eyes on the man who he was certain recognized his van. "Fallon, I'd like you to stay here." He opened his door, wishing she would listen to him, for once.

"Michael, I'm sorry. I'm going with you." She got out on her side.

Damn stubborn woman, Michael thought as he walked toward the man, his hands hanging loosely at his sides. The big guy watched their approach, his face revealing nothing. Michael stopped a good ten feet away and felt Fallon move up behind him, clutching the phone. "Are you Wesley Greiner?" he asked, trying to keep his voice even.

The man gripped a wrench in one greasy hand and narrowed his eyes. "Who wants to know?"

"I'm Michael Redfield and this is Fallon McKenzie. We're looking for her sister, Laurie. They're both from Colorado. Would you happen to know where she is?"

"I don't know what you're talking about." He studied them both for a moment, then turned back toward the car, dismissing them as he peered under the hood as if they weren't there.

In a move that Fallon was later to think of as faster than a lightning bolt, Michael charged Wesley, wrenched the tool from his hand, tossing it to the ground, and twisted the man's arm behind his back before shoving his face under the open hood of the car.

Wesley Greiner howled in surprise, then in pain over his arm being all but twisted off, and in fear as he realized he'd badly underestimated his visitor. "What do you want with me?"

"The truth would be nice."

"I don't know nothing."

Michael increased the pressure on his arm and forced the man's belly to the radiator and his cheek to the air filter as he gazed up at the metal prop rod that held the raised hood in place. "It wouldn't take much for me to jar that and let this hood drop on you, Wesley."

The big man grunted, trying an awkward backward kick to catch his captor off guard, but Michael was too fast for him, moving his feet aside while he used his free hand to deliver a sharp blow to Wesley's back in the vicinity of his kidneys. The man's shriek was even louder this time. "You don't want to make me mad, Wesley."

Fallon glanced around at the other houses, sure someone would run out to see what was happening. Not a door opened nor did she catch sight of anyone near a window. It was truly a neighborhood where people minded their own business. Tough luck for Wesley.

"All right, man, just don't break my arm."

Michael let up on the pressure, but only slightly. "You know Laurie McKenzie, right?"

"Yeah, yeah, we met."

"At the Rodeo Bar. You gave her an envelope of money, right?" He watched the dark head nod. "Who hired you to give her money?"

"Some guy."

Michael tightened the man's twisted arm and gave him a quick punch in the back. "Give me a name."

"Okay," Wesley groaned. "Guy named Gifford. Roy Gifford."

Michael's eyes slid to Fallon and saw that she was listening intently. "Tell me how you got involved with Gifford."

"He traced me through the an ad I put in the Yellow Pages a long time ago. I used to do private investigating. Gifford didn't mind that I'd had my license pulled. Said he needed someone who could keep his mouth shut because he wanted to get rid of someone."

Michael heard Fallon's gasp. "Those are the words he used?" he asked Wesley.

"Yeah, but he didn't mean murder. A payoff so she'd go away and never go back to Colorado." He grunted again. "Hey, man, let me up. You're breaking my damn arm."

Michael kept his hold firm. "Not until you tell me all of it. So this Gifford called you from Colorado and asked you to find Laurie McKenzie and pay her to go away and never return. Is that right?"

"Yeah, I already told you."

"Why did he want you to impersonate a private investigator from Colorado? Why not just use your own ID?"

Greiner let out a raspy breath. "Gifford told me his other daughter was in San Diego and he wanted a cover, just in case. He had Tompkins's card from when the guy did some work for the IRS and he mailed it to me. I got some made up at the print shop. The guy's paranoid. He had me check in at a motel so there'd be no connection to my real identity in case someone snooped around. Okay, I told you everything, now let me up."

"Not quite yet. How much money did he send you and how'd you get it?"

"Five grand sent through Western Union for the girl, five hundred for me."

"So you found her, met with her at the Rodeo and gave her the money, right?"

"Yeah, only I had a helluva time finding her. Took me weeks. I called Gifford at his work number, reported in every day like he told me to. Finally, I told him I needed more money. After all, my time's worth something."

"Did he send you more?"

"Yeah."

"How much more?"

"Another grand."

"He tripled your payment just because it was taking longer? You're leaving something out, Wesley." He pressed the man's head hard into the dirty filter, grinding his cheek. "Tell me the rest and let's stop playing games. Why did Roy want Laurie to get lost?"

"Hey, man, how should I know? He didn't say and I didn't ask. That's all I know."

"No, there's more. Come on, Wesley. Why did Roy give you another grand?"

Michael thought he knew exactly what Roy had paid extra for, but he wanted Wesley to say it out loud, wanted Fallon to hear just how rotten her stepfather was.

"Ouch, damn it. All right. He wanted me to find you and disable your vehicle. Nothing serious, just enough to warn you and to scare the girl's sister into giving up and going back home."

"So you punctured the brake line on my van, didn't you?"

"Yeah, but only a little hole. I figured you'd notice before anything bad happened. And you did or you wouldn't be here."

Michael ached to give the big creep a good going-over at how easily he dismissed their accident. "We were on the highway when the brakes gave out, going downhill. We could've gotten killed, you son of a—" He gave one last twist to Wesley's arm, then let go and stepped back. "Never mind. You're not worth it."

Moving slowly, Wesley Greiner straightened and carefully brought his arm forward. On his face was a painful grimace replacing the pugnacious look he'd worn before. He wouldn't meet Michael's eyes, but instead glanced over at the wrench that had been taken from him with such ease.

"Don't even think about it," Michael warned him. "I imagine you know I could use that phone and have the cops here in minutes. I think they'd be real interested in how handy you are at disabling cars."

There was helpless fury in the look Wesley sent Michael.

"I'm not going to do that, *this time*. But if I *ever* catch you near either of us, my house or my vehicles, or if I hear that you're looking for Laurie again, I'll be back. You'll have a whole lot more than a sore arm to contend with then." Still watching Wesley, he motioned Fallon to get in the van. "And I wouldn't be calling Roy Gifford about this, if I were you. Let's just keep this friendly visit between the three of us. I know where you live and I have a good memory."

Michael got behind the wheel. Even as they pulled away, Wesley just stood there holding his painful arm, his eyes once more radiating impotent fury.

They were back on El Cajon Boulevard before Fallon released a nervous breath. "I had no idea you could be so tough and unafraid."

"Who said I wasn't afraid? Only someone truly stupid wouldn't be afraid of a hulk like that without a conscience who'd do most anything for money."

"You moved so fast, I was amazed." She replaced the phone, still awestruck that things had gone as well as they had.

"Did you forget that I lived on the streets for years? You learn how to defend yourself quickly, or you don't make it. A street fighter can be a dangerous man because he knows how to fight dirty."

"Did you ever get hurt badly?"

He tapped his nose. "Been broken twice. A couple of cracked ribs. Nothing that time didn't heal." But he didn't want to talk about himself. "How do you feel about Roy being willing to pay five thousand to get Laurie out of his hair?"

"Awful, of course. But that still doesn't tell us *why* he'd want her gone so badly. I mean, I know that raising a teenager is no picnic these days, but to *pay* to have her gone! That's terrible. If Mom only knew."

"Are you going to tell her?"

Fallon was thoughtful. "First, I'm going to confront him. I want to hear if he's going to try to weasel out of this. Knowing him, he'll just say he never heard of Wesley Greiner and that the man lied."

"I don't think he lied, do you?"

"No, I believed him. It's Roy I don't believe." She noticed that he was heading back to Michael's House. "What are your plans for this afternoon?"

"I've got a staff meeting I must attend since I've postponed it several times. And tonight, I've got that fund-raiser that I promised Jonathan I'd attend. He's been really good about getting donations. I can't let him carry the whole load."

"Of course not."

"What about you?"

"I'm going to nose around some more. I can't just sit by and do nothing. Maybe someone's seen the poster and spotted Laurie. Maybe Sherlock will come through again." She leaned her head back, wondering just where they hadn't searched. It seemed to Fallon that she'd personally visited every hill and valley, every street and alley in San Diego.

"I don't like you going alone. Some of these areas are no place for a woman alone, even in the daytime."

Fallon shoved back a fall of her hair. "Michael, please, understand. I've *got* to find her. You know I'm careful."

"All right, but I'd like you back around four so we can get dressed for the fund-raiser dinner. It's being held at the Del Coronado. Very elegant. Dressy, tuxes, all that."

Inwardly, she groaned. She didn't feel much like an elegant dinner with people she didn't know, no matter how worthy the cause. She hadn't packed with a party in mind. "I don't know. We'll see."

He reached over and took her hand. "I'd really like you to be with me."

She turned to look at him. "Why?"

That stopped him. He swung his eyes back to the traffic to buy a little time. "Do I have to have a reason beyond the fact that I want to be with you?"

And she wanted to be with him. But she wanted more, and she doubted if what she needed from Michael would ever be forthcoming. Fallon sighed. Well, he hadn't lied, had never promised a thing; had in fact warned her that he didn't want and didn't need love or a permanent woman in his life. She'd been the one reading more into his words than he'd obviously intended.

No easy answers. "Let's wait and see," she said again, noncommittally.

"Hello, Mom," Fallon said into the phone in Michael's office. "How are you?"

"Oh, Fallon, it's so good to hear your voice." As usual lately, Jane Gifford's voice held a trace of tears. Except when Danny was home. "I'm all right. How are *you?*"

"I'm okay."

"Have you found any trace of Laurie?" A small sob escaped. "All this time with no word. I can't believe it."

So Roy hadn't told her mother about her call to him at his office when she'd mentioned finding Laurie, then having her take off again. Fallon hadn't expected he would. "Still nothing, Mom," she answered, keeping up the charade. It wasn't a lie, after all. She saw no reason to offer her mother false hope until she found Laurie a second time.

"Are you just looking there, in San Diego? Maybe she's gone elsewhere. Maybe...maybe you should just come home." There was a sense of hopelessness apparent in each slow word.

"I feel sure she's here, Mom. And I *will* find her." She shifted to the real reason for her call. "May I speak with Roy?"

"He isn't here, dear. He had to go out. Is it anything I can answer for you?"

It was Saturday afternoon, a day that Roy always spent at home. "Do you know where he is?" If he was working overtime in his quest to stockpile the almighty dollar, she might reach him there.

"No, I don't. He just said he had an errand to run."

Of course, Roy Gifford came and went as he pleased, not feeling it necessary to inform his wife of his whereabouts or his business. Despite Michael's warning, maybe Wesley Greiner had let him know about his unexpected visitors and Roy was out rounding up still another shady character, this time to finish the job by making sure their van went over a cliff. She shuddered at the thought, well aware that Roy was a dangerous man who'd paid someone to commit a crime that could have ended with two dead, possibly more.

"So you don't know when he'll be back?"

"No, but I can ask him to call you."

"Better not. I'm going to be in and out. I'll call him later."

"Are you really all right, dear? You sound, I don't know, kind of funny." Again, Jane's voice cracked.

"Well, Mom, this hasn't exactly been a picnic for me."

"I'm sure, and I feel terrible. Both of my girls not home."

Fallon loved her mother, but knew she had a propensity for hand-wringing and a tendency to hide from ugly realities. She wished she could indulge in that herself right now. "I'll be talking with you again soon, Mom. Bye." Slowly, thoughtfully, she hung up the phone.

Michael was upstairs in his staff meeting. It was already two. She didn't have much time before he would corral her into attending that charity dinner. She had too much to do to spend time making nice with the upper crust.

Fallon rose and grabbed her shoulder bag. She would take her car and go to Balboa Park and see if she could pick up some leads. Anything was better than sitting around and worrying.

The meeting lasted longer than Michael had planned for, but he couldn't exactly blame the staff. He'd been the one who hadn't been around to help with the problem-solving lately. He owed it to each and every one to hear them out. Which he did, but when they finally filed out of the conference room and he saw that it was ten to five, he hurried to find Fallon.

She wasn't in the third-floor room she sometimes used, nor in his room, and not in his office. The kids were already out of classes for the day, so he asked a couple if they'd seen her.

None had. Nor had Sukey or Opal. Damn!

On the off chance that she might have quit for the day and gone to the beach house, he called there, thinking that would be where they would dress for tonight's event. Sure enough, Eldora told him Fallon had called. But the news wasn't good.

"She said to tell you to go without her," Eldora told him, "That she doesn't feel like stopping right now and she'll catch you later."

Michael frowned into the phone. "What time did she call?"

"About four, I think," Eldora answered. "You two going out tonight?"

He had certainly thought so. "Don't plan on us for dinner, Eldora. I'll talk with you later." Hanging up, he tried to puzzle it out. Fallon could have phoned him here at the house, knowing he would interrupt his meeting to take her call. But no, she'd phoned the beach house where he would get the message, but wouldn't have a clue where to find her. Clever woman. Maddening woman.

He checked his watch again. Nearly five-thirty. He was to meet Jonathan in an hour. He would barely have enough time to get home, shower and change into his tux before the very prompt judge would be ringing his doorbell. He didn't want to go tonight, wanted instead to go looking for Fallon who was looking for Laurie. But his priority had to be Jonathan.

Priorities. His, it seemed, had shifted somewhat over the last few weeks since Fallon had come into his life. It had been years since a woman had had him in such knots that he wanted to turn from his obligations and go to her. That was *not* good news.

Digging in his pocket for his keys, he hurried to the van. He had to do what he had to do. He would just have to pray that Fallon would take care of herself.

"Sherlock, are you sure?" Fallon asked. "I mean, how good is the word of a pimp?"

Sherlock stroked his shaggy gray beard. "Shadow wasn't bragging. He was just talking, shooting the breeze, you know. And I didn't ask him about your sister. He just volunteered the information that he had a new young girl who would soon be joining his stable, and she had green eyes and long hair the color of yours. He was real tickled that she was only sixteen." The big man shrugged. "You can believe that or not. Don't matter to me. But I thought you were looking for leads."

Fallon sighed. "I am, and I'm sorry to sound so skeptical. But I...I can't bear the thought that Laurie would be working with a...a pimp. That has to mean that she's..." She couldn't complete the thought.

Sherlock wasn't without compassion. "Why don't you ease your mind and go find the man, see for yourself? If it's so, maybe you can coax her home. Maybe it's not too late. At least, you can try."

Fallon drew in a deep, bracing breath. "All right, tell me where I can find this Shadow."

"You know—downtown, same area I told you about before. You can't miss him. He's black, about six-four or -five and thin. He usually wears white slacks and a white silk shirt. And he's got a gold tooth in the front on top."

Oh, God, Fallon thought. Never in her wildest dreams had she thought she'd be looking up a pimp. "You said 'stable.' Does he have a lot of girls working for him?"

"Yeah, sure. Half a dozen, maybe more. You'll see them around on the same streets, but Shadow looks out for his girls. He keeps a careful eye on them."

"Why don't I find that a comforting thought?" Fallon tucked her hair behind her ear and felt like crying.

"You want me to go with you?" he offered. When she looked up at him with those big green eyes, he shrugged, embarrassed. "I don't usually, but you look like you're hurting. And that's not a real good neighborhood."

She gave him a weak smile. "Thanks, but I'll be all right." She wished she believed that. She also wondered if she would ever be all right again.

Sherlock touched her arm. "Maybe you should wait until tomorrow night when Michael can go with you. He's not going to like you going down there." Michael sure picked the wrong night to go meet with his fancy friends in La-Jolla. Sherlock wondered if he even knew she was out searching without him.

Fallon was certain the man was right. But she'd wasted too many days and nights already. If she could save her sister from—God forbid the thought—getting involved in prostitution, she would take the risk. "Don't worry. I'll be fine." It galled her to have to pay this man for information, but she supposed she should. "How much do I owe you?"

Sherlock waved a meaty hand. "This one's on me. And good luck."

Fallon nodded her thanks, swallowed around a lump in her throat and headed back to her rented Mustang.

Moments later, driving along Park Boulevard, she almost weakened and turned toward Michael's beach house. He'd probably gotten her message by now and was madder than a wet hen. She squared her shoulders. No, she had to do this and do it alone. She owed it to Laurie, to her mother and to herself. If she backed out when she was this close, she would never forgive herself.

That decided, Fallon aimed the car toward the seedy side of town.

* * *

His face hurt from smiling, Michael realized, and he forced himself to relax. He'd shaken dozens of hands, sipped wine, kissed a few cheeks and shored up his argument on behalf of runaways with several heavy contributors brought over to him by Jonathan.

And he'd checked his watch every few minutes, wishing he could look up and see Fallon walk through the double doors, having changed her mind and decided to join him, after all. But no such luck. Excusing himself from the small group having predinner cocktails, he wandered toward the bank of phones, wondering if he should call.

But *whom* would he call? He had no way to locate her. The frustration of having his hands tied had him frowning.

"Something wrong, Michael?" Jonathan asked, coming alongside.

"A lot on my mind, that's all." He gave the older man a smile. "You're looking good. Still playing tennis every week?"

"Don't try to divert me. What's bothering you, son?"

Michael could never resist Jonathan when he talked with him like a concerned father. So he took the older man aside and brought him up-to-date on what had been happening between him and Fallon, regarding the search for her sister, not their personal relationship.

Winding up, he shook his head. "I have to admit, I'm worried about her." He looked again at his watch. "It's getting late. If she's out there, she... Well, she's thinking with her emotions and not her head."

Jonathan fingered his mustache thoughtfully. "What about you? Are you thinking with your emotions when it comes to this young woman?"

A frown flitted across Michael's features briefly, then disappeared. "Of course not." He jammed one hand in his pants pocket. "It's just that I feel responsible. Her sister had been with us and we hadn't been able to keep her there long enough to discover what's bothering her, what caused her to run away in the first place. As you know, that's the key."

"Yes, indeed it is. Where do you think Fallon's searching this late?"

"I wish I knew."

A waiter approached Michael, stopping in front of him. "Mr. Redfield, there's a phone call for you. You can take it in Booth Number Three."

Michael sprang to attention. "Did you get the caller's name? Is it Fallon McKenzie?"

"No, sir. Someone who called himself Sherlock."

Jonathan looked questioning. "Do you know someone by that name, Michael?"

Fear clutched at his heart, fear for Fallon. "Yes, I do. Look, Jonathan, this may mean I have to leave. Can you handle things here without me? I hate like hell to do this to you, but . . ."

"Go. Do what you have to." Jonathan placed a hand on Michael's arm in reassurance. "We *all* have to do what we must."

But Michael was already sprinting toward the phone booth.

It was dark out, but the lights of several bars along the strip as well as a hotel that was doing a thriving business and a brightly lit theater marquee advertising a soft porn film gave the illusion of a vividly colorful day. Heart in her throat, Fallon walked slowly along the sidewalk.

A tall girl who couldn't have yet reached her eighteenth birthday was standing under a dim streetlamp wearing a skirt shorter than most of Fallon's shirts, along with mesh stockings. Just like in the movies, Fallon thought. Farther along were two slightly younger blond girls, smoking and watching the cars slowly drive by through jaded, bored eyes. A short middle-aged man in a black outfit with red suspenders lingered on the corner chewing gum.

But where was the tall man in white she was seeking?

She passed on by, daring to look everyone in the eye, hoping to find Laurie among them, yet dreading it as well.

She wasn't really afraid, although if she thought about it more, she might be. She'd acted quickly, driven here and parked, then started out on foot before she could change her mind.

The words that Roxie had said that day by the television came back to Fallon. *Did you ever love someone enough to feel their protective presence, even when they're not with you?* Yes, she did. Michael, his strength and his courage, were with her even though he couldn't be.

Fallon walked on, crossing the street, to the next block.

It took her half an hour to cruise the whole area, but on the way back, she spotted him. He was just like Sherlock had said—very tall and thin, wearing sleek white slacks, a white silk shirt—and he was smiling at someone, flashing his gold tooth.

Shadow.

Fallon swallowed hard and walked slowly toward him.

It seemed to take forever, but finally, Michael spotted Fallon's car parked under a streetlight. Jonathan had picked him up for the drive to the Del and he'd offered the use of his Lincoln when he had to leave, but Michael had declined. In this neighborhood, that car might not have lasted too long. So he'd grabbed a cab.

On the ride over, he'd sat on the edge of his seat, worried anxious and afraid. He never should have let Fallon out of his sight. If anything happened to her, it would be his fault. The thought of losing her had his palms sweating as he got out of the cab and paid the driver.

"You *sure* this is where you want to go, mister?" the cabbie asked, taking in Michael's tux and the fact that he'd brought him from the Del Coronado.

"Yes, this is the area. Thanks." Michael stepped up on the curb and looked around. The place was jumping, cars cruising, girls offering their wares, couples strolling arm in arm, music blaring. Saturday night in the big city, or at least in this section of the big city. Hands in his pockets, he started out walking.

He went into the first bar he came to that was nearest where Fallon had left the Mustang. One or two people gave him the eye, including a redhead seated on a stool who smiled invitingly, but most ignored him despite his out-of-place formal attire. Not seeing the one he was looking for, he left and walked on.

He was nearing the end of the second block when he saw several people clustered around a tall man involved in some sort of commotion. Cautiously, he approached, looking over the shoulder of a solidly built man wearing a garish blue blazer.

What he saw had him almost reeling.

"No, you listen to me," Fallon said, looking up into the face of the black man with the gold tooth. "I want you to tell me where my sister is right *now*."

Shadow's smile widened. "Sure, little lady. The Shadow knows everything." He dared to slip an arm around her slim waist. "You just come with me and I'll take you right to her."

"No, I will not." Eyes blazing, Fallon swatted away his arm. She'd about had it with this jerk. He'd been fencing with her ever since she'd approached him, trying to distract her first, then to persuade her to leave. Fallon was persisting because one of the girls hanging around had overheard her describing her sister to him and had spoken up.

"You must mean Laurie," the girl had said. "Sure, I know her." She'd looked up at the tall man. "Shadow, tell her where Laurie is."

"Shut up, Jasmine," Shadow had told her without taking his eyes from Fallon. "Get back to work."

Her heart had plummeted about then. If these people knew Laurie, then she had to be working with them. Fallon would think about that later. "I don't want to have to get rough and call the law in on this, Shadow," she went on. "But Laurie's underage and . . ."

His coarse laugh rippled out. "Down here, sweet lady, we don't talk much about age." His bold, dark eyes skimmed down her and back up. "Matter of fact, I think I could use you. You could make big money with Shadow backing you up."

Fallon felt a repulsive shiver take her as fierce anger rose in her. Made desperate by fear, she held her ground. "Tell me where she is. I have friends in the police department."

Shadow's smile slipped and his eyes took on a mean cast as he leaned down into her face. "Don't you threaten me, bitch. I ain't afraid of no cops, either." He scowled past her, his glance taking in several of his girls watching the little scene with grave interest. He ran long fingers down the girl's arm. "Let's you and me go somewhere private and—"

"Get your hands off her!" Michael, having just arrived and seen what was going on, stepped between two women who'd been standing with the short, stocky man. Sherlock had told him whom and what to look for. He owed the fat man big time for this one.

Surprised, his shrewd eyes measuring, Shadow glanced at Michael. "Hello, brother. She with you?"

"Yes, she is." Michael took Fallon's hand and pulled her to his side. "Don't you touch her again."

"I'm not leaving until I talk with Laurie," Fallon insisted.

Shadow brushed imaginary lint from his sleeve with manicured fingers. "Better go while the gettin's good, sweet lady. Your sister, she ain't here."

Fallon glanced at Jasmine who dared to give an almost-imperceptible nod. It was all she needed to dig her heels in. "She's here. Now, you produce her or I *will* call my source at headquarters." From her handbag, Fallon retrieved Michael's cellular phone.

"Fallon," Michael said in a low tone as he scanned the interested faces of those gathered around, "let me talk with Shadow alone and—"

"No! I want my sister here and now. I know she's in the area." She spoke directly to Shadow. "You call her or find her or whatever you have to do. But I'm not leaving until she shows."

Shadow apparently had had enough. He grabbed Fallon's arm and his eyes turned mean and ugly. "Go home, little lady. You got no business here." Then he turned his back to them.

It was a mistake. Again, Michael moved so swiftly that several people were shocked into jumping back. He whirled Shadow around, punched one fist into his stomach, then followed with a clip under the chin.

Shadow slid to the pavement and gave a loud grunt. Michael wasn't even breathing hard. "I told you not to touch her again." He reached for Fallon's hand. "Let's go."

"No, not until he brings Laurie to me."

"Dammit, Fallon," Michael said, his voice low and impatient, "I don't think he knows where she is."

"Yes, he does," she insisted, gazing down at the woozy man as he sat up, clutching his stomach. "Where is she?"

From the direction of the narrow alleyway behind them, a voice interrupted as heads turned. "I'm right here, Fallon," Laurie said.

Fallon sat in the front seat of the Mustang while Michael drove and Laurie rode in the back. They'd said scarcely a word since the encounter on the sidewalk. Fallon had hugged her sister, grateful that she was alive, then hustled her into the car. Laurie hadn't asked where they were taking her and Fallon hadn't, either, letting Michael drive, although she saw now that they were going to the beach house. That was probably best, since there they would at least have privacy.

She had a great many questions stored up, yet was fearful of asking most, sure that Laurie would bolt again. Drawing in a shaky breath, Fallon resigned herself to the fact that that might be the case. But not until she learned why her sister had left in the first place.

Laurie hadn't been dressed like the other girls who'd been hovering around Shadow. She had on black slacks and a red shirt, nothing slinky or sexy. Dared she hope that Laurie hadn't gotten involved too deeply yet, that she'd found her in time?

Michael pulled the Mustang into the carport and went upstairs to change clothes after showing them both into the living room that faced the sea. Fallon sat down and watched Laurie squat by the window, petting King who'd taken to her immediately, and staring out at the waves gently rolling in under a moonlit sky. She waited but when nothing seemed to be forthcoming, she decided to plunge in.

"Laurie, I . . ."

"No, let me." Laurie straightened, turned around and walked over, the dog following along. With her face clean of makeup, she looked unbearably young. "I didn't really think you cared about me, not really. I thought you just wanted to drag me back and get me off your conscience. But tonight, when you went after Shadow like that . . ." Her eyes filled with tears. "I knew you must care."

Fallon pulled her down to sit with her, taking her into her arms for a long hug, her own eyes moist. "Of course, I care. God, Laurie, I've been nearly crazy looking for you. I left my home, lost my job, got everyone mad at me. But I wouldn't give up because I have this gut feeling that you really don't want to live on the street."

Laurie sniffled into a tissue she dug out of her pocket. "You're right. I don't."

"Then tell me, please. Why did you leave in the first place? What happened back in Colorado?"

Laurie wadded up the tissue, then studied her hands in her lap. "I don't know if I can tell you. You probably won't believe me if I do."

"You can tell me anything, and I certainly will believe you. We don't lie to each other. Was it Mom? Or school? Some boy at school? What? Just tell me. Why don't you want to go back to your home?"

"Because I was *raped* in my home!" Laurie's voice was quivery, followed by a dry sob.

"Oh, God!" Fallon all but rose off the couch. "I'm going to kill Roy. You told me he hadn't touched you, but he did. I'm going to—"

"It wasn't Roy. It was Danny."

Fallon's mouth opened in stunned surprise. A sound from the kitchen had her looking up to see Michael standing in the archway.

"I was going to make some coffee," Michael explained. "I can go back upstairs."

"No, that's all right," Laurie said. "It's time I talked this out."

The coffee was made and served on the low table in front of the couch where Fallon sat near Laurie, with Michael seated on the floor across from them. He was there to lend support and to listen, but he would let Fallon lead the way. He had more experience, but this was her sister. He sat rubbing King's thick fur and listened.

"It happened the week before Danny was to leave for the academy," Laurie said, her voice hesitant, then growing stronger. "I was in my room with the CD player on sort of loud and I didn't hear him come in. It was late afternoon and Mom was at the library doing her volunteer work and Roy hadn't come home yet. I thought Danny was in his room packing. We'd had a party for him the night before—all his friends and some neighbors. As usual, he was strutting his stuff. You know how he does, Fallon."

Leaning back, her hand touching her sister's, Fallon nodded. "Yes, I know how he does."

"He startled me, so I turned down the music. At first, he just horsed around, kidding me, talking. I was on the bed where I'd been doodling in my notebook and he was sitting on my desk chair. I've talked with him dozens of time like that before, so I didn't think anything unusual. Then the next thing I knew, he came over to the bed and asked for a goodbye kiss. I laughed because, well, it was such a stupid suggestion. I mean, I always thought of him like a brother, you know."

Again, Fallon nodded encouragingly.

"Well, he didn't like it that I laughed. He decided he'd take what I didn't want to give. I didn't realize he was so strong. He pushed me down, kissing me, holding my hands down.'' She shuddered, remembering. ''I fought him, turning my head, then kicking my feet. That really got him steamed.''

Fallon leaned forward to take a sip of her coffee. No one else spoke. Laurie picked up her story. ''No matter how I struggled, I couldn't overpower him. By then, he was all worked up. He tore my shirt, ripped off my slacks and...and...'' Her lips trembled. ''I was a virgin, Fallon!'' And then came the tears in earnest.

Fallon took her into her arms and let her cry it out. Over Laurie's head, she looked at Michael.

''The bastard,'' he whispered.

''Why didn't you tell Mom?'' Fallon finally asked Laurie.

The young girl shrugged. ''She wouldn't have believed me. Don't you remember, she always took Danny's side against either one of us, me more than you. Besides, there was Roy.''

''You told Roy?'' Fallon was incredulous.

''I didn't have to. He found us when Danny was still on me. I've never seen him so mad. I thought he was going to kill his own son.''

''I can't blame him,'' Michael added. ''But then, he didn't do anything about it?''

Slowly, she shook her head. ''He sent Danny to his room to shower and change after telling him that if this got out, his chance at the academy would be ruined, his future gone. Finally, he looked at me. I was huddled in the corner of my bed with the blanket around me. He looked at me like I was something that had crawled out from under a rock.''

''What?'' Fallon couldn't have been more shocked. ''What did he say?''

''He said it was my fault. That I strolled around in skimpy clothes and what else could I expect from a healthy young man. Then he warned me that if I ever told Mom or you, he and his son would stick together and no one would believe me, that I'd been a problem child for as long as anyone could remember and they'd probably send me to some institution for wayward girls."

Disgusted, Fallon reached for her hand. "Oh, if only you hadn't believed him and called me. I'd have told you to get yourself to the hospital. They have something called a rape kit. They examine you and take samples, then use DNA testing to identify the rapist. Oh, dammit, why wasn't I there!"

Michael wasn't going to sit by and let her take this on. "Fallon, you weren't to blame anymore than Laurie was. Danny is the criminal here, and his father, too, for covering up the crime."

Her head knew that. Yet her heart had trouble handling the guilt. But Fallon nodded in agreement. "I want to get them both, Michael. I want to make them pay." She swung back to Laurie. "Did Roy suggest you run away?"

"Not in so many words, but the next few days whenever we were alone, he kept saying how much happier everyone would be if I'd disappear. So I heard about this private school where you could live on campus. I figured that if I didn't have to see Roy or Danny, maybe I could handle things. But when I suggested going there, Roy absolutely refused, saying it cost too much and that if I didn't like living in his house, I could just leave."

Fallon closed her eyes. "I want that man punished."

Michael wanted to tie up all the loose ends. "And then when Roy learned that Fallon was here looking for you, he hired a private investigator to offer you money to stay gone, is that right?"

Laurie nodded. "I didn't know he was a detective. He just told me that Roy sent him. I knew I shouldn't have taken the money, because I wasn't sure if I could stay away forever like he said I had to. He made me sign a piece of paper, can you believe it?"

"And you gave all that money to T.J., five thousand?" Fallon asked.

"We spent a little of it together," she said, looking downcast. "And then one morning, when I woke up, he was gone and so was the rest of the money." Laurie snifled, her eyes filling again. "I knew deep inside that T.J. wasn't all I wanted him to be. But I . . . I just wanted someone to love me."

Fallon drew her close, meeting Michael's eyes over Laurie's head. "That's what we all want. Don't blame yourself. We *all* make mistakes, honey."

"But mine are whoppers."

"No, Laurie," Michael interjected. "You had no reason to distrust a boy who'd lived alongside you like a brother since you were a baby, nor the stepfather who'd helped raise you. Don't blame your judgment. As for T.J., I imagine you were feeling pretty low when you landed here, and he was the first kid who was nice to you."

She almost smiled. "How did you know?"

"Because he's been there, honey. Michael was a runaway who lived on the streets for years. That's why he got into working with kids who are like he once was."

"Yes, and I trusted someone when I was just a little older than you, and got hurt pretty badly, too. It happens to the rest of us, Laurie."

"Wow, I had no idea." Laurie looked at him with new respect. "It's not easy out there, is it?"

Michael smiled. "You've got that right."

"I want to ask you something," Fallon said, "and I want you to know I won't judge you, no matter what your answer. Have you been working for Shadow since leaving Michael's House the second time?"

"No. I waitressed awhile, then I got fired when they found I'd lied about my age and I was serving alcohol. One of the girls introduced me to Shadow and he's been trying to recruit me. He always starts out, I was told, by giving you some money, setting you up with some clothes, a place to stay. Then when he has you in his debt, he starts demanding you work it off. If you hadn't come along when you did . . . Well, I don't know if I could have held out much longer. No one wants to hire kids with no papers, no experience."

"Yeah," Michael said. "I remember. I lied about my age, too, but I looked older."

Fallon had to know it all. "Niko hinted that T.J. was a pimp, too."

Laurie frowned. "Not while I was with him. He wouldn't have had to steal from me if he was making money like that. T.J.'s got a drug problem. That's where his money goes."

"Thank God you were strong, that you survived," Fallon told her. "I've been so worried."

"I'm so glad you didn't give up." Laurie smiled at her sister, then stifled a yawn. "So what happens now? Don't tell me, please, that you're going to make me go back there. I don't ever want to see Danny or Roy again. I miss Mom, sort of, but you know, Fallon, she's just never in my corner."

"Don't worry, I wouldn't dream of making you go back."

"Except maybe to testify against both Roy and Danny."

Michael looked at Fallon. "I hope you're planning to press charges."

"I'm going to try. After all this time, and with their word against ours, it might not be easy to prove. But at the very least, we're going to make a very large stink, hopefully get the wonder boy tossed out of the academy. If he's raping at eighteen and getting away with it, what will he do next? That boy needs counseling badly. As for Roy, I'm going to go straight to whoever he answers to. I'll muddy up his precious reputation until he won't be able to show his face at the IRS ever again." Fallon's fury knew no bounds. To think they'd nearly wrecked her sister's life.

"What about Mom?"

Fallon ran out of steam. "I'll have to explain things to her, too. Then it'll be her decision who to believe and what to do next." She met her sister's eyes. "I think we need to get you some counseling, too, honey. You've been through a lot. Those people can help you deal with the anger and all the rest you must be feeling."

"That's a good idea," Michael agreed. "Laurie, I've known other girls who've been through something similar. We're behind you. I know you'll make the right decision."

"As long as I don't have to go back to Roy's house, I'll do anything you say." Again, she yawned.

"Right now, I think you need to get some sleep. Michael's got a wonderful room all fixed up for you." He'd used the cellular to phone ahead and Eldora had taken it from there. "I don't have to lock you in, do I?"

Laurie smiled. "I won't run again. Fallon, I'm so glad you believe me. I didn't think anyone would."

"Oh, honey, of course I do. I love you."

Michael got to his feet, taking in the scene, his thoughts in a jumble. But about one thing, he was suddenly quite clear. "Maybe what you two ought to think about is staying right here in San Diego. With me."

They both looked at him in unison, but it was Fallon who spoke. "Why would we do that?"

"Well, because you don't have a job to go back to, and we have lots of stores here. I also have plenty of room here—four bedrooms. And a couple of other reasons I'll go into later, after you tuck Laurie in." Moving to her side, he hugged the slender young girl briefly. "Sleep well and I'll see you in the morning. If there's anything you need, you have only to ask."

"Thanks, Michael, for everything."

With a puzzled glance at Michael over his cryptic statement, Fallon led Laurie up to her room. King rose from his napping by the fireplace and trotted up with them.

They were snuggled in Michael's bed when she finally brought up the subject. "All right, tell me what other reasons."

"Only one other reason that counts." Skin to skin with her, Michael realized anew that this was exactly where he wanted to be. Instead of the thought being frightening, there was a feeling of rightness, of peace. "While I was driving to look for you after Sherlock called me at the Del, a lot of things went through my mind. Mostly, I was afraid. And I haven't been afraid for a long while. Afraid that something might happen to you, that I'd lose you."

Silently she let him speak, hoping this would lead up to what she wanted to hear.

"I know I've mentioned repeatedly that I don't want to care too much, to get too involved, because if they betray you or you lose that one person, it hurts too damn much. But I've come to realize that people who never take risks protect themselves from the lows in life, but they never experience the true highs." He shifted so he could look into Fallon's wonderful green eyes. "Since you've come into my life, I've gotten hooked on those highs, Fallon. I know I can live without you, but I won't ever be *complete* without you."

"Oh, Michael." Her eyes were once more filling.

"I love you, Fallon. Please, marry me. Move here. We can work the job thing out somehow. I want you here, in my life, in my home, or I'll build us another house if you don't like this place."

"I love this place. But most of all, I love you."

"One more thing. About kids. It isn't that I don't want any. It's more that I'm afraid I won't be a good enough parent. Children are so important and I see so many who've gotten screwed up by their parents."

"We'll do it together, Michael. I think you'd be a wonderful father because you know the pitfalls. And we have enough love to share, don't we?"

"Yeah, I guess we do." Michael kissed her then and knew for the first time ever that he truly was home.

Epilogue

Michael straightened when he heard the key turn in the lock, setting aside his memories. Rising, he went to greet his wife. His hug was a bit awkward.

"Another month and I won't be able to get my arms around you," he said, leaning back to gaze at her very pregnant belly.

Fallon smiled. "I have a feeling you'll think of some way." Married two years and big as a house with their first child, yet she was thrilled that Michael's ardor had never cooled. Nor had hers.

She glanced at the grandfather clock in the marble foyer as King sauntered in to greet her, then she reached up to stroke her husband's stubbled face. "Time for a shave and shower, my lord and master. The preview opening of California Hope is scheduled for seven and, though I just left utter chaos, both Opal and Sukey assured me that everything would be ready and presentable by the time we get there."

At last, the day they'd worked so hard for had arrived and his second facility would be a reality, Michael thought. This one would be more of a structured rehab center for treatment of more serious teen problems and addictions with a full-time psychologist on staff. With the judge's help, he'd been able to hire some specially trained personnel, as well. Tonight's reunion party was for the graduates—the kids who'd left and gone on to become good citizens over the years. The grand opening for patrons and press would take place next week.

Fallon had worked alongside Michael since even before their wedding, as had a recovered Laurie who'd graduated recently from high school and was living with them and working at Michael's House part time while taking college courses. The two women, along with Opal and Sukey, had spent all afternoon decorating the place. He was anxious to see it.

Only right now, he had another pressing matter on his mind. Sliding his arm around his wife, Michael led the way upstairs to their master bedroom. "There's something we need to talk about."

"Sounds serious."

"It is. I watched the tape you left for me."

She slanted a look up at him. "I thought you'd find it interesting, but unsettling. Are you all right? It must have been a shock."

"It was, but I'm definitely all right. Thank you for taping it." He gazed down at the child she carried, waiting to be born. "I think our little one's about to get another carload of relatives."

And then he sat down with her to discuss the television show that would change their lives forever.

* * * * *

Where are her children?
Finally Julia's search comes to a happy end
next month in KEEPING KATE, coming in October
from Silhouette Special Edition.

There's nothing quite like a family

The new miniseries by
Pat Warren

Three siblings are about to be reunited.
And each finds love along the way....

HANNAH
Her life is about to change now that she's met
the irresistible Joel Merrick in HOME FOR HANNAH
(Special Edition #1048, August 1996).

MICHAEL
He's been on his own all his life. Now he's
going to take a risk on love...and
take part in the reunion he's been
waiting for in MICHAEL'S HOUSE
(Intimate Moments #737, September 1996).

KATE
A job as a nanny leads her to Aaron Carver,
his adorable baby daughter and the
fulfillment of her dreams in KEEPING KATE
(Special Edition #1060, October 1996).

Meet these three siblings from

Silhouette SPECIAL EDITION®
and

▼ INTIMATE MOMENTS®
™ *Silhouette*

Look us up on-line at: http://www.romance.net

A Funny Thing Happened on the Way to the Baby Shower...

When four college friends reunite to celebrate the arrival of one bouncing baby, they find four would-be grooms on the way!

Don't miss a single, sexy tale in

RAYE MORGAN'S

Only in

BABY DREAMS
in May '96 (SD #997)

A GIFT FOR BABY
in July '96 (SD #1010)

BABIES BY THE BUSLOAD
in September '96 (SD #1022)

And look for

INSTANT DAD, WILL TRAIN
in November '96

Only from

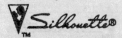

RMBS

Who can resist a Texan...or a Calloway?

This September, award-winning author
ANNETTE BROADRICK
returns to Texas, with a brand-new
story about the Calloways...

CLINT: The brave leader. Used to keeping secrets.

CADE: The Lone Star Stud. Used to having women
fall at his feet...

MATT: The family guardian. Used to handling
trouble...

They must discover the identity of the mystery
woman with Calloway eyes—and uncover a
conspiracy that threatens their family....

Look for **SONS OF TEXAS:** Rogues and Ranchers
in September 1996!

Only from Silhouette...where passion lives.

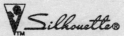

SONSST

**What do you get when you take a
reluctant dad and match him up
with a determined mom?**

A Baby?
Maybe

Discover how three couples are brought together
because of a baby and find that a little love goes
a long way.

Three complete stories of instant families by some
of your favorite authors:

RELUCTANT FATHER
by Diana Palmer

BORROWED BABY
by Marie Ferrarella

PASSION'S CHILD
by Ann Major

Available this October wherever
Silhouette and Harlequin books are sold.

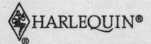 

Look us up on-line at:http://www.romance.net   SREQ1096

A woman with a shocking secret.
A man without a past.
Together, their love could be nothing less than

Scandalous

The latest romantic adventure from

CANDACE CAMP

When a stranger suffering a loss of memory lands on
Priscilla Hamilton's doorstep, her carefully guarded secret
is threatened. Always a model of propriety, she knows that
no one would believe the deep, dark desire that burns
inside her at this stranger's touch.

As scandal and intrigue slowly close in on the lovers, will
their attraction be strong enough to survive?

Find out this September at your favorite retail outlet.

MIRA **The brightest star in women's fiction**   MCCSC

Look us up on-line at:http://www.romance.net

FORTUNE'S Children™

Bestselling Author
MERLINE
LOVELACE

Continues the twelve-book series—FORTUNE'S CHILDREN
in September 1996 with Book Three

BEAUTY AND THE BODYGUARD

Ex-mercenary Rafe Stone was Fortune Cosmetics cover girl
Allie Fortune's best protection against an obsessed stalker. He
was also the one man this tempting beauty was willing to risk
her heart for....

MEET THE FORTUNES—a family whose legacy is greater than
riches. Because where there's a will...there's a *wedding!*

*A CASTING CALL TO
ALL FORTUNE'S CHILDREN FANS!*
If you are truly one of the fortunate
few, you may win a trip to
Los Angeles to audition for
Wheel of Fortune®. Look for
details in all retail Fortune's Children titles!

WHEEL OF FORTUNE is a registered trademark of Califon Productions, Inc.©
1996 Califon Productions, Inc. All Rights Reserved.

Look us up on-line at: http://www.romance.net

FC-3-C-R